COME DIE WITH ME

A ROXY HORNE NOVEL

VANESSA M. KNIGHT

Come Die with Me

Published by Inked Publishing

Cover Art © 2023 by Qamber Designs & Media

Edited by Nancy Canu

ISBN: 978-1-7344206-8-5

To Bill for all the love and support you have freely given. You fill my life with joy and inspire me to be better. I couldn't ask for a better friend and partner. I love you.

You & Me.

ROXANNA HORNE always wanted to be a private investigator. She'd had visions of magnifying glasses and big reveals while she twirled the ties of her deerstalker cap. She'd pictured a Watson—who looked suspiciously like Justin Timberlake—nodding while she said, "Elementary, my dear Timberlake."

Okay. The catch phrase needed a bit of work.

But the look she'd imagined in his eyes while he watched her brilliance made her heart pitter-patter. She couldn't wait to graduate college and get out there in the real world.

Well.

She was out there. In that real world. Talk about a disappointment.

There were no big reveals, and JT wasn't anywhere to be found. Because she didn't have the experience or the Nevada license to be a full-fledged PI, she worked for

M&J Investigations in Las Vegas as a process server. That could be her problem.

She edged her red Z28 Chevy Camaro to the curb. The car sputtered and gasped just before she turned off the engine. *Please don't die.* She rubbed the dashboard of her baby. Her parents bought the car for her high school graduation, when they'd both had a desire to run. Which was good news, bad news. Good news because she couldn't afford anything else on her minimum wage job. Bad news because the car was on its last tires and finicky as a cat near water.

She remembered to take the clipboard out of her bag on the passenger seat before getting out in front of a small manufactured home. Gray shutters flanked the windows on the front. Potted plants lined the stairs on the side of the doublewide. It was a well-kept rarity in a questionable neighborhood.

Her gym shoes sank in the gravel path across the brown and crispy front lawn as she approached the door. It was too hot in Vegas to keep grass alive. Not without money. The sun hung high as she hopped up the three steps and knocked.

No answer. Another knock.

She leaned toward a window and looked inside. Nothing. She'd been trying to find this guy for almost a week—keeping track of his work schedule and his excursions. He should be home, especially since his truck was sitting there. She knocked again. "Hello?"

A crash came from behind the door.

"Mr. Simpkins?" She tapped on the doorjamb.

"Who's there?" a scraggly male voice called out from inside.

"Mr. John Simpkins? Can you open the door?"

More crashing from inside. "Why? Who are you?"

"I'm Roxy Horne—"

"Horn? Can I blow you?"

Like she hadn't heard that one before, Captain Obvious. She rolled her eyes, metaphorically, because she had a job to do. But really? "I'm your meter reader. We think your meter is overcharging you." Surprisingly, no one wanted to open their door to get served papers, but they couldn't refuse a chance for free money from a faulty meter. It had only taken her a month on the job to figure that out.

"Damn straight." The door rattled open. White Einstein-hair shot out over Simpkins' narrow sun-blown face. A beer bottle bobbed in his hand as he talked—almost spilling on his bare chest and half-zipped faded blue jeans. "I better be getting a refund."

"Are you John Simpkins?"

"Yeah." He ran a dirty hand along his lip before he lifted his beer to his mouth. At least he'd waited till noon to start drinking. Maybe. "Want a drink?" Given the slight slur and the stench wafting from his mouth, he might have continued drinking from yesterday.

"Thank you, but I can't drink on the job. I have work

to do." She shook the clipboard as she freed the envelope from the clip. No one ever questioned the validity of credentials when you carried a clipboard. She'd learned that two months into the job.

"I got something you can do, pretty thing." His stare travelled up the black jeans that snugged her legs and landed on her chest. She was wearing a blue button down that made her hazel eyes pop, but he'd never know.

His free hand rubbed at his bare stomach and lodged in the waistband of his jeans, while a sneer landed on his lips. She needed to do this and get out, before his hands got other ideas. She stuffed the envelope she was holding into the hand in his jeans.

Desperate times and all.

"You've been served."

She ran toward her car. She usually had a good twenty seconds or so before the servees figured out what happened. Then they'd chase her or swear. One guy pulled a gun, but thankfully he couldn't figure out how to disengage the safety. Given this guy's state of alcohol consumption, she probably had a good minute or so before he realized he held a summons.

She angled into the car. The seat was leather fire because she forgot to put the damn heat shield in the front window of her car. Again. At noon in the desert, that was just asking for burnt thighs.

She twisted the key in the ignition. *Sputter. Sputter.* Nothing.

"No. No. No." She glanced at the house, but beer-baby wasn't coming after her. He was still squinting at the pages in the envelope. Thank goodness. She tried the key again. More sputtering, and then an unfulfilling silent ending.

Darn it.

Breathe in. Breathe out. She jiggled the key and kissed the top of the steering wheel before rubbing the dashboard. "Come on, baby."

Roxy flinched as something hit her car and dirt splattered the driver's side window. A bare-chested John Simpkins ran toward her. Yelling obscenities. Summons crumpled in one hand and a potted plant in the other. He threw the planter at the car, taking out her side mirror.

"Stop that," she screamed at the window and turned the key in the ignition. The engine sputtered. "Please start."

Another terracotta pot hit the hood. Dirt sprayed everywhere and a round cactus lodged in the windshield wiper. More sputtering and then—thankfully—the engine caught with a rumble. She threw the car into drive just as Simpkins stumbled back to the steps to his house.

He picked up a dying ficus from the bottom step and ran into the street. More swearing. The pathetic tree flew through the air and hit pavement. "You lying...."

As she raced onto Rainbow Boulevard, she avoided the words coming out of his mouth. She didn't need an active imagination to know what he was going to say.

She turned onto Lake Mead Boulevard, veering toward the high-priced homes in the Summerlin area of Vegas and pulling into the lot of a nondescript strip mall with a black-tiled roof and gray stucco. Although that pretty much defined most strip malls in the area. M&J Investigations was propped between a chiropractor and a day spa. If it wasn't for the ice cream bar on the corner, she never would have found the place.

She got out of the Camaro, hanging her bag on her shoulder, and tugged at the cactus attached to her windshield wiper. She pulled, but the roots were wrapped around the wiper like a boa with its prey. Roxy finally dislodged her new hood ornament and crossed the lot, passing large gray flowerpots filled with red phlox and banana yucca. The doors and window frames were painted a soft blue, and looked nice against the gray stucco. The walkway along the front of the building was reddish-brown pavers.

She opened the door to the agency, its bright blue sign stating *M&J Investigations. We Serve Your Papers in 7 Days or It's Free.* A burst of cold air slapped her in the face as her eyes adjusted from the sunlight to the fake indoor lighting. She dropped the former hood ornament into the garbage can next to the front counter, where her best friend Sarina West's voice sighed into the phone. "...we find things... just not coyotes. Have you tried the Humane Society?"

Or Ace Ventura. Roxy gave Sarina a sympathetic

smile as her best friend slanted the phone farther and farther away from her ear. If the person on the line got mad at the Humane Society suggestion, he'd bust a valve with the Ace Ventura thing. And Roxy knew it was a him. His voice was loud enough for the coyote to hear, no matter where the pup was hiding. So much for a sneak attack—good luck to whoever got stuck helping him.

Roxy walked past all the desks until she got to hers, in the center of the main room. It was an open-concept floor plan, or at least that was what one of the owners called it when Roxy asked for a cubicle wall. Apparently, privacy was out and collaboration was in. Why a bunch of process servers and skip tracers would need to collaborate, she had no idea. Instead, the room was filled with the loud hum of people talking on the phone. The string of desks faced each other, which led to weird staring contests. Offices lined the far wall, where the firm owners had nooners with their spouses or various strangers, depending on the owner.

She sat at her desk and booted up her laptop, nestled in the center of the paper-storm that had hit her desktop. Who had time to deal with all the paper? She had another guy to serve today, but first she had an affidavit to write—to prove she'd served John the plant-chucker his summons. You'd think a picture of her car covered in dirt and plant life would be proof enough.

Unfortunately, courts didn't take photographic proof of car violence. One would think it would be a thing.

The front door opened and Sarina appeared. At some point, she must have gotten off the phone and walked outside. Maybe this was why the boss was so against making Roxy a private detective. Her detecting skills were lacking.

"So." Sarina swished into the main room and claimed the chair next to Roxy's desk. Her black Prada mini skirt looked amazing on her skinny frame. The red tank brought out the green in her eyes. "Do you want to tell me what happened to your car?"

Did Roxy want to tell her? Not really. But since Sarina would just keep asking, she had better some up with something quick. "My car had an accident." That was quick.

"With a landscaping company?" Sarina's eyebrow arched like she didn't believe Roxy. Well, after being friends for twenty-five years, Sarina knew Roxy way too well.

The front door opened, again. This time, Roxy detected it. And the man who entered. He looked to be in his early thirties. Short light-brown hair cut shorter on the sides. Five o'clock shadow along a strong jaw. Dark jeans and a white shirt that appeared to cover a body worth licking.

If she was into that type of thing. She hadn't found anyone worth licking in a long time. Not that she'd been searching... much.

"I'm Detective MacAuley." He showed the badge

on his hip to Sarina, who, somehow, was already greeting him by her desk. "I'm looking for Roxy Horne."

"Uh, Roxy, someone to see you." Sarina's cheeks flamed as she turned to Roxy and made a face that said "hot guy in the vicinity". Her usual MO. Guys made her nervous—especially hot ones. Which was probably why she was stuck with her on-again off-again boyfriend. She could talk to him. Too bad he liked to do more than talking with most of the ladies of Vegas.

Roxy stood up from her desk and walked toward the nice-looking detective. "I'm Roxy."

"Miss Horne. We've had a complaint from a Mr. John Simpkins. He claims you stole his potted plants."

Stole them. "Is this some sort of joke? I'm being punked aren't I?" She looked for the hidden cameras, because c'mon.

He didn't respond. Didn't start laughing. Apparently, not a joke.

"I just left that guy like twenty minutes ago." Her hands flew to her hips. "Does he have you on speed dial?"

"He can be persistent." The detective still wasn't smiling.

"If I give you the plants back, will this be over?"

"How did you get the plants?"

"It's easier to show you. Follow me." She plucked the cactus from the trash on her way out the front door and walked over to her car. She turned to make sure he followed. He had. Roxy dangled the cactus by the roots. "Here's the first plant."

"What am I supposed to do with that?" He didn't move to take the cactus, so she tossed it on the hood of her car.

"Here's another one." Roxy untangled a lump of soil with three green leaves from the broken side mirror. She put them on the hood next to the cactus, in a happy little pile. Then she pried a piece of terracotta from the passenger-side wiper. "Here you go. Please give him my regards when you return his plants."

"Why are his plants on your car?" The detective's lips quirked at the edges.

"I went to John Simpkins' home to serve him, since I'm a process server and all. Apparently, he was so thankful for being served, he threw his plants at my car. You can see how I thought they were a gift."

Detective Stoic's lips curved upward. "What happened to your mirror?"

"One of the pots didn't break before it hit the side."

"Do you want to press charges?" The smile had disappeared, but his eyes sparkled. They were nice eyes. Light gray with dark gray edges.

"No thanks."

"Then my work here is done." He nodded to the foliage on the hood. "I'll let you keep that." Those nice eyes roamed her body. She resisted the urge to check that her brown hair wasn't a complete disaster. And unlike when creepy beer-baby did it, her skin warmed and her body burned. Although that could be the Vegas sun beating down.

"Nice to meet you, Miss Horne."

"Call me Roxy."

A full-blown smile appeared on his lips. "Nice to meet you, Roxy." He strutted away, giving her a nice view of his backside. Just because that wasn't her type of thing didn't mean she couldn't appreciate a great butt.

"Do you have a first name, Detective?" she called after him.

"MacAuley." He opened the door to a black SUV.

"Your name is MacAuley MacAuley?"

Another smile. "Have a good day."

She watched him drive out of the parking spot and into traffic. Probably watched him too long. Who cared? It wasn't like she'd ever see him again.

CHAPTER 2

ROXY HEADED BACK into the office, hands full of dirt and plants. She dumped them in the garbage as she passed Sarina's desk, and then slapped her dirt-crusted hands together. Nothing happened. She needed a sink. "Good news. I'm not going to jail."

"Being arrested by him might not be so bad." Sarina stared out the front window. Maybe hoping to get another glimpse.

That girl had definitely won the genetic lottery. Blonde hair from her Finnish father. Perpetually sun-kissed skin from her Puerto Rican mother. It was like if Jennifer Lopez and Thor started making babies. But somehow, she didn't realize she was every man's naughty-librarian fantasy. It was part of her charm.

Roxy was more of a scratch-off ticket. Her parents were Dutch, but no one believed her from the back. Her long, wavy dark brown hair gave her an exotic Italian or

Greek look. Then people saw her face. Pale as Bella in *Twilight*—but no gorgeous vampire in sight.

Sarina waved at the door. "What happened with him? Did you get his phone number?"

The loud and proud office hum from earlier was now silent. All eyes were on Roxy. Nothing like a little gossip to quiet a room. She pretended she didn't notice. "I didn't get his phone number, but I gave him a little handy to keep him distracted from writing me a ticket."

"You did not." Sarina actually looked shocked. Like there was a small piece of her that believed it.

Roxy shook her head. "Like I would stroke a stranger in the parking lot." Giving handys in the afternoon wasn't exactly her thing. There was that one time—but, never mind.

"Don't forget, you promised to go out with me tonight," Sarina said.

Going out meant drinking and pushy tourists. Maybe she could blow this off. "Inconceivable."

Sarina crossed her arms over her chest and puffed out her bottom lip. "No. You can't use *Princess Bride* to get out of this. You promised."

Roxy looked at the calendar hanging behind the front counter. Was it her birthday? Why else would they go out?

"That new club opens tonight." Sarina was either getting better at reading Roxy's mind or she'd said that out loud. "I have to be there as the assistant promoter."

Ahh. Sarina's dream job. She'd been working as an assistant to this local promoter for six months, hoping to get off the front desk at M&J. But so far, assistant just meant free help. Her boss, Doug, called it an unpaid internship. Tonight, Sarina was rolling out the red carpet to a bunch of local celebs for a new club—like Vegas needed more clubs—located in the Imprint Hotel, out in the suburb of Henderson. The hotel was old-Vegas elegance. The club was rumored to be old-Vegas meets new-brothel. Roxy wanted to check it out as much as she wanted to check out the cost of a new side mirror.

Roxy shrugged. "I have to track down Donnie Dunne, the disappearing investment banker." Every time she heard the guy's name, she wanted to call him Double-D—the pain in the butt. The guy was either Houdini or he'd left town. Either way, Roxy needed to get creative, and she didn't have time to go clubbing. The sign on the door said she had seven days, so she was three days away from another write-up. Her personnel record couldn't take any more red.

Sarina frowned at her. "I thought that was Skip's job?"

"Skip is taking his girlfriend to the hockey game in San Jose. I told him I'd help him out. Can't we go tomorrow?" Maybe if she just kept pushing it off, eventually Sarina would forget.

"No way. You blew me off when that club opened in the Aria Hotel. You swore you'd go with me. You know I hate these things." The puffed-out bottom lip was now thin and angry.

"Why are you trying to be a promoter if you hate parties?"

"I like to organize things and make them happen. It doesn't mean I want to participate."

Roxy was sure there was logic in there somewhere. She wasn't sure where, but who was she to squash Sarina's dreams?

"Find Donnie and meet me after. Cliff's meeting us there," Sarina said.

Cliff. The on-again and off-again boyfriend. When they were on, he was attentive and kind. When they were off, it was usually a *Jerry Springer* kind-of-thing. He slept around indiscriminately, and Sarina sat at home and cried.

If he was meeting them at the club, they were on again. There was no way to get out of it—without appendicitis or an equally intense emergency room visit. But maybe... "I have—"

"No. You're going or I'll hire Pennywise, the party clown, for your next birthday."

One problem with best friends that knew all your secrets was they used them against you at random times. Roxy hated clowns. They wore creepy makeup and made horrible balloon animals. She hated balloons too. They popped and scared the crap out of people—namely her.

"What time?" Roxy sighed.

"Yay!" Sarina did a little golf clap. "We're going to have so much fun. Let's meet in the Imprint lobby at eight."

"Sure." Roxy trudged back to her desk with less excitement than her counterpart.

An hour later, after Roxy's affidavit was written, she pulled her car into the parking garage at the Pura Vida hotel on the Vegas strip. Darn Double-D. She hated dealing with the strip. Between the cars and the pedestrians, she could barely keep her road rage in check. That didn't even touch on the morons who didn't know how to behave because they truly believed what happened in Vegas, stayed in Vegas.

Yes. Yes, it did. Okay, the women of Vegas think you're a pervert for showing your happy-stick—unprovoked. But the guys who can't handle their Vegas will go back to their homes, their lives, their wives with no one the wiser what a deviant they truly were.

But the locals of Vegas knew. They always knew. That was why they avoided the strip.

After she parked, Roxy made her way through the casino. Lights blinked. Machines whirred and dinged. It was time to get serious about this guy. He couldn't elude her forever—in theory. If she didn't deliver this subpoena soon, she'd be looking for a new job. So, what did she know...?

A. He was some big-shot investment banker whose partner was suing him.

B. He wasn't bad looking, if you overlooked the thinning reddish combover and his green suit. He'd actually worn a green suit for his website picture. It might work on some people, but somehow, it made him look like he was guarding his Lucky Charms.

And, C. His secretary said he was at a conference at the Pura Vida, a Costa Rican-themed hotel here on the strip.

Roxy exited the casino and crossed the lobby, heading for the registration desk. A woman in brown safari-wear carried a sloth. A slew of greenery lined the counters and walls. Roxy had never been to the rainforest, but she had a feeling this was the theme park version.

The young woman behind the counter smiled as Roxy approached. "Welcome to the Pura Vida."

"I'm trying to find the investment banker conference." She probably should have found out the actual name of the conference. Investment Bankers Conference... Investment Bankers Gone Wild... 101 Things to Make You Nap— take your pick.

The woman's smile never faltered. "I'm sorry. We don't have any conferences here this week."

"None?"

"No, we're preparing for the *Supernatural* convention next week so all the convention space is closed right now."

"Are you sure? I really need to reach someone at that conference. It's an emergency." Okay, it wasn't an emergency-emergency. But she only had a few days. She liked paying her rent, and she'd like to keep doing that. So, it was an emergency in her book.

"Hold on." The woman picked up a phone as customers lined up behind Roxy. "Do you have a minute for customer assistance?" the woman said into the phone. She set the receiver down. "Someone will be right up."

Roxy stood off to the side while hotel business swirled around her. She thought Donnie's secretary said he had a convention. Maybe if she'd found out the name of the actual convention, she could trust her *thought*.

"She has some questions." The woman at the front desk pointed to Roxy and then went back to clacking on a keypad.

A man in a black suit swaggered up to Roxy. And by man, she meant *oh man*. Black hair that fell to his collar, a body made for sin, and caramel-brown eyes that could make you forget your diet. His lips curved in a smile that melted panties and brain cells. *What?* She actually felt her brain cells shrivel up. Don't get her started on her panties.

"Roxanna Horne?"

Holy smokes. She knew this panty-melter. She almost didn't recognize him. Rafe Amato was the bad boy every girl in Vegas wanted to get with in college—the one she'd almost gotten with except the gods of probable regret and avoiding bad decisions saved her ass.

Time had been kind to him. And that was understatement on a massive scale. Roxy pasted on her most innocent grin. One that said I-didn't-just-picture-you-naked. Where was that god when you needed her? "Rafe. What are you doing here?"

"I'm working as a tactical commander." His sultry eyes swept up her body.

That look alone made her want to ride him like a pogo stick. But she didn't—so bonus points for discretion. "Not a cop anymore?" she asked. And no, she did not lick her lips. He'd gone from being the bad boy everyone wanted, to the cop everyone wanted. Seriously. He had those arms and he carried arms.

"Keeping tabs on me?"

"No." She couldn't help but grin. Even as he made fun of her, he was too darn cute. "I just don't know whose name to give to get out of tickets, if you're not on the force."

"Get a lot of tickets, do we?"

"Not really." She was pretty good at talking her way out of tickets... and felonies. Detective MacAuley MacAuley ran through her mind. Maybe she could use his name to get out of jams, if that was really his name.

Rafe raised his eyebrows. "Why are you here today? Did you just stop by to say hi?"

"I need to serve a summons to someone here." Roxy shrugged. "He's at some investment banker conference."

"Well, we don't have any conferences here." His hospitable disposition disappeared. "And if we did, I couldn't let you near any of my guests."

"Why?" She glanced down at her dark jeans and button-up shirt. Not couture, but they were clean. She thought she looked adorable.

"If I start letting you harass my customers, they'll stop staying at the hotel."

"But I have a legal right to serve him."

"I have a legal right to ask you to leave." His lips quirked. It was like he was trying to smile again. He almost seemed to get joy out of asking her to leave.

Funny, last time they were together, he was asking her to stay. She didn't listen to him then, either. "Weren't you a cop for like, ten years? Shouldn't you be for the purveyance of justice?"

"Eleven years, and I'm still for justice. Just not on this property." He motioned to the buffet across the atrium as he pulled something from his pocket. "Why don't you check out the buffet?"

She took the ticket he held out. A free buffet. She didn't know if she should be offended or thankful. Who didn't like free stuff? It was a scientific fact that food tasted better when it was free. "Does this mean he's in there?"

"No." He held out one more and snapped it back

when she reached out. "These are to remind you to not engage. If you find your investment banker, do *not* serve him on any of my properties."

"What am I supposed to do, stand outside and wait for him to leave... when I don't know where he is?"

Rafe narrowed his eyes at her. "Works for the paparazzi."

"Whatever. I have work to do." She really did. Sitting here talking to the subpoena-blocker wasn't helping her cause.

"Good luck with that." Rafe smirked. "It was nice seeing you again, Horne."

She wished she could say the same. But she left the hotel with the subpoena in her pocket. No Double-D. With three days left.

Although she had managed to get two free buffet tickets. When she was living on welfare after losing her job, she'd get to eat. For a couple days.

CHAPTER 3

HIGH HEELS ARE PLEASURE WITH PAIN. ~
CHRISTIAN LOUBOUTIN

ROXY STROLLED into the atrium of the Imprint Hotel at around eight. Her shoes tapped on the marble floors. Her flared mini-skirt swished at her knees as she passed a seating area fit for a 1930's prohibition sit-down.

Pink walls and dark cherry ceiling panels. Floral drapes behind the check-in desk. Brown camelback sofas and chaise lounges all around the room, plus leather chairs and mahogany side tables.

"You made it!" High heels clattered as Sarina flew at Roxy.

"I wouldn't miss it for the world." Although, an hour ago she was thinking about missing it because she didn't want to wear shoes or a bra. #bestfriendproblems

"Thank God." Sarina wrapped her hand around the crook of Roxy's arm. "Cliff brought his friends."

His friends? He didn't have many friends, just... ugh. "The jackasses from college?"

Sarina nodded. Fantastic. Dancing in a loud, over-crowded room with a bunch of strangers while Sarina chased after her boy-toy. Great news.

Sarina dragged her to the other side of the atrium, where two he-men in dark suits stood guard at a door. They moved to the side and opened the door.

The inside of the club was dark. The music thumped through Roxy's body as a DJ mixed two beat lines, segueing into the next song. She angled through the crowd, hanging onto Sabrina's hand until they hit a leather booth in the back. A booth with a bunch of bubbly twenty-somethings wearing sashes and sucking down shots without the use of their arms.

"Where is he?" Sarina yelled over the bass as she spun her head around like it was on swivel. Given the "he", Roxy could bet Cliff was missing.

"Maybe he ran to the bathroom," Roxy yelled back.

"I can't find his friends either." Sarina's eyes flamed. "I told him no drugs tonight."

"Is that normally a problem?" Adding drug use to Cliff's list of undesirable qualities left him with few desir-able qualities, except that he was hot and he made amazing pancakes. Roxy could vouch for the hot. She had to take Sarina's word on the pancakes.

"No. He doesn't normally do drugs, but..."

The old college friends. They weren't from Vegas, so they were the poster-men for not handling their Vegas. "But if he's in the bathroom..." Roxy locked eyes with

Sarina. They both knew what a group of guys in a bathroom meant, and it wasn't fluffing their hair and applying lipstick.

"Why don't we go get drinks?" Roxy asked, looking around. Bodies gyrated on the dance floor. People surrounded tables and chatted over the hard rock beat. More people stood in lines to get booze.

Sarina shook her head. "I'm going to walk around a bit. Try to find him. Can you grab me a wine spritzer and I'll meet you back here?" Sarina disappeared through the crowd before Roxy could reply.

Roxy headed in the opposite direction and found the bar. At least, she thought it was the bar. It was hard to see with the wall of people standing around it. She waited, slowly moving to the front of the line as she watched for Sarina to come back.

"Hey, baby." A man with slicked back hair and a creepazoid mustache leaned into her. "Can I buy you a drink?"

"No, thanks." She smiled, but she had a feeling it came out more like a cringe. It didn't scare off slicky-dude, though.

"Come on, baby. One drink."

"No. Thanks." She moved forward, trying to inch away.

"It's Vegas, doll. You don't have to be frigid." His breath scurried along the side of her face. Although, that might have just been her skin crawling. "It's party city."

"I'm waiting for my boyfriend. He likes to buy my drinks." She angled herself closer to the bar and tighter into the gaggle of people, blocking her slick new friend from getting closer.

He elbowed the girl next to her and scooched in. "What he don't know won't hurt him."

That breath was on her face again.

"I have mace and I'm not afraid to use it." Not exactly a lie. She had mace. It was in her purse. At home. But she'd gladly fight traffic to go get the darn thing and return to use it on this guy.

"Bitch." He turned to the woman he'd elbowed. "Hey, baby. Can I buy you a drink?" Roxy moved to the bar. "Can I get two white wine spritzers?"

The woman behind the bar grabbed two glasses and poured the white wine and sparkling water, adding a bit of lemon peel and a cherry to both drinks. "Thirty dollars."

Roxy paid for the drinks—almost crying since she could buy a few bottles of wine for thirty dollars instead of two half-filled glasses of frou-frou. She removed the lemon peel—yuck—and took a sip. This thing was pretty darn tasty. This wasn't the liter-jug wine she kept on hand when she was channeling Sex in the City.

Sarina parted the crowd like a Kardashian. "Let's go." She snatched the drink from Roxy's hand and downed the contents. "I'm ready to go."

Roxy jogged after Sarina toward the front entrance,

trying to keep the expensive, delicious drink she was carrying from taking a header onto the dance floor. If ever she wished for a beverage doggie bag, it was definitely right now.

They made their way out of the dark club and into the atrium. People sat around, milling and talking. Roxy took a sip from her glass. Still tasty. "What was that all about?"

"Cliff is a—a jerk," Sarina spat.

"What happened? Drugs?"

"I wish. Blow job."

"Getting or giving?" Both options were bad when talking about one's boyfriend.

Sarina laughed and then hiccuped. She'd be crying soon. Poor girl. "I suppose things could be worse. He was getting it from some skank."

Skank? That was the equivalent to swearing in Sarina's world. She must be mad.

"I'm so sorry, sweetie." Roxy wrapped an arm around her best friend just as Cliff yelled for Sarina from the door to the club.

Fire burned in Sarina's eyes as she turned to face him. "Go away."

"Wait. Give me a chance to explain." His blond hair recently finger-combed. His boyish good looks marred by the concern on his face. That was what happened when you let a skank run their fingers through your hair. Definitely a "The More You Know" moment.

Sarina crossed her arms. "I don't want to hear it."

Was there really a plausible explanation for why another woman's mouth was on your man's junk? *She had a tickle in her throat, and I was scratching it. My lungs collapsed, and she was trying to blow them back up.* Hopefully, he wasn't dumb enough to try that one.

"I was confused. I thought it was you." He should have gone with the collapsed lung. Idiot.

"Just go. Please." Sarina's voice was flat with resignation. The please was a nice touch. Always polite. Well, at least Sarina was.

Roxy? Not so much. "Why don't you take your crab-infested slut stick far, far away?" Roxy stood in front of Sarina. He would get access to her best friend when Roxy's hands were cold and lifeless. "Go home. Take a few rounds of antibiotics and clear up whatever you just contracted."

"We're done." Sarina leaned over Roxy and took the spritzer before gulping it down. "That's really tasty."

Cliff slunk away, his head down, his shame following him like slug slime. Roxy would feel bad for him but... Nah. Her best friend had just downed two fifteen-dollar spritzers like a shot of cheap bourbon, and their very public, very loud production seemed to be entertaining the gawking guests.

"We should go." Roxy glared at the spectators.

"No. I can't leave Doug, and Cliff will not ruin my

job." Sabrina's lip pushed out and she looked about ready to cry.

"Fine." Roxy couldn't say no, not to her best friend, not after everything that happened with Cliff. She moved toward the club, but a red tuft of hair stopped her. The leprechaun, Donnie Dunne, sat on one of the couches. He wasn't wearing green, so his leprechaun power was diminished.

Roxy pulled Sarina back a few feet and whispered, "That's him."

"Who?"

"Donnie Dunne. My summons." Roxy tried not to watch him too closely. She had to play it cool. If he knew she was looking for him, he'd run—and she'd finally tracked him down. She wasn't losing him now. "Can you get the summons from my car?"

"Now?" Sarina flinched, but she knew the timeline. "Can't you go?"

"I'm not letting him out of my sight." Roxy was inches away from sitting on his lap to keep him in place. There was no way she could leave him here alone.

"I'll go, but then you owe me a drink."

"I bought the last drink."

Sarina tilted her head and stared. Delivering this summons was well worth the fifteen bucks plus tip.

"Fine." Roxy handed over her keys and leaned against another set of couches.

Sarina disappeared as Roxy pretend-studied her nails instead of outright staring at Donnie.

"Find something interesting, Horne?"

She jumped at a man's familiar voice. Rafe. "Are you stalking me?"

"I was going to ask you the same thing. You've showed up at my hotels twice in the same day."

"You work for this one too?"

"I work for a lot of hotels. Crowd control, defensive tactics, training, keeping people safe. What are you doing here?"

"Club."

His eyes drifted up and down her body, making her pulse throb—other body parts were throbbing too—from one look. To be fair, that one look could start forest fires. "You're wasting that outfit on the morons in there?"

"Do you have a better place for me to wear this?"

"I can come up with a few." He rubbed his thumb along his lower lip and smiled.

Holy crap. Where did men learn to do that? That smoldering grin combined with big manly hands...dead. She was going to drop right here.

"Are you alone?" he asked.

"No. My friend is with me." The friend who was grabbing the summons. The summons Rafe said she wasn't allowed to serve. "So, I'll see you later." She looked over at the flapping red hair as Donnie stood.

Rafe shook his head. "Stay away from him."

Her discretion must have been on the fritz. "From who?" She tried to play dumb, batting her eyelashes. It rarely worked on cops trying to give her a ticket. It wasn't working here.

"Dunne. He's a customer of this hotel. You can't go near him."

"I wouldn't dream of it." She motioned to her clothing. "Do I look like I'm dressed to chase after some guy? My friend and I came here to dance."

Sarina stumbled into the atrium, her breath stuttering. She must have run. In heels. A for effort. "Do you know how far the parking garage is—"

"Sarina." Roxy cut her off before she could say something that would get them in trouble, or worse, thrown out of the hotel. Sarina wasn't holding an envelope, which didn't bode well. If Roxy accidentally left the paperwork at home, she'd lose her shit. "Do you remember Rafe Amato? He was the quarterback at Vegas University."

Vegas rich kids didn't associate with public school riffraff unless said riffraff were part of the popular crowd. Roxy and Sarina were so far removed from the popular crowd, they were their own crowd.

That didn't stop them from showing up at a party at Rafe's house one night sophomore year. It wasn't the first time Roxy had seen Rafe, but it was the last time she tried to get noticed. When you hear a guy actively disavowing a relationship with you after you've spent the night together, you tend to lose interest.

Sarina must have forgotten the history. The drool practically hung from her open mouth.

"Nice to meet you." Rafe went to shake her hand, but her arm didn't move.

Sarina still had that stunned look on her face and then she lifted her hand. "You brought me a beer."

"What?"

"At that party." Sarina's mouth had somehow found a way to close and the drool appeared to be gone.

"That was the party after we beat Colorado College." He obviously remembered.

She was surprised. It was the night they'd met. One of the few times their social circles had happened to cross. The fact he remembered that night said something. She wasn't quite sure what it said... Sarina had talked Roxy into going to that party on a fact-finding mission. Long story that led to Sarina getting suspended. It was also the party that led to Rafe and years of unrequited-lust-slash-disgust. Not that she wanted to think about any of this right now.

"And you scored the winning touchdown," Sarina said, still looking stunned.

"Well, this has been fun, but we should run to the bathroom and head back to the club." Roxy looped her arm through Sarina's and dragged her toward the women's washroom. Rafe stood in the center of the room with his arms folded.

Roxy saw the little leprechaun slink from the couches toward the washrooms. Except instead of turning into the opening, he went to the elevators.

Bingo.

With one final wave, she tugged Sarina into the little recess near the women's washroom door. Roxy shifted far enough so Rafe couldn't see her.

"What are we doing?" Sarina asked.

"Rafe said we couldn't serve the papers in the hotel. We can't let him see us." Roxy watched as Donnie pressed the up button and got inside the elevator. The lighted numbers stopped at the forty-fourth floor. "Do you have the summons?"

"It's in my bra with my phone." Sarina slid a folded envelope from her chest-purse.

Roxy crooked her head around the wall to see if Rafe was still there. He was. Thankfully, he was talking to another employee and didn't appear to see her head pop out. She needed to lose her tail. "We'll head over to the club and then, once we lose Rafe, we're going to find Donnie's room."

"Do we have to lose Rafe?" Sarina pouted. "He's cute and I've had a bad day. I can watch you flirt."

"He's stopping me from getting my man. So, yeah, we need to lose him. Ready?"

"Yeah." Sarina stepped out of the doorway. "But I

don't see why you don't want that man. Is it the thing in college?"

Of course it was. "No. I'd forgotten we even knew him in college. It's because that man's questionable stance on process-serving in his hotels doesn't mesh with me keeping my job."

Her gaze found Rafe as they headed for the club. His arms were still crossed over his broad chest. The arrogance on his face should have been a turn off, but he still looked pretty darn edible. But that could be because his arrogance was completely misplaced. He thought he'd won.

Silly man.

"Sarina." He tipped his head as they passed him. "See you around, Horne."

"You too, Amato."

They clicked-clacked along the marble floor, and Sarina grinned like a teenager with a fake ID. "Let's grab another drink while we wait."

Roxy checked. Rafe still stood there. It might be awhile before she could get upstairs.

"Yeah. Let's get a drink."

CHAPTER 4

THREE DRINKS, two hours, and one indecent proposal later, Roxy felt pretty good. Did she mention the three drinks? She came off the dance floor looking for more refreshments, but she also needed to find Sarina—who'd been lost somewhere during the switchover from spritzers to vodka neat.

Finding Sarina wouldn't be easy. She ran errands for the DJ, and kept things going, so he could focus on the music. Which was awesome. The club was hopping. The dance floor a bunch of gyrating sardines. Even the VIP area was packed. There were rumors of a Kardashian sighting. There were also rumors a big light show would be starting up soon.

Not that any of that mattered. Roxy still had a summons to deliver. At this rate, she'd be too drunk to deliver it.

She used an empty chair as a step-stool and looked

over the gyrating bodies. How hard could it be to find a five-foot-six blond in a sea of darkness? Evidently, pretty darn hard. Roxy spun around and angled her hand above her eyes. Everyone else did that when they tried to see far away. Maybe it would help.

It didn't.

She jumped down and stumbled back, hitting someone. "I'm so sorry," she yelled as she turned.

Sarina.

Who held her hands up, steadying Roxy. "Whoa. I found you. We should run up and deliver that summons before you're too drunk to walk."

They should. But something about the look on Sarina's face said she might need a few more drinks. Either it was remnants of the Cliff situation or work was stressful. It could go either way. "We should get another drink," Roxy said.

Sarina smiled. "One more..."

The music stopped as flashing lights splashed across the ceiling. "Welcome to the Imprint Hotel," a disembodied voice boomed at the same time a waterfall of glittering sparks spilled down the side of the stage. "Are you ready?" The crowd's response echoed off the walls, and people surged forward to see the faux fireworks.

Roxy tugged Sarina off to the side to keep from being shoved. There was a weird *zzzt* right behind them, and the fireworks cut off—replaced by a puff of smoke that didn't look like part of the show. Something crackled and white sparks flew up from the power supply, right toward the curtains on the side of the stage. Then all the lights went out.

All noise stopped. Blackness cloaked the room. People gasped. Sarina crushed the feeling out of Roxy's hand.

"I'm here." Roxy squeezed her hand. Ever since Sarina's brother locked her in the closet when she was six, she'd been afraid of the dark. Roxy wasn't a fan, either. Especially with the frantic voices and the anxiety amping up the heat in the room.

"Everyone remain calm," someone said from over by the bar area. Red lights popped and sputtered along the floor. "Please follow the lights to the exits in an orderly fashion."

People didn't do either of those things. Which wasn't much of a surprise. Everyone screamed and stampeded toward the doors along the front and back walls of the club.

Roxy pulled on Sarina's hand. "We have to get out of here."

The two of them followed the crowd out the front door and into the parking lot. People stood around, watching as firetruck after firetruck sped up to the building. Ten minutes later, the lights in the bottom half of the hotel flickered back on. Thirty minutes later, the firemen exited the building. The people from the club peeled off, heading to cars. Roxy surveilled the group of spectators, looking for Donnie.

No Donnie. Just the bartender who served her earlier.

"Hey." Roxy walked over to the bartender. "That was insane. Are the hotel guests outside, too?"

"Nah, they didn't evacuate the hotel rooms. Just the main floor."

Which explained why she couldn't find Double D.

"Can we go home?" Sarina asked, rubbing her bare arms and shivering. It was a little cold.

"Why don't you go wait in the car?" Roxy suggested.

"Are you going in the hotel?"

"I have to deliver this."

"Fine." Sarina pouted. "But I want pancakes."

"After we deliver this, you can have all the pancakes you want."

"Promise?"

"Cross my heart."

A man in a black suit whistled to get everyone's attention. There were still at least a hundred people milling around. "We're closing down the club for the night," black suit guy announced. "We're sorry for any inconvenience. For those staying at the hotel, we'll start letting everyone in."

Groans echoed between the cars as clubbers must have realized they didn't have to go home, but they couldn't stay here.

"Time to party!" a group of girls squealed next to Sarina. A bridal party, if the eighties outfits and sashes were to be believed.

"Oh, crap. You got your key? I gots no key." A woman with a gold tiara and a sash that read Bride slapped at the spandex on her legs. She giggled and then yelled, "I'm getting married." Apparently, she only spoke English when talking about her wedding. Otherwise, her sentence structure was lacking.

Sarina leaned in. "Do you see Rafe?"

"No." Roxy stepped up on a planter and watched as people filed into the hotel, security holding the doors open. The employees checked that each person held a room key. Roxy focused on the bridal party. Half the women had key cards. Ergo, Sarina and Roxy needed to be in that half.

"Excuse me." Roxy stumbled into the bride. "You're getting married!"

A chorus of screams and woots filled the air as her posse followed behind. Their plastic hats and lei's whipped over their heads. "Let's go up to the room and party!"

"Party!"

"Time for shots!"

"Sarina, follow me. Stay with the group." Roxy turned to one of the bridesmaids. At least, that was what her sash said. "Can I try your hat?"

"My hat?" She shrugged. "Sure."

Roxy put on the hat and ducked as she ran with the bubbly bridesmaids. The women bounced and screamed like cheerleaders at nationals. Roxy didn't bounce or scream or bubble. She improvised. She raised her hands, yelling sporadically about weddings, marriage, and the occasional ode to booze.

The security personnel at the door waved them all in. "Make good choices, ladies."

Roxy, Sarina, and the gaggle made it across the atrium and stood at the elevators. A man in the center of the room directed traffic. Rafe. His gaze moved to the wedding party. Roxy swore he could see her. She waited for him to stomp toward her, but he just kept staring until a man in a suit grabbed his attention.

The elevator door swung open and the wedding party slipped inside. They hit the button for the thirty-fifth floor. She inched to the back of the elevator, pulling Sarina with her. When the women staggered out the door, Roxy and Sarina waited. The door shut before anyone seemed to notice they hadn't followed.

Roxy hit the button for forty-four. "They have cameras, so we'll have to be quick."

"What exactly are we doing?"

"We have to knock on doors."

Sarina looked at her like she was out of her mind. "Knock on doors? It's after one. People are probably sleeping."

"We'll be fast. It's Vegas. No one comes to Vegas to sleep."

The elevator doors opened onto a small vestibule with a mirror and a walnut side table. All was quiet, except for the hum of a soda machine and the clink of cubes from the ice machine. Hallways—multiple—branched out to the right, left, and center.

Sarina voiced Roxy's next question. "Which way do we start?"

"I don't know." Roxy pointed to the various hallways. "Eenie meanie minee moe?"

"Really?"

There had to be a more scientific way to get this done, but Roxy couldn't think of one. She blamed the vodka. No one stood in the halls. No open doors. "Do you have a better idea?"

"No. But do it quick." Sarina rubbed her hands over her arms. "I'm tired."

Roxy's finger bounced as she mumbled and counted out the rhyme, landing on the hallway to their right. "That one."

"Fine. Let's go."

Roxy knocked on the first door. "Let's split up. Can you take the evens?"

"Sure." Sabrina knocked on the second door. "What does this guy even look like?"

No answer at the door. Roxy approached the next door. "Five-five. Red flyaway hair. Pale."

"Paler than you?" Sarina laughed as she retreated from her first unanswered door.

Roxy knocked on the next one. "Funny."

The door flung open. "What?" A woman in a floral muumuu hovered in the opening, hair sticking up in peaks. Her eyes were heavy lidded. And glaring.

Roxy's mouth dried. She probably should have had a plan—what to say, what to do. But instead, she stood in front of this poor woman, who was half asleep. *Think, Roxy. Think.* Why would she be knocking on random strangers' doors? "I'm looking for my father, Donnie."

The woman glared.

"Smallish man, red hair."

"Do I look like your father?"

"No, ma'am?" The door slammed in Roxy's face. This was going well. In all the mayhem of muumuu lady, she hadn't noticed another door was open.

"We're looking for her father, Donnie. Have you seen him?" Sarina stole Roxy's excuse. Although, it was probably good that they had the same story.

"No, man." A guy with a Black Sabbath T-shirt and boxers leaned against the door jam. Skunky smoke billowed out of the room as someone called out, "You girls wanna party?"

"Sorry." Roxy pulled Sarina back from the door opening. "We need to find my dad."

"Oh, yeah. That sucks." Stoner shook his head. "Good luck, man."

"Thanks."

They knocked on the next set of doors. Nothing. They were halfway down the hall, and Roxy slapped her palm on the door. What? Her knuckles felt like she'd just left fight club.

The door popped open. "It's after one o'clock. The building better be on fire." An elderly man in button-down pajamas blinked. His white handle-bar mustache swished as his nostrils flared.

"I'm looking for my father?"

"So you knock on random doors. What's wrong with you?"

Roxy backed up. She wasn't sure his question was meant to be answered. Because if she answered what was wrong with her, they could be here for a while. Instead of jumping on his couch and revealing her darkest secrets, she said, "I got the room number wrong. I'm so sorry, sir."

Which could be true. He was freaking out about a wrong knock, but she could be genuinely lost. He didn't know. "You're sorry? Pfft. You young people have no concept of common decency. Too busy playing on your phones." He sighed.

"We're so sorry..." Sarina put her hand on Roxy's arm —in comfort or to pull her away, Roxy wasn't sure.

"Another one? What is wrong with you two?" Again rhetorical.

"We didn't mean..."

"I need my sleep. I'm calling security." He slammed

the door as Roxy and Sarina begged him, "Please don't." But the door was shut, and his bushy lip was probably yelling into the house phone as they stood there.

"We have maybe five minutes." Roxy knocked on the next two doors. "Go two at a time."

Sarina nodded and ran down to the next set of doors. Nothing.

Roxy approached the next set and realized a sliver of light glowed along the edge of the door. "Sarina, this one is open." She knocked. No one answered. "Should we go in?"

Sarina moved to the next door. "Just check. I'll knock on this one."

"Fine." Roxy nudged the door and it opened with a creak. The lights were on. "Hello?" She stepped inside.

The room was huge. A large foyer led to a living area, where the TV on the wall played music videos with the sound muted. An L-shaped red couch, bigger than Roxy's entire living room, sat in the center. On the coffee table were two champagne flutes, filled half-way. An open bottle of Dom Perignon chilled in a silver ice bucket. Someone had to be here.

"Anyone home?"

No answer. To the right was a door to another room, probably a bedroom. To her left was a kitchenette with... Holy crap. There were round trays with enough sugary pastries to put a toddler into diabetic shock. In the center of one tray was a giant cake covered in strawberries. The first tier had been cut, revealing bright pink cake.

She loved strawberry cake, but it was rude to take cake, right? Individual pastries were fair game, though. She picked up a brownie square. The white chocolate circle propped on top had a weird crest painted on it. Roxy took a bite. Heaven. Maybe she should try a bit of the strawberry cake—soak up all the booze in her system. *Yeah, that's why.*

"Any luck?"

Roxy heard Sarina's voice before she saw her. And she felt like she was caught with her hand in the cookie jar—or pastry plate, as it were. She walked around the counter and across the room to the couch. Gauzy pink material hung on the red armrest. Maybe he threw a party and they all got stuck on the roof. Sometimes even locals couldn't handle their Vegas.

She turned toward the door of the bedroom and peered inside. "Hello?"

Quiet. She slid her hand along the wall next to the door and found a switch. With a flick, light flooded the room. A large king-size bed stood against the far wall. Emptiness and quiet. She went to flip off the light, and paused.

There was nothing in the room... until there was.

A bare foot angled around the edge of the far side of the bed. Or maybe not. Maybe it was flesh-colored clothes. She inched closer.

Please be flesh-colored clothes. Please be flesh-colored clothes. Or towels.

"Hello?" She asked the ... the sweatshirt?

But it wasn't a sweatshirt. Her vision went black as her heart raced.

Red liquid splattered along the side of the bed. Before she could tell her feet to stop, they carried her around the bed. A scene from *A Nightmare on Elm Street* played out on the floor. Donnie's red hair was caked in blood. His eyes wide. Red pooled on his shirt and had seeped into the carpet. Her feet reversed direction, trying to get away before whatever was on the ground jumped onto her. A good plan, except she hadn't counted on the bedspread wrapping around her legs like a polyester kraken. Flailing her arms did not help as her ass hit the floor with a splat.

Blood coated her hands. Her dress was soaking in a pool of Donnie's life force. There was a scream. Apparently, it was her. The brownie in her belly was on the verge of full-fledged mutiny.

"What's going on... Oh my God," Sarina said from behind her, followed by an ominous thud.

Roxy scrambled back, her bloody hands smearing on the rug. Not her blood. Donnie's. All. Over. Her. A gag stuck in her throat. She'd never seen a dead body, let alone swam in one.

Oh, she was going to hurl.

"Security!" A man in a suit slammed the door open,

gun drawn. Another man in a suit followed behind. The first suit was Rafe. Thank goodness. She wanted to jump into his arms and climb him like a howler monkey. He could carry her away and she could pretend the past few minutes didn't happen.

Rafe kept his back against the wall as he slid toward Roxy.

"He's here." Roxy raised her hands into the air and pointed a finger at the bed.

Other suit guy moved to the bathroom and flipped on the light. "Clear."

Rafe made his way into the room and opened the closet. He swiveled toward the room. "Clear." He holstered his weapon, stepped over Sarina, and avoided the blood. He put two fingers on Donnie's throat.

"Is he..." The wobble in her voice went all the way to her toes. She couldn't bring herself to finish that question.

"Yeah." Rafe nodded, unclipping the walkie talkie at his hip. He clicked it and said, "Amato here. We need the police and an ambulance in room 4428." He leaned over Sarina and felt her pulse. "What happened here?"

"She fainted."

"And you?" He ran a hand down Roxy's arm as his eyes travelled up her body. No leering, just concern. "Are you okay?"

She wanted to say yes, nod her head and pretend this wasn't the most horrifying thing she ever saw. But her head wouldn't lie, and the tears poking at the back of her eyes wouldn't stop.

He must have understood her inaction. His arm snaked around the back of her body. "It'll be okay."

He was warm, and big, and strong. She almost felt like she was safe. Almost. She laid her head on his chest. His heart was steady. Hers pounded a heavy metal song. His hands were sure. She could feel their strength on her back. She shook like a tweaking meth addict. "We found him like that," she told him.

"Shh. It's okay." His lips lingered at the top of her head, his breath along her hairline anchoring her. "We'll talk later. Just relax."

"What happened?" Sarina propped herself up on her elbows and dropped back down. Thank goodness. She didn't need to see any of this again.

"Stay there," Roxy said, pulling away, but Rafe held on tight.

"I'm not going anywhere. I'm dizzy." Sarina's hand flopped onto her face.

"Sir, the cops are in the lobby. They'll be here in three." Another suit guy stood in the doorway. He might have been there the whole time.

Rafe pulled back but kept his hands on her arms. Maybe he was afraid she'd float away.

Or maybe that was her.

"Let's go wait outside," he said.

There was nothing more she wanted than to get out

of that room—away from the man staring with dead eyes. But she couldn't leave. "Sarina needs help getting up."

"The EMTs will be here in a minute."

"I can't leave her here." Roxy's best friend might not be covered in blood, but Donnie sure was—and so was Roxy— dammit. Sarina needed to get out of the room without seeing Donnie, or she might go down again.

Rafe looked at Roxy like he wanted to argue. But instead, he nodded at the security guard at the door. "Can you let Roxy in to 4430 and prop the door open?" Rafe rested his hand on her back and guided her toward the door.

She stood by the guard and watched Rafe rescue Sarina. He slipped his arms under her shoulders and knees and lifted her. Careful not to hit her head on any walls or door frames, he carried her out of the room down to room 4430. He laid her on one of the beds. Gently. It was super-sweet and super-hot.

"I have to meet the police." Rafe straightened and turned to Roxy, sliding a hand along Roxy's cheek. It was strong and warm. She wanted to lean into his hand like he was a homing beacon. "Are you going to be okay?" he asked.

She nodded. It was the most logical thing to do. She didn't feel okay, but he didn't need to know. From experience, she knew she'd be fine, eventually. Although her experience never included a dead body before.

"I'll be right across the hall if you need me." His hand

hadn't moved as it softly held her head in an upright position. He was close. Too darn close. He wet his lips, and her body seemed to forget that her best friend was on the bed and a dead guy was in the next room.

She kept her eyes on his—eyes that were hooded, hazy, like any minute he would kiss her until the whole night just disappeared. It almost looked like he didn't want to leave her.

Join the club.

He shook his head and the haze parted. "I have to deal with this." He went to the open door and turned. He was such a nice guy. "If I tell you to stay, will you listen this time?"

This time? Had to get in that jab, didn't he? Good thing he left. She had so many responses to that comment. So many. Good ones, too. But she had a best friend that needed her.

Roxy sat on the bed and ran a hand over Sarina's arm before taking her hand. "Sarina, honey, are you okay?"

Sarina tilted her head to the side, squinting a little. "He carried me in here."

"He did." She squeezed Sarina's hand.

"I think I'm in lust with those arms." Sarina's lips tipped up at the edges.

Roxy could understand. "I want to cut off those arms and dip them in gold."

"Are you Roxy?" A woman carrying a giant bag with a medical symbol stood at the door. She looked hesitant to walk in. Her eyes kept snapping back and forth between Roxy and Sarina.

"Yes."

"Did you hit your head?" She approached Roxy, staring into her eyes in a "have you lost your mind" kind of way. Or maybe she was just checking for a concussion.

"I'm fine."

"I should probably check you out." The EMT stepped over near the bed, but her eyes were on Roxy—namely the blood on Roxy's hands.

She'd forgotten about all the blood. "It's not mine. I slipped and fell near the victim." Roxy rubbed her red hands down the side of her skirt. It was a lost cause—dried and crusting. Her skirt, however, was wet and sticky. Roxy didn't want to look. "My friend on the bed passed out and fell."

The EMT hesitated before sitting on the bed and opening her bag. "Do you remember what happened?" The EMT shone a light in Sarina's eyes and checked the back of her head.

It was easy to see the moment Sarina remembered. "Dead guy?"

"Yeah." Just thinking about him made her stomach clench.

Sarina must have gotten a good look at Roxy, because her skin turned a Lady Liberty shade of green.

"How does your head feel?" The EMT was still all business, pushing aside blond hair.

"Fine." Sarina started to get up as the EMT pulled away.

"Go slow." The EMT turned to Roxy. "Are you able to make sure she gets home?"

"Yes."

"She doesn't appear to have a bump, but she shouldn't drive and needs to be watched for the next twenty-four hours to make sure symptoms don't pop up. Confusion. Headache. Vomiting. Mood changes."

"I can do that."

"I'm fine." Sarina stood. No wobbling or tripping.

"I'll keep an eye on her." Roxy nodded to the EMT as a cop entered the room. Detective most likely. White shirt, dark jeans and a badge at his hip. Kind of like the clothes MacAuley MacAuley had on earlier today, but this guy was black, with a buzz cut and fade.

"Do you have a minute for some questions?" He had a deep tenor that made her insides go gooey.

Until she heard the next voice.

"Roxy Horne. Twice in one day." As if he was conjured up just by thinking of him. Detective MacAuley walked in right after the sexy baritone.

Rafe followed.

"You know each other?" The scowl on Rafe's face told her the next half hour would be interesting.

And by interesting, she meant worse than a clown popping balloons while feeding her lime wedges.

CHAPTER 5

ROXY NEVER THOUGHT she'd be part of a murder investigation. At least, she thought it was murder. With all the blood... She shook her head. She didn't want to think about that. She had bigger issues. Like Rafe looking at her as if she kicked his puppy.

"You two know each other?" Rafe's large, defined arms were crossed over his chest. At some point, he'd lost the suit coat and was sporting a white button down, with the sleeves rolled up to the elbows. It was like arm porn—complete with bulging muscles.

MacAuley's lips curved into the barest of smiles before tilting back down. "We met today."

"There was a whole thing with a servee throwing cacti at my car." She sighed and sat on the bed. She never thought she'd wish the worst thing a servee would do was throw pottery at her car.

"I'm Detective Geary." Baritone motioned to Sarina, then Roxy. "Can I get your names?"

"Roxanna Horne."

"I'm Sarina West."

"So, let's start at the beginning." Geary wrote on a little pad of paper. "What were you doing at the hotel tonight?"

"I was working the opening of the club downstairs." Sarina looked tired. But after all that happened tonight and the whole passing out thing, she should be.

"Then how did you get up here?" MacAuley didn't have a pen and paper, but Roxy had the feeling he was remembering everything.

"We saw Donnie Dunne in the lobby." Roxy said, and avoided meeting Rafe's stare. "I needed to serve him a summons, so we followed him up to the forty-fourth floor."

"You followed him up?"

"Well, not really followed. We watched him push the button for the forty-fourth floor and then went back to the club."

"Why did you go back to the club?" Geary's pen hovered over paper.

"Because we were told we weren't allowed to follow him."

"By whom?"

"Mr. Amato," Roxy said.

"It's against hotel policy for anyone to harass or intimidate my guests." Rafe's arms were still crossed in angry-man fashion.

"I didn't harass anyone." Roxy felt the pout grow on her lips. She wasn't harassing.

A loud *hmm* came from the wall where Rafe stood. "Well, you're not intimidating."

Like those were the only two options. She could think of lots of perfectly lovely things to call herself. Just not right now, with the cops hovering.

"How long did you stay in the club?" Geary asked.

"Thirty minutes or so."

"Then what?"

"Then Sarina and I came up to the forty-fourth floor and knocked on doors, looking for Double... Donnie." Since the poor guy was now gone, she should probably stop calling him Double D or the leprechaun. Respect for the deceased and all. "We noticed the door was open."

"We?"

"I noticed it. It was on my side of the hall. I volunteered to go in so Sarina could keep knocking. We didn't have time to stop because one of the hotel guests threatened to call security."

"How long were you in there alone?"

"A few minutes?"

"What were you doing for those minutes?" Rafe's shoulders bunched and he looked like all the scary.

"I walked into the room and no one was there, and there was all this food just sitting on the counter. I love strawberry cake, but I didn't want to cut someone's cake because that's just rude. But there were brownies."

"You stopped to eat?" Now MacAuley was looking at her like all the crazy.

"No." She so was not coming out of this story looking normal. "Okay, fine. I ate a brownie. I didn't know there was anyone in there. No one answered."

"He was dead." Geary's face had gone from chick-be-crazy to chick-be-guilty. The judgement in his eyes was obvious.

"I know that now," Roxy protested, waving a hand. A bloody hand, Not a good idea. "I didn't know it then. I didn't do this. You know that, right?"

Geary didn't answer, just repeated, "So, you were alone with the body for a few minutes."

"It might have been less. I don't know. Can't you check the video tapes?"

"What video tapes?" Rafe sighed. "We don't record in the rooms. That would be illegal."

MacAuley didn't seem to have judgey eyes for her, but the way he looked at Rafe said there might be a story there. "After the brownie, what happened?"

"Sarina came in and passed out. Then Rafe, I mean Mr. Amato, ran in and found us."

"How long after Ms. West came in did Mr. Amato and his team arrive?"

"Seconds. It was right away."

"We had multiple complaints of someone knocking on doors." Rafe glared at Roxy.

Like it was her fault all this happened and like there were multiple people complaining. "Multiple? Only one guy said he'd call."

Rafe shook his head. "Not everyone opened their door."

"Why not?" She'd said she was looking for her dad. What if it had been an emergency? Well, what if she'd actually been looking for him and there had been an emergency? They didn't know she was lying. Yet they ignored her knock.

"Probably because a crazy woman was knocking on their door at one AM." MacAuley smiled. It would have been adorable if he wasn't calling her crazy.

"Then what?" Detective Geary asked.

"Rafe told other suit guy to call the police and they moved us to this room."

"Why?"

Roxy got that all information could be important, but this was ridiculous. Who cared what happened after she found him? "The cops were here."

"You saw the cops?"

"No, suit guy said they were here."

"Suit guy?" MacAuley looked at Rafe.

"Gabe Martin," Rafe explained.

"I think we have everything. If you can think of any

more details, please call me." MacAuley handed Roxy his card. "Don't leave town."

"Am I a suspect?"

"Everyone is until we get some answers." Geary stuck his notebook into his pocket. "I'm going to check on the M.E."

MacAuley watched his partner leave. Then he turned to Roxy. "Are you okay?"

"I've been better."

"Two incidents in one day."

"I have a gift." Roxy rotated her neck as exhaustion slipped through her entire body. "I'd be happy to give it back."

"Are you done, MacAuley?" Rafe growled. "She needs to go home."

MacAuley's attention switched from Roxy to Rafe. "You're not leaving, Amato."

"Wouldn't dream of it." Rafe still leaned against the wall, his arms still crossed. His hands must be numb by now.

"Do you need a ride?" MacAuley reached out a hand and helped Roxy stand. So chivalrous. Too bad Rafe looked about ready to take his hand off. MacAuley, naturally, found it amusing, if she read the smirk on his face right.

If they whipped it out and started measuring, she was so out of here. "I have my car."

"Are you sober enough to drive?" Rafe's scowl hadn't moved.

It had been a few hours since her last drink. Something about death sobered a girl right up. "Yes. I haven't had a drink since the club. And I ate."

MacAuley lips quirked up. "A brownie?"

"It was really good. You should try one."

"No thanks." MacAuley gave one of his full-fledged smiles. Nummy.

Nummy? Okay maybe she was little bit tipsy yet. But the room was filled with so much testosterone, she could feel it in her ovaries. Her ovaries? Definitely tipsy. Thank goodness the hotel had a great hamburger joint.

"I'll walk you to your car." MacAuley waved toward the door.

"Not necessary. I've got it covered." Amato pulled away from the wall.

She avoided them both. It was almost cute watching two men act like Neanderthals. Although, it usually ended with the girl getting clubbed and being dragged by their hair. Her roots didn't need that.

"It's been fun, but we're not leaving quite yet." Roxy swept past the two men and stopped at the door.

"We're not?" Sarina bumped into Roxy, who grabbed at the edge of the door to keep from falling.

She almost forgot Sarina was there, what with all the testosterone flying around. Or it could still be a remnant of the vodka. "No, I need a burger."

"Yes." Sarina practically licked her lips. She'd been unusually quiet. "And maybe a drink."

Rafe wrapped his arm around Roxy's shoulders and led her out into the hall. He pulled out a business card with one hand. "Give this to the front desk. They'll set you up with a room and something to eat."

She flipped the card over in her hand. It wasn't a free room ticket or anything with the Imprint logo. It was a business card with Rafe's name and a local Vegas number. That was it. "Why would they believe me?"

"They will."

"Are you sure? Have you done it before?"

"Yes."

Why would he give out cards? Then it hit her like a ton of erotic books. "You give these to the women you sleep with, don't you? Like 'sorry the sex was mediocre, but here are some pancakes to make up for it'. The least you can do is give them a coupon for Hash House A Go Go. Give a good meal. Although the room is a nice touch."

MacAuley laughed out loud as he passed them and slipped into Donnie's room.

"I don't do mediocre. I don't give out cards to make up for anything." Rafe's lips were at her temple. His voice low. If it wasn't so charged with sexual energy, she would call it menacing. But as it was, it was hot. "I would do things with you that would make your eyes roll to the back of your head, while you scream for more."

Her body leaned into him. It wasn't her fault. It just kind of happened. She was melting into a pile of need and his body was right there to catch her.

Until he wasn't.

He stepped back. "Enjoy the room." Amato knew what he'd done. He knew he'd gotten her all hot and sweating. He knew walking away would leave her cold and fretting.

He did it on purpose, because he was sexy and mean and because he knew he could. He disappeared into Donnie's hotel room without looking back.

And she knew he didn't look back. She watched.

She couldn't even blame the alcohol on that bad decision.

CHAPTER 6

ROXY'S EYES closed as Rafe ran his hand along the front of her body.

"I want you." His voice was heavy with need. His hands were demanding.

Her eyes rolled to the back of her head as a loud chirp pierced through the sexy haze.

"Do you want brownies?" MacAuley stood over the bed.

"No." She wanted to say yes, but Rafe's hand was roaming along her body, and she had a feeling he'd stop if she started eating MacAuley's brownies.

Another chirp, but it somehow sounded closer. Her phone.

She felt the arm before she heard the snores. A snore that blew at the side of her face. Last night pieced together in her mind. Clubbing. Sneaking. Finding a body. Questioning. After the police-party, they'd gone to the front desk and checked in. Apparently, Rafe's card worked at securing a bed for the night. Then she'd cleaned herself up while Sarina bought her a new outfit with the hotel insignia. They'd grabbed a burger and pancakes before coming up to their room, where Roxy had checked on Sarina throughout the night to make sure she didn't have a concussion.

Well, Roxy had checked on her most of the night until Sarina threatened to knock Roxy in the head if she touched her one more time. The threat didn't really hold up, though. If Sarina gave Roxy a concussion, then Sarina would be up all night checking on Roxy.

The room was dark, except for the light sneaking through a crack where the curtains met the bottom of the windows. Not bright, just enough to see the blond hair covering Sarina's face ripple as she exhaled with the grace of a rhinoceros. Sarina's arm sat on Roxy's chest—but not in a front-facing spoon kind of way.

No. Sarina's arms were open wide like the Jesus statue in Brazil. She slept on her back, her hand resting on Roxy's boob, ready to fight-club the speed-bag.

Roxy edged the arm off her chest—stopping all breathing because that would apparently keep Sarina from waking up.

A gasp and a jump and Sarina opened her eyes. Scowled. "Where are we?"

"Hotel."

Sarina ran her tongue over her teeth and grimaced. "Did we knock on doors in the middle of the night?"

"We did."

"Did we actually see a dead guy?" Sarina's grimace deepened.

"We did."

"Darn. I was hoping that wasn't true."

"Sorry." Roxy yanked back the blankets. She'd stripped down to her new hotel-bought underthings when they'd come up to the room. If you had to do a walk of shame, you could at least be wrinkle free. "We should get dressed. We might have time to pick up breakfast before we head in to work."

"Oh, I want breakfast. I have the weirdest craving for pancakes."

"We had pancakes last night." Roxy's feet slogged across the plush carpet. She picked up her gift-shop clothing—an Impact T-shirt and Vegas sweatpants.

"One can never have too many pancakes." On that they could agree.

Dressed in her gift-shop haute couture, Roxy checked the mirror and cringed. The sweats actually sucked the sexy out of her body. With hair sticking up like she'd French-kissed a light socket and makeup running away from her eyes, she was past tough night and onto rode hard and put away wet. But she hadn't been ridden hard at all. One shouldn't look this bad without all the fun to get that way.

Roxy gave up and washed her face, shoved her wet fingers through her hair.

"We should have brought a change of clothes." Sarina said as she slipped her skin-tight dress back on. And because life wasn't fair, she was basically catwalk ready. Her hair was still blond, a little flat maybe, but her face didn't look like a knockoff Pollock painting.

Roxy frowned into the mirror. "To the club?"

"It's not such a weird thing. We could have gotten lucky and needed something to wear."

"Has that ever happened?" Roxy couldn't remember Sarina ever needing a change of clothes after a night at the club.

"No." Sarina stepped up to the mirror. "I'm a mess." She fluffed her flattened hair, getting a little bit of height, which gave it life.

"Sure you are." Roxy made one more try at smushing her bedhead into submission.

Sarina grabbed her purse. "Pancakes."

"Pancakes."

Twenty minutes later, Roxy sat across from Sarina in a black booth. Wood beams lined the ceiling, and black drapes with a gold design covered the windows.

Their server ambled over and set two golden plates on the table. Both covered with three giant pancakes.

Sarina's three giant pancakes had blueberries mounded in the center and dripping down the side.

Roxy dumped syrup over her equally huge three non-fruit-covered pancakes. If the pancake didn't float, there wasn't enough syrup.

"You shouldn't put that crap in your body." Sarina, the sugar hater, cut a piece of pancake and topped it with fruit.

"Are you sure there's not a recall on blueberries? I swear, I heard about a recall."

"That was strawberries." Sarina cut at the stack on her plate.

"You know what never has a recall? Syrup."

"Yes, but your food has no food. At least, throwing on some fruit gives you antioxidants and potassium." Sarina picked up one blueberry. She slipped the perfect bite past her lips. "Nummy."

Roxy cut her cakes with a fork and folded a bite in her mouth. "I'm on a high carb diet, focusing on the glucose group." At least, that was what she meant to say. It might have come out as "Armon ricar iet oh gon da guco goup."

Sarina shook her head and kept shoveling in her real-food. Not that Roxy was judging, her elbow was bending in double-time.

"It's good to see you haven't lost your appetite after last night." The voice was not only recognizable, she'd also heard it in her dream last night. It had been a great dream.

So great, Roxy could feel heat pool in her cheeks. She took a sip of coffee to hide her flaming face.

Rafe sank into the seat next to Roxy with a sigh. He wore the same suit pants and white button up shirt he'd worn last night, but the shirt was unbuttoned to the collar bone. His sleeves were pulled up to the forearm. He looked exhausted, but still edible.

A server hustled over—not their server. No. *Their* server was a fifty-year-old man with male-pattern baldness. This server was blond with brazen-patterned boldness. "Can I get you anything, Mr. Amato?"

"Coffee and oatmeal, Ashley."

She actually preened when he said her name, more than a cat who'd just caught the canary. "Be right back." She swished her hips.

Rafe was either too tired to notice or completely unimpressed. He sat back in the booth. "How did you sleep?"

"Fine, except someone kept waking me up." Sarina finished the last of the fruit, leaving most of the pancakes. Sacrilege. She pushed away the plate and tossed her napkin on top.

Couldn't even save them now, even if Roxy wanted to. "I slept fine, except for trying to check an ingrate for a concussion."

"The ingrate appears to be fine." Rafe gave a pathetic

excuse for a smile to the server as she set a cup of coffee on the table.

"She almost didn't make it through the night." *Without pictures on her face.* Roxy had been so close. So close to drawing a giant penis on her best friend's forehead. Thankfully, Roxy was too good a person for that. That was the story she was sticking to, anyway.

Rafe yawned and took a deep drink from the cup. The spark was gone from his eyes. He looked like he'd been up all night binge-watching *Game of Thrones*.

"Have you been up this whole time?" Roxy almost felt bad for the guy.

"Yeah. The cops just left." He ran a hand down his face as the server put his oatmeal in front of him.

"Cops are still here, Amato." MacAuley strolled across the restaurant looking like he'd spent the night binge-watching next to Rafe. "Mind if I sit?"

"Sure." Sarina pushed herself closer to the wall, letting MacAuley slide in.

The waitress miraculously reappeared, dimples popping for the detective. Given her tight blouse, it wasn't the only thing popping in her repertoire. MacAuley nodded to the brazen one. "Cup of coffee, please."

"Sure thing." The waitress wiggled as she disappeared. Where was the old-man waiter when you needed him?

"What are you still doing here?" Rafe ate his oatmeal. "Don't you have police work to do or something?"

"I'm done for the night. Or should I say morning? Don't you have a drunk to escort out of the building?"

The edge of Rafe's mouth tipped up. "They're all sleeping it off. Anyway, I'm too busy dealing with a murder on my property."

"Was it murder?" Was it wrong that Roxy found that exciting? She'd never been part of a real murder before. Which—come to think of it—was probably pretty normal.

MacAuley reached for the cup that the waitress put on the table. "I can't discuss an ongoing investigation."

"Especially with a suspect." Rafe motioned to Roxy, like she was the suspect.

Wait. "Am I the suspect? I thought Detective Geary was just trying to scare me."

"Cops don't go around scaring people. And I can't discuss the case." MacAuley glared at Rafe.

Roxy sighed. "What *can* you discuss?"

MacAuley sucked down a gulp from the cup. "The coffee here is fantastic."

"See." Rafe sat back, draping his arm on top of the booth behind her. "Being on Las Vegas PD means they tie your hands. You're under their control twenty-four seven."

"Is that why you left?" MacAuley leaned back. "I always thought you realized you couldn't cut it."

"See, MacAuley, that's your problem. You tried to think."

Really? They were back to the manhood measuring? Sarina and Roxy's eyes met as they both rolled them.

A hollow laugh spilled from MacAuley's mouth. "So, throwing away eleven years of experience and becoming a card-cop was you thinking? No wonder you avoid it so much."

Eleven years. She'd assumed they knew each other, being in the same department, but that was the exact number of years Rafe had been on the force.

"Is there something going on here? Do you two know each other?"

"We took the detective exam together." MacAuley grinned. "I was best man at his wedding."

Wedding? Roxy stared at his bare ring finger. "You're married?"

"My ex-friend was the best man at my wedding to my ex-wife." Rafe was now glaring at MacAuley, his fingers flexing.

So much to unpack here—and she hated that saying. Rafe and MacAuley had been best friends. Why did they stop? What happened? Rafe had had a wife. Did she leave him, or he her? How long were they together? What did she look like?

Was Roxy hotter? Not that it mattered, but a girl could wonder.

"I should get going. I need to sleep." MacAuley slid out of the booth.

Wait. She had questions. A lot of them.

He dropped a twenty on the table. "It was nice seeing you again, Sarina. Roxy." He acknowledged Rafe with a nod before leaving.

Rafe tipped the coffee cup back and rose. "I should go, too."

"You can't just drop all of that on me and leave. You were married?" Roxy put her hand on his arm. She'd physically hold him back if she could get answers.

"First? I didn't drop it on you, he did. Second? I don't want to talk about it." Rafe sat back down.

"But, who did you marry? What happened? Why aren't you and MacAuley friends anymore?"

"How about this?" Rafe sighed as he peered into the bottom of his empty coffee cup. He was either wishing there was more or wishing he could get swallowed up by the thing. Either way, his fidgeting and frown said he was uncomfortable. "We drop the questions about my life, and I'll tell you what I know about Donnie Dunne."

"Like why I'm a suspect?"

"That one's easy. You were in the room alone with him for an indeterminable amount of time and covered in his blood. In theory, you could've been the last one to see him alive."

In theory. Indeterminable. Like they couldn't determine what she'd been doing. But she'd told them. There were brownies. "But you know, *in reality*, I didn't do it. Right?"

"We're waiting on the forensics, but it looks like he was stabbed seventeen times."

"Seventeen?" Roxy thought about the night before. She hadn't noticed how many times he'd been stabbed. She'd just noticed the blood. "Seems like overkill. Pun intended."

"Or someone who was really ticked off. They're bringing in his wife for questioning, but no one saw her on the premises." Rafe ran hand over his face with a sigh. "That dammed club opening. I told them they needed cameras that backed up real-time. But that was too expensive. We'd have camera footage if the power surge hadn't happened." He shook his head, the dark around his eyes somehow darker.

"You should go home before you fall asleep at the wheel." Roxy had more questions, but she'd find a way to ask them later. When he was awake.

"Yeah." He stood and threw a twenty on the table. Apparently, that was the going rate for crashing a person's breakfast. "See you later."

"We should get to work." Roxy left the two twenties on the table and inched out of the booth. She wasn't jumping up and down about going in to work, but maybe serving a few summonses would keep her mind off the cluster she'd found herself in.

"So far, this is a great day." Sarina got up and smiled. "Free hotel room and a free breakfast."

Roxy would agree if she wasn't a suspect in a murder.

CHAPTER 7

ROXY AND SARINA walked through the front door of M&J Investigations and the normal buzz of the room disappeared. Roxy was having that effect lately.

Sarina stopped at the edge of her desk and whispered to Roxy, "Why is everyone looking at me?"

"I don't think they're looking at you. I think they're looking at the prime suspect in a murder investigation." Roxy felt the word prime all the way to the bottom of her gut.

"You're not the prime suspect."

True. Like anyone cared.

"Roxy, can you come here for a minute?" One of the owners stood outside his office. He was the J in M&J Investigations. As long as you weren't married to John Sherwood, he was great. His fourth wife was currently in negotiations to separate their record collection, and he was on the hunt for the next ex-Mrs. Sherwood.

The M left after he'd been caught with his hand in multiple cookie jars. He'd decided to fix things with his wife, which included moving near her family in Utah. John still didn't have the heart to change the name—even after he brought on additional owners. It probably didn't hurt that they had brand recognition and billboards all over the city.

"Sure." She slunk past the gawking staff. Somehow there were more people here then yesterday. She hoped that was a coincidence. She closed his office door and sat in the chair across from his desk.

Maybe if she pretended this was normal, it would be normal. Not that she'd never been called into John's office before, but this time felt different.

"Are you okay?" John looked concerned. Not mad. Not terminating-like. Good start. His dark skin glowed under the fluorescents. His brown eyes were assessing. They were always assessing. He was a brilliant man who saw everything. Probably why he became a PI and built an empire.

"Yeah. I guess you heard about what happened last night. I tried to serve Mr. Dunne his subpoena, but I got there too late."

"I'm concerned as to why you were serving this subpoena. You're on probation. I gave that to Skip." Yeah, Skip was a PI who did skip tracing. Unfortunate.

"Skip took Melody to the Knights game in San Jose

for their anniversary. I was just helping out. It's not a problem for the firm, is it?"

John sighed. "Don't worry about that. Let's talk about you, and how you're doing. The whole ordeal must have been scary."

Scary—not really. Just disturbing. Not that she'd tell anyone that. It was bad enough she became a blubbering mess in front of Rafe. Okay, she didn't blubber, but she'd held on to him like a koala. "It was a long night, but I'm fine."

"It's okay if you want to talk, with the murder and then being the primary suspect."

Primary. There was that word again. "I didn't do anything. I swear."

"Oh, we know." John steepled his hands in front of him. "It must be so hard for you with all this going on. You should take some time and relax. I see you have vacation time available."

"I do, but I think getting back to work would help keep my mind off things."

"I'm sorry. The paper mentioned your name. It's only a matter of time before they mention where you work. Our clients trust us. We need to maintain that trust." He actually looked upset as he said the words. Didn't change the awfulness of the message. "So, while the police investigate, we want you to take some time off."

Time off. "Like paid time off?" Sitting around

watching soap operas and eating bonbons sounded pretty good, if she was still getting paid.

His wince told her "paid" wasn't in her future. Which meant food and shelter were on the fence, too. "You have some vacation you can use."

"I only have six days left."

"I'm sure they'll figure out who did it before then." He attempted a smile, but it fell flat. "We're putting you on a leave of absence."

Leave of absence. She'd read somewhere that forty percent of cases never got solved. She wasn't getting fired, but it was pretty darn close. It didn't matter how she wasn't getting paid. All that mattered was she wouldn't have the money to pay her rent.

"Is there anything I can do to change your mind? I can keep a low profile. Work skip-tracing." The thought of sitting behind a desk gave her hives. She actually scratched at the back of her neck, but it didn't seem to reach the itch.

"I'm sorry. We don't have any open positions at the desks. I'm sure they'll figure out it wasn't you, and you can come back to work." He stood up.

"All I need to do is prove it wasn't me?"

"All the police need to do is prove it wasn't you." He shook his head, and his eyebrows drew together. Pity was written in the curl of his lips, or that could just be her interpretation. "This is a murder investigation. Let the police handle it."

"Sure." She was totally lying. She didn't know if he knew or not, but she didn't care. She had one week to prove her innocence. One week to put all this behind her before she had to rethink her career choices.

"Please come to us if you need any help." If he meant help with the investigation or paying her rent, she had no idea.

Either way, she had a feeling he was totally lying, too. She was on her own.

CHAPTER 8

ROXY KEPT her head high as she left M&J. Thankfully, Sarina was on the phone when Roxy left, so she wasn't able to ask questions. Roxy didn't know what she'd say. And she certainly didn't want to say it in front of everyone.

At least, that was what she kept telling herself as she slid into her car and dreamed about the largest glass of wine known to man—and how she would be drinking it tonight.

She twisted the key in the ignition. Nothing. The longer she sat there, the more likely someone would come out of the office and ask her questions—if the rumor mill hadn't already broken the news to everyone. Not something she wanted to think about.

She patted the wheel and tried the key again. Sputter. Luck must have been on her side, because even though the engine coughed up a hairball, it still turned over. She pulled out of the parking lot.

She had no idea where she was going. If she was smart, she'd stop at the grocery store and grab some chocolate long-johns, hide in her apartment and watch cable TV in the dark. But no one ever accused her of being smart.

She had a name to clear. Hers, to be exact. She needed a plan.

Her cell phone rang from the passenger side. She looked at the screen. Her mom. She didn't want to have this conversation—or any conversation right now. But Mom probably saw the news. Explaining it all over again wasn't high on Roxy's list. But if she didn't answer, Mom would think Roxy had joined the mole people in the flood tunnels. Against her better judgement, Roxy accepted the call.

"Your office is on the news." Why waste time with pleasantries like hello?

"Olivia?" Danielle's voice came across the line. Roxy's mom, aka Olivia, met Danielle twenty years ago, when Danielle set her broken arm. They'd been together ever since. Between Roxy's deadbeat father and his teenage bride and Mom—Danielle was her favorite by far.

"Don't *Olivia* me. Her office was on the news in connection with a murder."

"Olivia, let me talk to her." The phone tapped and sputtered as it must have switched hands.

"Roxy honey, are you okay?" See? Danielle. Favorite.

"I'm fine." If they didn't count the Lifetime movie her life had become.

"You shouldn't be alone tonight. I have to work a double at the hospital. Why don't you come by? Your mom has to stop at the Schmidts' house to feed their cat and then you two could go to the club for dinner." The golf club in Lake Las Vegas was her mother's nirvana. Perfectly coifed men and woman comparing the size of their money stacks.

"She's feeding their cat?" If there was one thing her mother hated, it was cats. If there were two things her mother hated, it was watching someone's house. Roxy would end up feeding the cat.

The thought of scooping up tuna and then sitting at the club with her mother was as enjoyable as being a murder suspect. She could only handle one of those things at a time. Her mom would have to wait.

"Sorry, with all the media attention, we're really busy at work." Someone was probably really busy at her work. Not exactly a lie. If she played her cards right, she'd be getting busy with a bottle of wine later tonight.

"Why don't you go see your father?" Danielle suggested at the same time Roxy's mother said, "She can see her father."

"It's okay," Roxy yelled into the phone.

More fumbling sounds, and then her mother said, "You can see your father. It's just—"

"I have to work." Roxy had no desire to hear what followed the "just." Probably how much her mom hated her father's teenage girlfriend.

"You don't have time to stop at the Schmidts?"

"I'm sorry, Mom."

"I don't have time either," her mom whined.

Roxy would tell her it's unbecoming, but her mom would find more things to whine about. There wasn't enough wine in the world to save Roxy from that. "Then why did you say you'd watch their cat?"

"Mrs. Schmidt is the head of the Blue Bonnets." The charity organization at the club. If the club was hell, the Blue Bonnets were the four horsemen of the apocalypse —but there were twelve. Absolute nightmare of cold uppity women, with cryogenically enhanced judgement skills.

Granted, Mrs. Schmidt had been an old friend of her parents, when her parents had been together. She was always nice. Not nice enough to want to scoop poop or schlep tuna. But nice.

"See you later, Mom."

"Fine. Call me if you change your mind."

About the schlepping? No thanks.

"And warn me next time you're on the news."

Because that was the highest priority right about now —how this all affected her mom. "I will."

Her mother disconnected. Thank goodness. Roxy had work to do. She needed to think like a PI. It was good practice. She needed to figure out who killed Donnie. There was a slight problem with that figuring, though. She'd never investigated anything before. But she'd seen her share of *Law and Orders*. She knew how it all worked and it was what she'd always wanted to do. This was the perfect opportunity. Too bad her own innocence hung in the balance.

So. Where to start...

What had Rafe said? The cops would talk to the wife sometime today. Maybe Roxy could get to her first. She waited till she hit a red light and opened the file she'd created when she was just serving a summons. His home address was in the Southern Highlands neighborhood of Las Vegas.

When the light changed, she drove the twenty minutes from Summerlin to the Southern Highland neighborhood. The roads became winding and hilly, and large contemporary houses stuck out from the sides. She pulled up to a gate, the Camaro's engine sputtering but holding on.

A white building with large windows sat off to the side. A gate that looked like it guarded the queen's jewels was in front of her, blocking the road.

If she wanted in, she needed to play nice with the robocop, frowning as he approached her window. He didn't seem impressed with her choice of vehicle. The guy was big enough to be the Rock's brother. He glanced at the clipboard in his hand. So naturally, she took him seriously. He had a clipboard, for goodness sake.

"Good morning. Address?" he asked.

What a weird question. "My address?"

The guard's pen hovered over the clipboard as he sighed. "The address of the person you wish to see."

"Oh." Yeah. That made more sense. "13267 Mockingbird."

"Name?"

"Donnie Dunne."

"Your name." He sighed.

"Roxy Horne." It wasn't her fault he kept changing the rules. First it was Donnie's address, then her name. Next, he'd want blood type—whose? She had no idea.

"Are they expecting you?"

She wanted to ask him which answer would get her through. But that didn't seem like the smartest move. So she went with honesty. "No."

"What's your business?" His eyes narrowed.

She was blowing it. Truth was meant to be bent for the common good. Right? Roxy handed him her business card. "I'm working with the Pura Vida hotel. She knows about what." Okay. Honestly, that wasn't a bending of the truth, more like creating a whole new truth. Fine lying. But who was counting?

His head bobbed as he wrote. Then he pushed the button on the walkie-talkie on his collar. He mumbled something and waited. More writing. More waiting. More mumbling. They were probably contacting Donnie's wife. Great.

He finally nodded at a guard manning the little white building, where there must have been a magic button because the gate swung open. "Do you know which way to go?"

No clue. But she'd finally talked her way in. She wasn't about to give him a reason to change his mind. "Yep."

He sighed. Apparently, her lying skills weren't as good as she thought. "Follow this curve and take a left at the first street past the golf club. Do you think you can handle that, or do you want a map?"

This was a classy neighborhood. There was a good chance they actually gave out maps. Wouldn't want the riffraff wandering around checking out their stuff.

"Got it. Thanks." She tapped the gas, passing the Rock II with a finger wave. She used all her fingers, not like a one-finger salute. No matter how much she wanted to for the whole sighing thing. But one-finger gestures might lead to a whole mind-changing thing. She needed to solve this in seven days. No He-Man wannabe would stop her.

She navigated the curvy streets till she found Mockingbird. The houses were all large, with brick facades, four car garages and giant front yards covered in lush carpets of real grass.

She pulled into the red brick driveway, following the curve to a green Porsche hybrid parked by the massive double front doors. One door opened as Roxy angled out of her car.

A redhead wearing a feather headband and a floral dress stood inside. "You're from the hotel?"

"I'm working with the hotel." She held out her hand. "I'm Roxy Horne."

The woman grasped Roxy's hand in both of hers. She stared at Roxy a little too hard. Held onto her hand a little too long. And weirded Roxy out a lot too much. "You have a good soul."

Roxy would like to think she did. Although if the woman knew she'd been weirded out, she might think otherwise.

"You have a beautiful blue aura. I can see the kindness all around you."

"Thank you?" Roxy wasn't sure what the common response was to a blue aura.

"It's in the eyes. Your eyes are kind."

"Thank you." Roxy knew the response to kind eyes.

"Come in. I'm Mandy, Adelaide's best friend."

The front of the house might have been gorgeous, but nothing prepared Roxy for the foyer. A grand marble staircase stood in the center. A large crystal chandelier stared down its nose at her. Probably wondering why department store gym shoes were tracking lower-class cooties over the Persian rugs.

They crossed the entry to a giant opening trimmed in dark wood. "Adelaide, it's the lady working with the hotel," Mandy yelled as they entered a room that could host a small wedding. A pool table and five full-size arcade games sat along one wall. The other side of the room had a large screen TV. The couches and tables had been moved to the side and Adelaide's body was pretzeling with a gorgeous hunk of man.

"Feel the stretch." Hunk ran a hand along her thighs. Now that was motivation to get in your exercise.

"Why is someone here?" Adelaide grunted as the trainer came up behind her to pull her hips back. Roxy wasn't sure if it was a grunt of appreciation or pain. Adelaide's brow was covered in sweat, but calling him a trainer didn't feel quite right. His "stretches" looked more like something the guys in the *Thunder from Down Under* show would do than aerobics and a warm-up. "I have a meeting with the police this afternoon," Adelaide added.

"I was hoping I could ask a few questions." Roxy turned to look out the sliding glass doors at the pool sparkling in the back yard. Anything to get her attention off the grieving widow tilted forward on her hands while her legs wrapped around the trainer.

He pushed into her with his hips. "Work those arms."

Roxy wasn't sure the woman was working her arms, but she was definitely working something. Her work had a smile on his face.

"You're doing great." He held her hips as she did inverted push-ups. "Three more... two, and one."

He lowered her legs to the ground. "I'll make your smoothie." Then he was gone.

Adelaide's face stayed planted on the floor and she looked content staying there.

"Get up!" Trainer hunk walked back in the room, carrying a light green drink that looked like it would taste like grass clippings and bark. "Keep moving or you'll tighten up."

Adelaide stumbled to her feet and took the drink from his hand. "Sorry."

"I'll see you next week." He slung a giant sports bag over his shoulder before heading out the front door.

Adelaide waited till he was gone before dropping to the couch with a groan. She splayed her body against the back and sucked on the grass clippings like it was her last meal. "That man is a genius, but I have no idea why I put myself through that."

"I keep asking why you continue with that man." Mandy didn't seem to approve of the trainer hunk.

"You know why." Adelaide shook her head. "I was trying to lose weight for Donnie."

"Well, he's not around to cheat on you anymore, so drop the trainer. Have a burger."

Cheating. Donnie. Wow, those were two words Roxy would not have put together. He was a weeble-looking leprechaun with thinning hair. Adelaide was a gorgeous brunette, probably in her late thirties, with legs that could wrap around a trainer. Yet she was trying to change so the leprechaun wouldn't cheat? The world was one messed up place.

"I'm sorry to interrupt, but I have a few questions about your husband."

"Ask away." Adelaide's eyes closed. The only indication that she was awake was the level of green goop lowering in the glass.

"Why was your husband at the Imprint last night?"

"Some conference." Adelaide sliced her hand through the air, but her eyes stayed shut. "For accountants or something."

"Or something." Mandy dropped to the couch next to her BFF.

Roxy addressed Mandy. "You don't seem to like Donnie."

"I didn't like how he treated the people in his life."

"He wasn't always that bad. There were times he was really sweet." Adelaide opened her eyes and inched up to sitting. She seemed to be begging Mandy to understand.

Mandy sighed and dropped her hand to Adelaide's knee. "I get it, sweetie." She turned to Roxy. "He did just enough to give her hope. But that didn't stop him from banging every hooker in Nye County."

"Not every single one." Adelaide sighed.

Somehow this conversation felt like it embodied déjà

vu. Like these two women had had the same discussion over and over again.

Mandy sighed. "Fine. He's banged half the hooker population in Nye County. Better?"

"No." Adelaide wiped a tear from her eye. "Any other questions?"

"Where were you last night?" Roxy asked.

"Everyone was here scrapbooking."

"Everyone?" Roxy had never scrapbooked. She never understood it. But then again, she hadn't realized it was a group sport.

"A few girlfriends. Enya, Patrice, Nia and Mandy. We scrapbooked in the dining room all day and stopped at six for dinner. After that, we drank wine. A lot of wine."

Roxy could understand a night of wine and friends. Maybe she needed to look into scrapbooking. "Did you stop at the hotel at all?"

"We did earlier in the evening. Mandy and I dropped by before dinner to give Donnie his phone. He leaves it everywhere."

"You went up to the room?"

"No. Just dropped it at the front desk."

"You didn't leave anything in the room?"

Heat crawled up Adelaide's face, but she smothered the anger simmering in her eyes. "No. If there was anything left in the room, it wasn't mine." She sighed again. "There wasn't really a conference. Deep down, I knew it was bogus. But I always thought I was being crazy. He was spending time in Reno trying to find us a house. You don't plan a huge move if you're trying to be with someone else."

Mandy sighed. "Sweetie, it's called a guilt-gift."

"I loved him." Adelaide shook her head. "Now he's gone. What am I supposed to do?"

"You'll sell the house and move in with me." Mandy's hand rubbed Adelaide's knee, slowly getting higher.

Adelaide didn't seem to notice. "Even if I sell the house, Donnie was in debt. It's all gone. The house. The cars. The money. I have nothing."

Nothing? That didn't sound like Donnie. He'd had a suite at the hotel and Dom chilling in the ice bucket. If he was keeping all the hookers knee-deep in college textbooks or jewelry, depending on their need, where did all the money come from? "Didn't he own an accounting firm?"

"It was more about wealth management, but they did some accounting." Adelaide wiped her brow, moving the hair from her forehead.

"Wealth management?"

"Investing in the stock market. Retirement planning." Adelaide shook her head. "It doesn't matter. It was going under. We were losing everything."

"That must have made you angry." Roxy could see how losing everything might make a bride a little stabby, maybe not seventeen times stabby, but everyone had their tipping point.

"I'm more angry at his partner. He just abandoned Donnie when he needed him most. It hurt Donnie. That's why we were leaving. He couldn't trust his friends."

Mandy snorted and Adelaide glared. Mandy covered her mouth. "My ex might be a jerk, but he didn't abandon him."

Roxy blinked. What? "Your ex?"

"Her ex was Donnie's partner." Adelaide leaned back. "He's a good man."

"He's a good man who's boring as lint. I swear I almost fell asleep when he spoke."

"But he didn't sleep around." Adelaide's tone was clipped.

"Yeah, but we still weren't a good fit. You, at least liked Donnie." Mandy sighed. "I don't know why."

"Donnie promised things would be different," Adelaide said. "It would just be us. It was almost a blessing. We were moving to Reno. No more extracurricular activities. I would have had him all to myself."

It was Mandy's turn to sigh again. "He was taking you away from your friends. From me."

"I would have done anything for him." The conviction in Adelaide's tone told Roxy she meant it.

And it made sense. He was having trouble at work. The whole hotel scene could have been business gone bad. With the two wine glasses, it looked intimate. But it could have been a business meeting. "One last question. Do you know who he might have met at the hotel?"

"Met?" Mandy's eyes said it all, as in who he might have met besides the multitudes of call girls. "I knew he was cheating. That was just who he was. I knew she deserved better."

Doesn't everyone deserve better than a cheater. But that didn't answer who could've been in the hotel room.

"Could he have been meeting someone from work? A friend? Coworker?"

"He didn't say anything. He could've met his business partner, Steve Brandt. Or his friend Harold was trying to find a way to fix everything. He could've met with him." Adelaide stopped and stared at the ceiling, lost in thought. When she spoke, her voice came out small. "Every time I caught him, he'd tell me they meant nothing. That they were all random. But I caught him twice texting with a girl named Presley."

"Last name?"

"I don't know. You don't think she could have done this?" A fire lit in Adelaide's eyes. "She tried to steal my husband, and when he wouldn't go, she killed him. I'm sure."

Given the scene in the hotel, there was definitely romance involved, but Roxy supposed he could've tried to cut off the relationship. "Thank you for your time."

"Does this mean I don't have to go down to the precinct?"

Roxy pasted on a smile. "Sorry, you do. This is a separate investigation."

She walked through the bright afternoon sun and opened the car door. Heat billowed from her car. Darn it. She forgot to put the sunscreen in the front window again. Now she would have red thighs. She slid into the burning leather seat that was more cracks than smooth leather.

That had been interesting. On the one hand, the wife had a motive. Her husband was about to lose everything. On the other hand, she didn't seem to care about that. She loved him. She wanted him around and faithful, if she was to be believed.

On the other hand... Mandy didn't seem to like Donnie at all. Honestly, Roxy couldn't blame her. If someone else was treating Sarina like that— and Sarina let him— Roxy would lose her mind. There wouldn't be a string of swear words long enough to describe her hate.

On top of that, Donnie wanted to take Adelaide away. Mandy didn't seem too happy on that front either. But was the aura maven mad enough at Donnie to kill him? That was the question.

CHAPTER 9

AFTER SOME BARBECUE at Lucille's restaurant and an hour trek across town, Roxy pulled into the parking lot of the Imprint Hotel. She thought about going home, but she'd never be able to sleep. She needed answers.

Once through the garage, she opened the door to a gust of air conditioning from the casino inside the hotel. Reels whirred as they spun. Bells dinged. A slight hum of conversation whirled around the room. Screaming came from the corner as whistles announced a lucky streak.

She reached the elevator banks without being tackled. No Rafe. She wasn't sure if she was happy about the missing hunk of man... or disappointed. Getting tackled by him sounded hot, but if he was here, he'd stop her from getting her job done. If he was against her serving his clientele, she could only imagine how he'd feel about her getting involved in the murder investigation.

Which meant she was happy he was missing. She

made it to the elevator without a sideways glance, and hit the button for the forty-fourth floor. The doors opened to tomb-like silence— like before she'd found Donnie. She needed to get in and get out. She turned the corner. A stone wall jumped in her face and she stumbled back.

"Hey, are you okay?" A man with dark dreads reached out and held her arm so she didn't fall.

"I'm fine. Thanks." Roxy smiled as she straightened. No harm, no foul.

"I can't believe there was a murder in there." A woman came up behind the mountain, the camera attached to her face almost hiding her bright green eyes. The shutter clicked as she noticed Roxy. "Who's this?"

"No idea. She just came running around the corner," the mountain said.

A bit of an over-exaggeration. Roxy was a lover, not a runner.

"Come to see the scene of the crime too, huh?" camera lady asked. "I've never been to a murder before. I've seen them on TV, but that's not the same." She took another picture. Her dark-skinned hands hit the button with a click. "Someone said they heard there's a ghost. I would love to see a ghost."

The sparkle in her eyes said she meant every word about the ghost theory.

"Ghosts kill people, babe." His dark skin grew pale right before Roxy's eyes. The guy didn't look like he wanted to see a ghost.

"They can't touch us. They're on a different spiritual plane." The woman took another picture. "Let's check out the restaurant. They said he ate there before he died. Maybe his spirit is lingering there."

"Great." The mountain's color didn't seem to be getting any better. Hopefully he wouldn't pass out. "Babe" didn't look like she could carry him very far. They headed to the elevator and disappeared with a ding.

The floor went eerily quiet again. The cops and other personnel were gone. The silence wrapped around her head as she caught sight of the door. The scene of the crime, as "Babe" called it. She'd never been to a murder before either. Not something she wanted to relive—yet here she was, getting closer.

Closer to the body and to the rumored ghost. Because if there was a ghost, wouldn't it linger around the body, waiting for someone from the living world to come by, so it could act out its fiery vengeance?

No more *Supernatural* for her. It was giving her ideas. And not good ideas.

She approached the door with the yellow police tape. Somehow, it felt like she was being watched. Like someone was waiting to jump out. Like that ghost hid in the shadows left by the overhead lights.

Relax. She was being silly. "There is no such thing as ghosts." Crap. Did she say that out loud? The ghosts might get the wrong idea. "I believe in you, ghosts, and think you're awesome, you got a bum deal..." She'd say whatever the ghost needed to hear so it didn't leave its spiritual plane and suck out her soul.

The door was closed. Not that she thought the door would be wide open, not with a crime scene behind it. But wouldn't that be nice? She reached around the tape and jiggled the handle.

It was locked. She needed a keycard. Again, why would they let anyone check in on a crime scene? It would be a zoo of "Babe" and other Vegas tourists taking pictures of blood spatter.

A bang sounded behind the door. At least, she thought it came from behind the door. Her heart raced as she looked around for the source of the noise. The banging could have come from the owner of the eyes she swore were watching her. Which made her skin crawl, and her feet back up from the door. Fast.

The yellow police tape mocked her. She needed to get inside, but didn't want to. The blood. The dead man on the floor. He'd taken his last breath in that room. If there was anyone who had earned the right to haunt these halls, it was him.

Maybe this was a bad idea.

She jumped at a crash down the hall. Really bad idea. The door clicked and flew open. A scream ripped from her throat.

Rafe reached behind his back and yelled, "Son of a... Roxy? Why are you screaming?"

"Why are you jumping out at me?" Roxy eyed the gun in Rafe's hand.

"I didn't jump out." He slid his gun back into the holster. "I opened the door."

"But you waited till I was right outside."

"Yes." He rolled his eyes. "I've been standing here all day behind this peephole waiting for you to come up to the door so I could open it. Why are you here?"

Now that her heart was thumping at a normal rate, and he asked the question, she remembered why she was here. She craned her neck to look past him. "I wanted to get a look at the crime scene."

"Why?" He kept his broad shoulders in the doorway, making sure she couldn't see around him.

Why? Good question. Telling him the truth could backfire in her face. If he knew how bad she wanted this thing solved, but still kept her out, she'd never get in the room. Then again, she needed him to get her into the room. If he didn't understand her desperation, he might still keep her out.

It was easier to just stick to the truth. She sucked in a breath and said, "My bosses saw the newspaper with me on the front page and there's all this speculation. So I have no job until I can prove I'm innocent. And without a job, I have no way to pay my rent. Or electricity. Or for food. And I like to eat. Having a roof over my head is pretty cool, too."

Rafe's eyes crinkled at the corners. His lips curled up at the edges.

Roxy shrugged. "I like electricity."

"Is your love of electricity why some woman interviewed Adelaide Dunne?" Rafe asked in a tone so dry Roxy thought she'd need moisturizer. Rafe's eyebrows rose just a bit. "Asked her questions on behalf of the hotel. Wouldn't know anything about that, would you?"

"How did you find out?"

"Cops talk."

She wanted to remind him he wasn't a cop, but she had a feeling once a cop always a cop. The smile he'd started with had somehow morphed to annoyance. She didn't want him annoyed. She needed information. "I have to clear my name. You understand, right?"

He sighed. "I get it. But why didn't you come to me first? Now I have MacAuley breathing down my neck."

"Why didn't he come to see me?"

"Because the women couldn't remember your name. They came into the precinct drunk off their asses." Rafe shook his head. "You're lucky they didn't remember you. You're still a primary suspect, and cops don't have my sense of humor."

"Are my future meals of ramen funny to you?" She would have joked about her future living in a cardboard box, but that felt more tragic and hit way too close to home—as in, her home would be a box.

"No, but that sure as hell beats your life in county

jail." His eyes travelled up and down her body. "You would be popular in general population. You could find a prison wife, settle down, and make a few shivs."

"Shivs?"

"Homemade weapons. I'm sure they'll teach you how to make them in county."

"I get it. County jail is worse than ramen." She hated this conversation. He totally lied—he no longer had a sense of humor. "But I have very few marketable skills—even for Vegas. I can't dance, so stripping is out. I need my job."

"Although watching you strip does sound like a lot of fun." Rafe's lips quirked. "I'll help you clear your name."

"Really? Why?"

"Why not?"

She glared. He laughed.

"Fine," Rafe said. "I want to help an old friend. I'd hate to see you end up in jail. I've seen what jail does and it's not pretty." He leaned against the side of the door jamb.

Roxy waited a beat. "That's it?"

"And maybe I owe you one. I heard what they called you in college after my party. I tried to tell everyone nothing happened, but they still ran with it." He truly looked sorry.

"You knew about that?" She didn't think Rafe had heard the rumors. Or more likely, she'd hoped he hadn't heard the rumors. After that night, she'd practically gone into witness protection. The girls in her class avoided her like bedbugs and the boys wanted to jump in her bed. *Roll-around Roxy.* A nickname she was hoping to forget.

"Yeah." He shook his head as if to clear it. The pity disappeared, and his cop face was back on. "So why did you need to see the room?"

"I wanted to take a look at the scene. I was a little shocked last time I was here."

"What are you looking for?" Rafe stepped to the side and let her in.

Roxy contorted her body to go under one strip of police tape and over another. "I don't know. I'm thinking I'll know when I see it."

"You'll know it when you see it, huh?" He looked so adorable when his lips quirked that way. Too bad it was at her expense. "Don't touch anything." He wrapped his hand around her arm, keeping her from going inside the room. "Horne, seriously, you cannot touch anything. Do you understand?"

Really? "I can understand basic English." She pulled her arm away and edged around him into the room. It was just like she remembered, or at least she thought so. It was like some kind of intense déjà vu. She'd swear she saw it before, but couldn't remember any details.

She walked to the kitchenette and laid her hand on the counter. The cake and desserts still sat there, still looking delicious, probably the consistency of cardboard by now. She edged her hand toward the tray of brownies.

"I thought you understood basic English." His hand slid along her arm. "Don't touch."

"I'm just looking."

He pulled her hand back and slid his fingers between hers. "Look with your eyes, not your hands."

She stepped back. "You did *not* just say that. I haven't heard that since I was five."

He laughed. "Really? Because your hands were on that counter, when we agreed you wouldn't touch anything."

She'd like to argue. They hadn't agreed. She hadn't touched anything. But really, she had—touched and agreed. She hated when he was right. He brought her hand to his lips. He didn't kiss her, just ran it along the edges. His breath tickled her skin, sending a pang of need through her body.

Her body forgot about him being right as it pulsed. Her head forgot he'd just talked to her like she was a toddler. All of that should've mattered, but she couldn't get on board. She couldn't get her heart to stop hammering out of her chest.

"Can you keep your hands off the crime scene?" he whispered into her knuckles, that warm breath shooting desire to her core.

"Hmm..." Her eyes closed. Every word and thought gone. All she could do was feel.

"Roxanna?"

"Hmm..." Every breath brought new feelings. Every

nerve ending twerked. She might not dance, but apparently her nerves were ready for Broadway.

"Roxanna? Can you hear me?"

She opened her eyes. The words didn't come with warm tingles even though her body had practically gone up in flames. She knew she had her bedroom eyes on. Which was a complete embarrassment, since he didn't.

"Are you okay?"

Mortified. Pathetic. Disgusted. She was so many things. Okay was probably not high on that list. Not that she'd tell him that. "I'm fine."

"You can look around, but don't touch." He kissed the tips of her fingers—like it was something he did every day. Her body went on a hormone rampage, and he acted as if he was kissing his baby cousin.

Crap. She'd completely misread the situation. Which made her want to run and hide. But she couldn't. She had a crime scene to analyze. There was a good chance this was the only opportunity she'd have to check it out. She had better make the best of it.

She scanned the room. The body was gone. Thank goodness. The blood wasn't. Two whiskey glasses sat on the table in front of an off-white couch. Draped on the matching chair was a black suit jacket with SBM embroidered on the inside pocket. "SBM?" She stretched her hand out. It was an automatic response. It looked soft. Sue her.

Rafe's hand found hers before she could touch the material. "We're thinking a monogram."

"Steve Brandt?" Donnie's partner. "But what's the M for?"

"His middle name?"

She needed to be sure. A rough finger drew lazy circles on the back of her hand and those nerve endings started a tango. She wanted to get lost in the touch. She had a feeling she'd forget all about the job, the suspect list and the ghost, if he laid that hand on any part of her body...

His face was unreadable. No haze. No "I wanna sex you up" vibe. His finger stopped moving. Her brain cells began to fire. This wouldn't fix her problems. She needed to solve this puzzle—then she could have the oblivion those hands promised. It might not be given by those hands, but she had a vivid imagination and a battery-operated-boyfriend.

She pulled her hand away. "Thanks, Amato." A chill travelled the length of her body, replacing all the warm tingles. Which was good. She needed to talk to Donnie's partner. Alone. Without distractions. Because distractions wouldn't help her get this case solved. They only messed with her mind and body.

"Anytime, Horne."

Somehow, she believed he'd help her with the case anytime. The hormones whipping through her body was all on her and b.o.b.

CHAPTER 10
FIVE DAYS TILL SELLING PLASMA IS MY FULL-TIME JOB. ~ ROXANNA HORNE

THE NEXT DAY, the sun glimmered like pools of glass on the streets of Las Vegas. Roxy turned into the Ridges, a neighborhood filled with million-dollar houses surrounded by trees and grass.

She pointed her car toward the cul-de-sac where Steve Brandt's house stood. Of course he lived in a monstrosity. Just like his partner had. White stucco. Red tile roof. A glimpse of Spanish-desert architecture among the modern-day black and white sharp-edged designs.

She pulled up to the curb and got the heat shield from the floor in the back seat, stuffing it in the front window. She remembered.

A for-sale sign hung in the front yard. She rang the doorbell and waited as a banging noise echoed from inside. A balding man in a red track suit with yellow piping opened the door. His gray hair stood at attention around a horseshoe of flushed red skin.

"Mr. Brandt?" Roxy asked. Really? This was Mandy's ex?

"Please, please call me Steve. I'm so sorry. I thought you wanted to cancel." He rubbed his face with a hand towel and tossed it onto a side table. He motioned for her to come in. Opened boxes were stacked haphazardly along the floor. "I'm in the process of moving."

He led her through a narrow trail of stuff to what was once the living room. Every square inch was covered with boxes, or stuff waiting to be boxed.

"Where are you moving to?"

He played with his fingers as he bit back a grimace. "To my daughter's house until I can find a house for myself. This place is just too big for a bachelor. Can I get you a drink?" He moved a pile from the couch and patted the cushion.

"No. I'm fine." She sat on the white suede couch. It was soft and gorgeous. There was no way anyone could live with this couch. How did you stop the Cheetos dust from getting in the fabric? "Is your wife home?" She hadn't heard much about Steve, but the pink and maroon curtains and various doilies suggested a woman's touch.

He sighed. "We finalized our divorce last month, but we'd been apart for a while now."

"I'm sorry to hear that." And she was. It looked like, no matter how he wanted to hide it, he wasn't quite over that loss.

"Don't be. She's happier now. I'm doing well, too."

"Dad, we need to sell this Chagall. Stop putting it in the keep pile. We need every dollar." A younger woman stormed in the living room carrying a small painting. Her peach spandex capris were covered with a large darker peach T-shirt and her red hair was pulled into a ponytail. The painting might be small, but that little framed picture could easily go for a couple thousand dollars. An original Chagall could cover a down payment on a new place.

Steve frowned. "I need to keep some things."

"You need to keep the necessities. This is not a... necessity." Her eyes widened, like she'd just noticed Roxy was in the room. "I'm sorry to interrupt."

Roxy didn't mind the interruption. It actually gave her a bit of insight. He wasn't selling the house because he wanted to. He was selling because he had to.

Steve walked over to his daughter and whispered in her ear. She dipped her head and scurried away.

"I'm sorry about that interruption. She's really excited to have me close to her. She's not taking the divorce as well. Anyway, Connie, you're here to talk about planning for retirement." He grabbed a pen and paper from a desk in the corner.

She wasn't, but she should really start to think about planning for retirement. It was something grownups did. She was technically grown. So why not? "I am." She just had to be Connie.

"I was so disappointed when my secretary said you'd

cancelled. But I'm glad you changed your mind." Steve sat in a chair across from the couch and grabbed a pad of paper from the top of a box.

"Retirement planning is important."

"What are your goals?" He grabbed a pair of reading glasses from his pocket and settled them on his face. His pen hovered over the pad in front of him.

What kind of goal was there outside of just retiring? Rambling about things she clearly didn't understand wouldn't get her the information she wanted. "I was hoping we could talk about your company first. If I'm going to be putting my money with you."

"Absolutely." He took off the glasses and set them on a box near his feet. "What questions do you have?"

"I want to know a little more about your partner, Donnie Dunne, if I'm going to invest with you."

"Donnie is not a part of this." His voice didn't seem to change. No anger. No sadness. "He passed away."

"I'm so sorry for your loss. What happened?"

"It was a shock." His mouth turned down at the edges. Maybe a hint of sadness... or maybe guilt. "He was found at the Imprint Hotel."

How diplomatic. "Found?"

He ran a hand over his face, obviously uncomfortable with the conversation. She needed to keep it going, though, without making him so uncomfortable he shut her down. That was an interrogation tactic—and she didn't really have any tactics on her side. What was a safe question? "Were you there?"

"No. I was at my daughter's for dinner." His gaze roamed the room. He couldn't seem to look at her all.

He was hiding something. She was sure of it. "Do they know what happened?"

"The police are working on it." He motioned to his paperwork. "If you don't have any more questions, we should probably start defining your future planning." From the look on his face, if those questions didn't include talk of his dead partner, he'd be just fine.

The doorbell buzzed.

"Sorry." He yelled into the other room, "Gretchen, can you get the door?"

Gretchen mumbled something as she shuffled past the living room to the front hall. Her mumbling didn't sound particularly flattering.

"Where were we?" Steve's gaze moved from Roxy to the hallway, clearly distracted by the noise at the front door. Roxy had a feeling nothing she said would penetrate the excitement of another visitor.

"There's someone else to see you." Gretchen returned to the living room, followed by a man in jeans and a white button-down shirt. His gun hung off his hip. He looked surprised when he saw Roxy sitting on the couch. Not quite as surprised as Roxy, but she did a good job of hiding it. She hoped.

"Mr. Brandt, I'm Detective MacAuley."

"Detective, I thought we were meeting later this afternoon." Steve stood and shook MacAuley's hand.

"I thought I'd stop by and talk to you where you're more comfortable." MacAuley's gaze was still on Roxy.

"I'm sorry," Steve said. "This is my client, Connie Dillon."

"Connie Dillon?"

Roxy nodded to MacAuley. "Nice to meet you."

Steve took his seat again. "We were just discussing her retirement planning. Can you give me an hour to finish up here?"

Roxy stayed in the chair. "We didn't get a chance to start, so if you need to talk to the police, go ahead." Maybe if she played her cards right, she could listen in. "I can wait here."

"Are you sure?" Steve looked at her like a cat about to run.

"Sure."

"Gretchen, is there any space in the kitchen for me to meet with the detective?"

His daughter shook her head and huffed. "There's barely a path to the kitchen. I'll straighten up the hallway."

"Give me a minute to clear off the kitchen table, and we'll go in there, Detective." Steve disappeared after his daughter.

MacAuley focused his cop-stare on Roxy. "Connie?"

"My middle name?"

"Really?" He raised an eyebrow in the universal *I call BS* move.

"Fine, it's not my middle name."

"Then why are you here?"

"Financial advice?"

His eyebrow arched.

She needed to stop answering his questions with questions. No wonder he didn't believe her. She sucked at this. "I wanted to ask him a few questions about that night."

"Which night?"

"The night Donnie was murdered."

"Why?" MacAuley didn't give away anything. He wasn't angry. He wasn't concerned. Just straight curiosity.

Either way, he didn't seem to have anything against her, even with her listed as a suspect—if she still was. She didn't even know where she stood. "Am I a suspect?"

"You're a person of interest."

Still. "What's my motive?"

MacAuley smiled. And it was gorgeous. Nice lips. Nice teeth. She almost got lost in the sparkle. "We can't find one. I don't suppose you'd like to tell us what your motive might be? Save us some time."

She decided to give him an eyebrow arch of her own instead of rolling her eyes and calling him an inappropriate word. Total grownup move.

MacAuley huffed. "I'm going to go on a limb and say you have no motive."

"That's a safe limb."

"But that leads back to the question, why are you here?"

"Fine." A burst of air left her lungs, taking all the fight with it. If he was going to use knowledge as power over her, too bad. She was done. "I've been put on leave because of all the press. I need to clear my name and get on with my life."

He ran a hand along the back of his neck, massaging the base. "This isn't TV. You can't just run around asking questions. A person is dead." Apparently he didn't like her answer.

"I get that."

"Do you? You're here when you should be letting the cops handle it."

"The cops think I did it." Anger burned in her veins. "How can I trust someone who is dumb enough to believe I would do this?"

"First, I don't think you did it." Finally, a chink in his poker façade. Except now fire steamed from his eyes and he leaned in closer. "Second, you don't have to trust us. You have to get out of the way so we can do our job." He wasn't nearly as cute when he was mad.

She didn't want to tick him off. She just needed to keep paying her rent. "I have no job until this is solved. No paycheck, but I still have bills. Let me help."

He sighed and ran that hand down the back of his neck, again. "What did you learn so far?"

"He said he was at his daughter's for dinner."

"Do you believe him?"

"He got real shifty when he said it. All of a sudden he couldn't meet my eyes. So, no. I think he's hiding something." No, not think. She knew Steve was hiding something.

"What?"

"I don't know. You interrupted my questioning. I didn't even get to ask about the jacket."

"What jacket?"

"There was a suit coat on the couch in Donnie's hotel room. I wanted to know if it was his."

"Suit coat?" MacAuley frowned, but then the light went on. His gaze moved back to her. "The jacket with SBM on the pocket. The initials don't match."

"Maybe he has another name he uses. Rich useless guys usually have a bunch of names."

"Maybe." He didn't look all that convinced. "But let me handle it."

"Will you tell me what he tells you?"

He sighed again. Like he had anything to sigh about. She was the one who was being shut out, here. "Go home. Enjoy a few days off. I'll ask the questions and get to the bottom of this. Okay?"

She retrieved her purse and passed MacAuley on the way to the front entrance.

"Where are you going?" he asked.

"Home." She paused at the door.

"You didn't answer my question."

"You didn't answer mine." She wrenched the knob. She might have sounded a bit perturbed, but she was. Why hide things if she wasn't a suspect?

He snuck up behind her, pinning her between the cracked open door and his body. She could practically feel his heartbeat on her back. He was so warm, and it took everything inside her to not lean back and seek comfort from the pain-in-the-butt man who made her need comforting. "Let me talk to him, and I'll see if there's anything worth sharing."

If there was anything worth sharing... More like if there was anything he was willing to share. Big difference. One meant he'd give her information to help, the other meant he'd give her the mushroom treatment—keep her in the dark and feed her horse droppings.

"Then let me go home, and I'll see if there's any reason to enjoy a few days off."

His hand rested on the door inches from hers. His body so close, she could practically taste him. "If you need a reason to stay home, I'd be happy to volunteer."

"Fine. Then you stay home and let me talk to him." She turned toward him. It might be a big mistake with him being so close and so hot and all, but she didn't care. If he was willing to play this game, she would call that bet.

He smiled. So pretty. So annoying. "Give me your phone. I'll call when I'm done."

She handed him her cell phone and he entered in some numbers. "Really?"

"Really." He hit dial and his cell phone chirped. After he handed her phone back, he pulled open the front door.

"Thanks." She slipped outside.

He'd given her his number. He said he'd call. He didn't seem like the type to lie.

She unlocked her phone and the screen opened to his contact information. At least she assumed it was his. Detective Volunteer. That was the new name in her contacts.

Still didn't get a first name for the friendly neighborhood detective, but she had his number and an offer that seemed too good to refuse.

Not that she was thinking of taking him up on it. She already had enough male drama with Rafe. Adding another testosterone-filled Neanderthal with a gun would only make things worse. Lord knew—right now— she was as *worse* as she wanted to be.

CHAPTER 11

ROXY DROVE TOWARD PARADISE, her own little piece of suburbia about a mile off the Vegas strip. If she looked in her rearview mirror, she could see the Westgate Las Vegas. But she rarely looked.

It just reminded her there were people here doing what happened in Vegas, with a yard-long margarita. She might be a bit jealous. But when you lived in Vegas, what happened here absolutely stayed here—with your family and your friends and your coworkers. Not that she didn't drink, but it generally wasn't with the abandon of anonymity.

Given her current situation with the police, anonymity sounded pretty darn good. She turned into the parking lot behind her building, pulling into a spot as far away from the industrial-sized garbage bin as she could get. Coming home late at night meant she had to park near the nasty smelling monstrosity all the time. But since everyone was at work, she lucked out.

Just when she thought nothing good could come from unemployment.

She sat in her car and tried to come up with something to do. But she had nothing. No new leads. She couldn't go out with friends. They all had jobs—like functioning adults.

But they didn't have the good parking spot. So there was that.

She left the car and walked toward the off-white ridged-concrete building. The reddish clay tile roof angled up, but instead of coming to a peak, it just stopped at the flat roof. The building itself was two stories, with four apartments per floor.

Once inside, she headed up the dark brown staircase. Before she got to the third step, the door to the apartment below hers opened. Gladys Potter stood in the doorway. She was a short, stocky woman, whose pink house shoes matched her muumuu. The sunlight bounced off her dark brown skin. Her dark-gray Orphan Annie curls covered her ears—not that the hair stopped her from hearing everything that happened in the building. She was like neighborhood watch and Enews combined. "Shouldn't you be at work? Are you on holiday? You been sacked? You still owe me rent for this month."

Every Harry Potter joke flew through Roxy's mind as Ms. Potter spoke in her British accent. She was a nice lady, with enough stories to fill a book. She'd done it all. From mountain climbing in Nepal to getting it on with one of the Rolling Stones. If she hadn't done it, it wasn't worth doing. She was like a composite after-picture of the most interesting women in the world.

"No, Ms. Potter. Everything is fine. You'll get your rent." *Don't let them see you sweat*—or they'll start eviction proceedings sooner rather than later. For the record, she hadn't been sacked—fired. Not yet anyway.

"Last week, Meredith in 2D came home early. She reckoned it was a simple stomachache and she ended up with salmonella. Went to hospital for liquids and everything. She's home now, having a bit of a lie in, but she can't run a marathon anymore. People only come home early when they're ill or they've been sacked." Gladys had been in Vegas for fifteen years, but that hadn't erased the British from her vocabulary. Not that Roxy minded. In fact, it was kind of cute.

"I'm not sick and I haven't lost my job." Not yet anyway. But there was no way she'd tell the poor woman. Mrs. Potter would worry a hole into the floor. Literally. A few years ago, the kid in 2A had chicken pox, and Gladys paced for a week and a half till the girl felt better.

Or worse, she would show up with a steak and kidney pie so Roxy wouldn't starve. A sweet gesture, but last time she shared one of her casseroles, Roxy ended up praying to the porcelain gods and wishing for a quick, efficient death. Death hadn't come, and nothing about that night had been quick or efficient.

"Want to come in for a bit of tea and biscuits?"

"I'm in a hurry." But she needed to change the topic before she accidentally told the woman everything. "How long has it been since you got a haircut? We might need to have a girl's day."

Dark fingers fiddled with the curl at her ear. "Not since we went last month."

"Let's schedule something for next Saturday?" Roxy wanted to ask her to go tomorrow, but then Gladys would know something was up. She'd worry, and Roxy would be tossing a gifted pie on the down low.

"Can we pop round the grocery, too?"

"Sure. Make your list of things you need, and we'll go." Roxy smiled.

"Rent?"

Roxy's smile disappeared into the desert, where her excuse for not having her rent money was hiding. "Yes. I'll bring it down later today." There was no way she had the money for rent, yet. But maybe, just maybe, she had some money lying around.

Gladys disappeared back into her apartment, closing the door. She probably had the pen and paper out already. She was nice a woman—a little lonely, but she was fun to hang out with. Her people watching skills were unmatched. She saw everything. And she shared everything.

Roxy liked their girls' days. It was nice for Gladys to get out of the apartment. Her kids were grown with jobs and children of their own, and Gladys, despite the fact that she still had her driver's license, was a menace on the road.

Anyway, Gladys seemed to like their girls' days too. It gave Roxy some entertainment on the weekends. She had something to do now. Looking for rent money gave her a purpose—even if it was only three minutes of purpose and probably fruitless. She'd try to fit it in between binge watching daytime TV and scrounging for something to eat in her fridge.

Three things to do. Her list was growing.

At the top of the stairs, she unlocked the brown metal door to her apartment and pushed her way in. Home sweet home. It wasn't big, just a one-bedroom apartment. In the living area, a large screen television sat on a TV stand. Along the side wall, a blue suede-adjacent couch faced the TV. A matching chair sat to the right, angled for a good view out the front window.

Heading to her bedroom, she pulled her phone from her pocket and checked the time. Somehow, an hour had passed since she left Detective MacAuley. He hadn't called. He was probably done, yet Detective Volunteer hadn't even sent a text.

She threw on a pair of yoga pants—the ones she'd only bought because Sarina forced her to try yoga. But they were comfortable and forgiving if she overdid the cookie dough. Cookie dough. She could go for some of that right now.

She slid into her Pink! T-shirt and Care Bear socks before shuffling across the light tan mock-wood-plank tile to the galley kitchen. She sifted through one of the dark brown cabinets lining the wall. She didn't have a pantry, so this was it. A box of crackers. Minute Rice. Questionable bread. An old bag of chips.

She ripped opened the bag of potato chips and pulled one out. Rubbery stale salted grossness slid along her tongue. The bag chip crinkled as she scrunched it shut and tossed it into the garbage can.

That didn't work.

Things weren't much better in the fridge. Soda. Ketchup. She didn't even have eggs to throw together an omelet. Maybe she accidentally left something in the crisper drawer.

Aerosol cheese food product. Score. She grabbed the fake cheese and a can of Coke, setting them on the white tile countertop. Roxy went back into the cabinet and got the crackers before scooping her not-so-gourmet snack up in the crook of her arm. All she needed now was a staged drama. She dumped her lunch on the couch and hit the on button for the big screen. Big screens weren't only for football fans anymore. They were also for watching a larger-than-life-size Jason Mamoa, sitting around grunting at the Dothraki in *Game of Thrones*.

She used the remote to find a tabloid talk show.

Although a Khal Drogo binge might be fun. Others' turmoil was always the best medicine when you had no direction, and the man you wanted to call wasn't blowing up your phone.

A pale woman smooshed into a short skirt, with giant nipples poking through her tank top, shook her finger at some guy missing his front tooth, while another woman in green spandex and a T-shirt screamed at the woman in the short skirt. "*.. he don't got no job. He needs someone who gonna take care of him. That's me, bitch. You don't deserve him.*"

Then there was slapping and hair pulling. Light brown hair extensions went flying. The censors earned their paycheck as beeps filled the air.

Roxy felt better almost instantly. Her life might suck, but she wasn't debasing herself on TV to get attention. That had to give her some karma points. Right?

Her cell phone dinged. Sarina. *They fired you?*

Not fired. On vacation. At least, she hoped it was only a brief vacation. Six days to be exact.

You should come out. A couple of us are doing a happy half hour on the High Roller tonight.

Who's going?

Three dots popped up and disappeared. The dots started a few times. She didn't want to answer. Which could only mean one thing.

Cliff, his friend and me.

More dots.

Don't be mad. Come with us.

Roxy could think of a million things she wanted to do with her newfound time off, and hanging with Cliff and his friend wasn't on the list.

Sorry. I have plans. Not lying. She had plans with spray cheese.

Roxy dropped her phone next to her on the couch and sprayed some cheese onto a cracker. The cold cheese came out reluctantly. She didn't have to leave the cheese in the fridge, but it felt unnatural for cheese to be in the cabinet. Thank goodness it tasted the same.

She slid the cracker in her mouth. So good. Fake cheese was awesome.

Her doorbell rang. Ms. Potter. She probably wanted her rent money. Which meant Roxy really should have looked for it. The one thing on her to do list that required action, and she hadn't even thought about it.

The doorbell rang again.

"Hold on." She set her lunch on the couch and opened the door. Not Ms. Potter. Detective MacAuley looked the same as he did that afternoon. That didn't explain why he was here, though. "Making house calls now, officer?"

"Only for some people."

"What makes me so special?"

He smiled with those teeth and sparkling eyes. "Are you going to let me in?"

"Sure." She stepped back just as a voice screamed

from the television, "You don't got nothing on me, whore."

Crap. She draped her body over the back of the couch, reaching for the remote. She hit the power button at the same time she realized she should have planned that move a little better. Her upper body slid until her thighs caught the top of the couch back, giving the detective a view of her ass. She tried pushing herself backward, but that was not going to happen. Roxy let gravity do its thing, sliding forward till her knees hit the floor.

MacAuley's eyes were on her as she popped up on the other side of the sofa. He had that smile on his face. The one that melted panties—which she was thankfully wearing under the thin yoga pants.

"Sorry. I had to turn off the TV." She checked the waist band and found it was still around her waist. Thank goodness. No free show.

His attention moved from her to the couch. "Is that your lunch?"

She could deny it, but the the cheese canister and box of crackers gave it away. "Yes."

"How about I buy you lunch?"

I don't think that's a good idea, ran through her mind, but she couldn't figure out why. Which was probably why it didn't seem to make it to her lips. She thought about her empty fridge and the free meal he was offering.

"We can go over the information I got from Donnie."

A potential new lead sealed the deal. "Let me get dressed." She reached for the box of crackers.

"Go get dressed. I'll clean up."

"Really?" The crumbs on the couch seemed to multiply when she stepped away. Embarrassment made her want to cover them all with a blanket. "It's not your mess to clean."

"It's part of the job." He picked up the cap for the spray cheese, clicking it into place. "I want to."

"Okay." She walked toward the hall entrance, but couldn't keep from watching him tidying up her house.

MacAuley rolled the bag inside the cracker box and pushed the tab shut. He swept the crumbs into his hand. The whole sight was somehow adorable. And hot. The man was cleaning up after her, so she could get dressed. Get dressed.

Her feet took her to her room where she whipped open her closet. This wasn't a date. She didn't need to dress up, right? She grabbed a pair of jeans and a silk collared-shirt—okay— she was dressing up a little.

Sarina had left the shirt behind after one of their nights out drinking. She shouldn't have left it here if she didn't want Roxy to wear it. Sarina would be on board with her wearing the shirt to impress the detective—if Roxy were hoping to impress him.

She ran a brush through her hair and slid on some lip gloss. She looked good enough to have lunch with a guy— a hot guy with a badge who cleans—or maybe she wasn't quite that good. She fluffed her hair and pushed up the girls. Better.

She popped her lips. Ready. Her body was getting warm and tingly just thinking about the nice guy wanting to buy her food and cleaning up after her. What was it about a man cleaning that was such a turn on?

That and a man with a puppy—and no shirt.

There went those tingles again. She needed to stop the tingles. She needed to get her head on straight. This was a business lunch with a guy who could be mistaken for a *People*'s hottest man of the year. Nothing more.

Libido. Checked.

Tingles. Checked.

Remembering the man could arrest her at any moment for a murder she didn't commit. Reality.

CHAPTER 12

THE ONLY PERSON WHO EVER WANTED ME FOR WHO I AM WAS THE POLICE ~ UNKNOWN

TWENTY MINUTES LATER, she sat in a booth at Hash House A Go Go, staring at the man across from her as he ordered chicken and waffles. She should order a nice salad. That was what women on dates ordered, right?

Thank goodness this wasn't a date. She didn't eat flora.

"What can I get you, sugar?" The older woman standing next to the table wore Super Girl knee-high socks.

"Cheeseburger with blue cheese and sweet potato fries."

"Great choice." The waitress slipped the oversize menus under her arms and dropped a straw next to the soda she'd put in front of Roxy. She lumbered across the wood floor of the restaurant toward the open cutout in the wall, where chefs hovered around steaming grills.

"I love this place." MacAuley drank from the coffee

cup in his hand. "It was the first place I found when I moved here."

"When did you move here?"

"Seven years ago."

"From where?"

"San Diego." He did have that dark blond surfer look. Which wasn't usually her type. He also had that annoying, non-talkative thing going on. Which, unfortunately, was always her type. But it would be nice to not have to pull every piece of information out one by one.

"Do I have to ask?" She sighed.

"Ask what?"

Apparently, she did. "Why did you move here?"

"I got a job offer at Las Vegas PD." He stopped talking when the server came by with plates bigger than their heads, with a steak knife stuck in the middle. The food was always pretty. It tasted even better than it looked.

"Didn't you have a job in San Diego?"

With a pained smile, MacAuley cut into his fried chicken. "I needed something different. What about you?"

"I've never worked in San Diego."

"Cute." He took another sip of coffee. "Are you from Vegas?"

"Born and bred."

"Is that how you know Amato?"

"We went to the same college. What about you and Rafe?"

"I worked with him." MacAuley dug his fork into a pile of waffles. The big plate of food piled high enough for a starving giant was disappearing fast.

Her food, however, had barely been touched, which meant she'd have food for a doggie bag. She could eat this tower of burger for a few days if she played her cards right.

"You just worked with Rafe?" The whole detective exam, best-man thing, and the way they acted around each other? There was a story. Even though she really should get him to talk about the case, that seemed way more interesting. Maybe there was a fight scene like the one in *Bridget Jones Diary*. The good guy fighting for his woman's honor.

Which one would be the good guy, though? MacAuley. Definitely MacAuley. She knew way too much about Rafe to call him good. "You worked with him, obviously, but there's got to be more. Didn't you say you were his best man?"

"You should ask Amato." MacAuley squirmed in his seat.

What the hell happened between these two? "I'm asking you."

"Rafe would want to be the one to tell you." The fork clinked on the plate as MacAuley put it down and finished his coffee.

Roxy had a feeling Rafe wouldn't care what MacAuley had to say. To Rafe, she was a nuisance. "Why would he care who told me?"

"Trust me. He'd care what I told you." MacAuley looked up like he wanted to say something, then shook his head. "Anyway, it's his story to tell."

"But aren't you afraid he'll paint you as the bad guy?"

MacAuley frowned. Really frowned this time. "I am the bad guy."

The cruel wife in Bridget Jones Diary popped into her head. "Did you sleep with his wife?" Holy moly. Was she sitting here with a wife-stealing, best-friend-back-stabbing jerk-hole?

"No." He laughed, but it fell flat. "I should probably get back to work."

His food was mostly gone, but she didn't want him to leave. She didn't want to be alone with her thoughts or the boredom that came with no job—and no leads to get back to that job. She wanted to push for more information about Rafe, but MacAuley acted like a skittish kitten, practically climbing up the curtains trying to get away. Maybe she could get him to stay if they stayed away from personal information.

She really needed a new lead. Or she'd be stuck eating leftover burger plus spray cheese and crackers, watching reality television for the foreseeable future. She tilted her head to the side and played with a wave in her hair. "I see what you're trying to do."

He tugged out his wallet and dropped two twenties on the table. "What's that?"

"Get away before you tell me what Steve had to say."

That smirk spread across his lips. He took the bait. The twinkle was back in his eye. "Maybe it's classified." The flirting was back in his voice.

"Then why did you offer to take me to lunch?"

"Could it be I just like your company?"

She'd buy that if he wasn't trying to gnaw off a limb to escape. A minute ago, he'd been looking at the door like it was the holy land.

She patted the opposite side of the table as she leaned forward in her chair. It was a woman power move. Her arms squished her chest, giving him a nice view of the Grand Tetons. Okay, her Tetons weren't all that grand. But they were big enough to get a guy to sit down, as proven by MacAuley dropping back into his chair.

"What do you want to know?" he asked on a sigh.

"Did Steve do it?" That seemed like the logical first question.

MacAuley laughed—deep and full—he was back. "He didn't sign a confession."

"Did you get any weird vibes, though?"

"Weird vibes?" He stared off to the side before shaking his head. "No. He said he was meeting Donnie for drinks that night, but Donnie never showed up. Steve stayed in the hotel bar till eleven and then left."

"That was around the time Donnie was in the lobby.

He was probably waiting for Steve. But then why did he go upstairs?" Roxy leaned forward. She couldn't understand why he'd gone upstairs—unless he knew the person he went up with.

"Not sure. He might have gotten a call from someone." MacAuley shrugged. "But we can't search the phone records because someone took the phone. We have a warrant out for the records, but phone companies are not very forthcoming."

"Anything else?" Because at this point, she wasn't getting anything she could use to move forward. If the cops couldn't get the phone records, there was no way she could.

"Steve mentioned Donnie's girlfriend, Amethyst."

"Was she the new one?"

"The new one?"

The server came over to the table and picked up his mostly empty plate. "Can I get you more coffee?"

"Please."

She juggled his plate in one hand while pouring more coffee with the other. This was why Roxy could never work food service. The plate would be in his lap and so would the coffee. No one wanted that. "How about you, honey?"

"A box would be great."

The woman disappeared into the kitchen.

"Where were we?" she asked MacAuley as he dumped a pack of sugar in his coffee.

"You said something about a new one?"

"Oh yeah, his wife didn't mention Amethyst. She said he was with friends-with-benefits with someone named Presley." She air-quoted friends-with-benefits, since they sounded more like benefits and not so much friends. Although the wife thought this one had been different. Could she have gotten the name wrong?

"He had a lot of friends-with-benefits. He could have had one named Amethyst and one named Presley." He didn't bother with the air-quotes, just took a drink of coffee.

"But she was sure that he was getting serious about Presley. Why would he keep seeing his side-side piece if he was getting serious about the side piece?"

MacAuley coughed and set the coffee cup on the table. After he finished laughing, he said, "I'm going to let you sit with what you just said for a minute."

"What?"

"Why would a man with a wife have a side piece, let alone have a—what did you call it—side-side piece? If a man is happy, why would there be any side pieces, let alone side-side pieces?"

"What?"

"See? It makes no sense." MacAuley shrugged. "Maybe Presley is a last name."

"Maybe." Roxy wasn't sure she bought that, but she'd follow the clues and keep Presley in the back of her mind.

"According to Steve, the girlfriend—whichever side piece that is—had been pressuring him to leave his wife."

The server brought a container and a plastic bag. "Take your time." She dropped the check on the table before shuffling off to assist other patrons.

"According to the wife, he had many girlfriends, usually of the by-the-hour variety." Roxy tried not to roll her eyes. It still killed her that he had multiple girlfriends while a good woman sat at home. "He had a regular he was getting close to, but he said he broke it off."

"That aligns with what Steve was saying. Donnie was getting pissed at his girlfriend because she wouldn't just let it go. She wanted him to leave his wife and he didn't want to. He was planning on breaking things off. He must have done it."

"So the girlfriend has a motive." Thankfully, that motive meant Roxy had a lead. No reality TV for her. She would meet some woman named Amethyst.

"She does."

"Does she have a last name?" Roxy put her burger and fries into the container and slipped it into the bag.

"Not that he knew of. He said her name was Amethyst. She's a dancer over at the Diamond Gentlemen's Club."

"At Pura Vida?"

"Yeah."

Which meant she had to go to another one of Rafe's hotels. She didn't know if that annoyed her or excited her. With everything going on, it would be stupid to be excited, so she'd stick to annoyed. She didn't think she'd see him again until she had more information on the jacket. Which begged the question... "Did that jacket belong to him?

"He said it didn't. Which makes sense if he never went in the room." MacAuley finished the cup of coffee and put the money on top of the check. "We should go."

He stood and, this time, Roxy followed. He still had a job and he probably wanted to keep it. He couldn't hang out with her all day. But wouldn't that be nice?

MacAuley held open the door as she slipped through. He smelled woodsy and manly and delicious. Not that he was delicious, or she felt that way about him. But there was something about a man who rocked the scoundrel/protector look all while smelling like a wet dream.

Nope. She didn't have any inappropriate feelings about him. None at all.

"Thanks for lunch." She meant it. He'd been nice enough to not only feed her but give her information on the case.

"Anytime." He started toward his dark green Ford Explorer but stopped before he reached it. "I know I'm going to regret this. But do you want to have dinner some time?"

He was going to regret it? She was already regretting it. She knew Rafe and MacAuley had a complicated history—well, join the club. She didn't want any more drama in her life. But he was nice. It didn't have to be a date.

"With that warm and fuzzy intro, how can I say no?" She could say no because she had to. She shook her head. "But I have to say no. It's not a good idea."

"Yeah." He turned toward his car before looking at her again. "Is it Rafe?"

Yes. "No. We're just friends. I mean we're not even friends. We're casual acquaintances that just... cross paths sometimes." *No. More. Words.*

"Then why?"

"I need to clear my name. I can't think about anything else right now."

Roxy could practically see the wheels in his head spinning. He might be nodding on the outside, but inside, he wasn't buying it. Hopefully, he'd let it go no matter what side he decided to listen to. "Then let's be friends."

"I'd like that." Outside it was.

Roxy opened the passenger door and got in the Explorer, settling her food for the week on her lap. MacAuley was nice. He'd given her so much information and hadn't asked for a thing—so yes, he was nice. He'd bought her food. Definitely nice.

Rafe might not be nice. But the things he could do to her and the way he made her feel was nice. Okay it wasn't nice, but it was hot and real. He'd offered to help her with her case—letting her in the hotel room when he didn't have to. So, yeah, he was nice, too.

She had so many new nice friends. Friends she wanted to get to know better. Friends she'd thought about naked. Well, she hadn't thought about MacAuley naked…

His arms bulged as he turned the car toward her house. His thighs bunched as he tapped the accelerator. All kinds of inappropriate thoughts ran through her head.

Oh yeah—now she'd thought about him naked. And nice wasn't even one of the first fifty words she would use to describe it.

CHAPTER 13

THE NEXT AFTERNOON, Roxy parked in a front spot in the large parking garage next to Diamonds Gentlemen's Club, behind the large drive-up lane reserved for valet and drop-offs—probably with some large limousine. Everyone became a baller when they came to Vegas.

She approached the tall gold door of the club, where normally a large hulking man loomed with an iPad, scowling at the world because he obviously hated his life of excluding the simple people. Or maybe he really liked it. Either way, there was no bouncer here now.

She tried the knob, hoping it wasn't locked. It was much easier to find a person when you could get in the building—and not walk through the hotel where Rafe would be watching the cameras.

The knob turned, and the door opened onto a dark, expansive room with red leather couches and chairs, plus a few small white tables. There were four raised platforms, each one with a silver pole in the center. It was too dark to see clearly, but Roxy thought there was a stepladder on the biggest platform, the one at the back of the room.

Soft lighting ran along the floor below the bar. A man wearing headphones mopped the floor, and given the way he shook his hips, he wasn't cut out to be a dancer any more than Roxy.

She needed to find a manager and get Amethyst's number or address. Then she could leave. Or maybe say hi to Rafe. It seemed silly to come all this way, not say hi and oogle his googles.

Not that she had time to oogle anyone's googles. Yeah, she heard the ridiculousness of it all—the words and the thoughts. She didn't need to be reminded. *Stop judging.*

"We don't open for twenty minutes."

Roxy jumped, and she looked up to see the man leaning on the mop handle, talking to her. "I'm not here for the show. I was hoping to see a manager."

He sneered. "Dave? Why? You want a job?" Whether it was an appreciative sneer or "you don't have the body of a dancer", she wasn't sure. Nor did she want to know.

She already knew she carried one too many donuts in the junk in her trunk. It wasn't a secret. No matter how much Victoria tried to hide it. "I need to find a friend of mine, Amethyst."

"I go by Amy when I'm not on stage." A woman's voice came from the stage with the ladder. She finished wiping the pole and stepped onto the platform. Her blond hair was rolled into curlers, and she wore a tiny red robe. Below the robe were black stockings held up by a garter belt. The red sneakers probably weren't part of her performance outfit. The woman eyed Roxy suspiciously. "Do I know you?"

"Not really. I'm sorry to bother you, but do you have a minute?" Roxy asked her.

"I just have to get my workspace ready." Amy-Amethyst rested her hand on her belly. A little pooch was beginning to show, and Roxy was sure if the lighting was better, she'd see a glow on the woman's skin. "I go on right after we open."

"I'll keep it short." Hopefully. "I wanted to offer my condolences. Were you dating Donnie Dunne?"

Amethyst winced and dropped the towel. "I was more than dating him. We were engaged."

Engaged, huh. So not broken up. "That's so hard." Especially on account of the bigamy.

"It has been." Amy climbed down the ladder and stepped down the stairs to the main floor. "I just miss him so much."

"When was the last time you saw him?"

"Saturday afternoon at the hotel."

"You were there?"

"He used my discount to get the room. I figured I'd take a nap before I went on that night. It's hard working that late when you're moving around for two." The maternal glow seemed to seep from her pores.

"Did you go back to the room that night?"

"I was going to go back after my shift. He had a meeting with some financier or something."

"Do you know the name of this financier?"

"Henry. Hank. Some old guy name with an H."

"Harold?"

"Yes." Amy giggled. "I should've remembered that. Like the crayon."

Roxy blinked. "The crayon?"

"Harold and the Purple Crayon. It was my favorite book growing up. That's where I got the name Amethyst."

"So is Amy your real name, then?"

"Yeah."

Since Amethyst was an Amy, there was little chance the jacket in the hotel room belonged to her. "How about a jacket with the initials SBM? Is that yours? Or do you know whose it could be?"

"SBM? Steve?" The lights over the stages flickered on and Amethyst squinted. "Who did you say you were with? I need to finish getting ready." Now she sounded distinctly unfriendly.

"I'm with the hotel." Roxy might have mumbled that

last part. Amethyst seemed to like to talk about the baby and Donnie, so Roxy just had to keep her on that topic and away from things that seemed to annoy her. "Were you and Donnie together long?"

"Four months. It doesn't seem like a long time, but it's the quality, you know? We were soulmates." A tear slid down her face. "He was everything to me. I don't know what I'm going to do."

Either she was telling the truth, or this woman was good. She looked heartbroken and the tears were flowing. The devastation was coating the air. This didn't sound a like a woman Donnie had left.

"Were you and Donnie still together?"

"What do you mean?" Amethyst swiped a finger under eyes and then placed her hands back on her baby-bump.

"Did Donnie break up with you?"

"No. Like I said, we were engaged. We were planning on leaving. He was selling his company so we could move closer to my parents."

"Where were you moving?" Part of Roxy hoped the answer wasn't Reno. Maybe he was going to actually choose one of these women and not lead some secret sister-wives thing.

"Reno."

Of course it had to be Reno.

"Donnie just had to pack up his office in Henderson

and then he was going to Reno to search for a place for us."

Well, at least she and the wife agreed on that. Roxy almost wondered if Amethyst knew the wife was moving too. "What about his wife?"

"They were getting a divorce."

"Did the wife know?" Roxy hadn't meant to ask that, but her mouth was moving faster than her brain. That happened a lot.

"I'm assuming she did. We were moving away." Amethyst's tone changed. Snippy. She didn't seem to like to talk about the wife.

Roxy needed a bit of redirection. "Is this your first?"

"Baby? Can you tell? I'm just a bundle of nerves." She giggled. "Donnie would tell me all the time how great a mother I was going to be. You know, his wife wouldn't give him kids. She didn't like them or something. What kind of person doesn't like kids? They're so cute."

Roxy tried to keep her face passive. Her thoughts on children weren't on trial here. It wasn't that she hated them. They were awesome and cute—when they went home with someone else. "He must have been so excited about the baby."

"Yeah." Amy rubbed her hands along her belly. "He called him his little running-back. He said with my athletic ability and his power, the kid would be a football player for the Raiders."

"You're having a boy." This woman's love for her child and her child's father gave Roxy a sugar-rush. It was too sweet. Too adorable.

"I am." A tear pooled in her eye. "My boy won't have a father. It's going to be so rough for him."

"Are you still moving back with your parents?" The question had nothing to do with the investigation. This had to do with a woman having her first baby alone, and grandparents who would probably love to help. If they were anything like Amethyst.

"I'm not sure. My friends are here. My life is here. I don't want to go."

A loud *ahem* came from across the room. Rafe sauntered closer, his black BDUs cinched at his waist and ankles, black boots, and a black button-down shirt. His dark brown hair was sexily disheveled, like he'd just run a hand through. He looked pretty bad-ass— and mad. But then again, Rafe was always mad when Roxy was around, so that wasn't anything new.

"Why are you here?" Rafe asked.

"I work here?" Amethyst wiped the last of her tears from her eyes. She picked up the towel from the little platform and folded the stepladder.

"I'm sorry, Amy. I wasn't talking to you." Rafe picked up the stepladder and focused on Amethyst. "Are you okay?"

"I'm fine. Just talking..."

"...with a friend." Roxy was being helpful. Hopefully,

Amethyst wouldn't contradict her exaggeration. Yes, exaggeration. Roxy liked the woman now that she'd met her. She even asked about her moving in with her parents. Total friend question.

"You're her friend. Since when?"

"Since..." Roxy didn't think *since five minutes* would go over very well. "Who cares?"

"What's her favorite color?" Rafe was so smug.

Roxy stared at Amy's robe. "Red." Her pre-stripping robe and sneakers were red. So that must be her favorite color and if not, she'd just said it with enough conviction that Rafe wouldn't question it.

Rafe lifted an eyebrow at Amethyst. "What's your favorite color?"

Or maybe he would.

"Red?"

He folded his arms. "What's her hobby?"

Stripping was probably not her hobby or her lifelong dream. Although, maybe it was. People had weird aspirations, but it was probably more a step to an aspiration. "Dancing."

Rafe looked at Amethyst.

She giggled. "I do like to dance."

"But is that your hobby? Is that what you like to do when you're not working?" Rafe kept at it, because—well, because he was a jerk.

"No, I like to read romance."

Read. Romance. Roxy's smile perked up. They did have something in common.

"Oh, my goodness, Amy. I love romance, too." Roxy could relate to sitting in bed from the moment she woke up till the sun dipped below the skyline. Forgetting to eat. Taking a Saturday to get lost in a book. "JD Robb is my jam."

"My jam?" Amy scowled, but in a cute way. "I don't think people say that anymore. But Rourke is my book boyfriend."

Roxy was so bonding with Amethyst. Which was nice. She didn't really have time to make any new besties, but it was ticking off Rafe. Bonus.

He sighed and turned to Roxy. "You should go. We have work to do."

"Fine."

"Amy Flannery?" Another male voice Roxy recognized. MacAuley and his partner, Detective Geary, came up behind Roxy and joined their happy little group. Great. It was bad enough Rafe and MacAuley were here. Now she had to deal with the partner. The partner who was glaring at her like she tit-punched his mom.

Geary and MacAuley pulled out badges. They were eyeing Amethyst, but they seemed to have enough eye to go around for Roxy and Rafe, too.

"I'm Amethyst," she said. Apparently, they weren't her friends. They didn't get to call her Amy. "Thank you so much for meeting me here, officers, but I only have a few minutes before I have to go on stage. That was the whole point of meeting here. I can't miss any performance, or they won't move me to host job when I get big."

"Why don't you get dressed? Take all the time you need, and I'll tell Dave." Rafe gestured to a hallway behind the main stage. "There's an office at the end of the hall if you want privacy," he said to the cops. "The music will get loud out in the main room."

Amethyst hurried away, presumably to the dressing rooms. MacAuley started for the door Rafe had pointed to, but the partner just stood there, looking at Roxy with his angry brown eyes. Seriously. She would have remembered if she'd tit-punched anyone. So there's no way she'd done that to his mother. But there was obviously a problem.

"Do you need something?" Rafe stepped between Geary and Roxy. Like a giant shield. It was incredibly barbaric—and hot. *Yes.* She realized barbaric and hot should not be in the same sentence. She'd have to forfeit her woman card if she didn't burn her bra or something after that comment.

"Miss Horne, you need to come to the precinct for questioning today." Detective Geary handed her a card. Like she needed the address to the police station. She'd lived in Vegas her whole life. She'd driven by them all at one point or another. And maybe been inside one or two of them.

"I thought we were going to do this later," MacAuley said to Geary.

"Well, I didn't think we'd be seeing her anytime today. But here she is. I don't believe in coincidence."

"You've already talked to her." Rafe's arms were crossed, and he didn't seem to like the direction the conversation was taking. Although maybe that was her.

"She failed to mention she was on probation from work a few weeks ago and wasn't given the Dunne case." Geary didn't quite sneer, but it was close.

"So? What does that have to do with anything?" She didn't realize she had to give them her whole life story. "I also punched Leslie Scott in eighth grade because she stole my boyfriend. I didn't mention that either."

Geary was definitely sneering now. "Mr. Dunne was the one who complained, causing your probation. You weren't allowed to work his case. Why were you?"

All six male eyes bore into Roxy. All of them with questions and judgement. Even the brown-eyed man who had just been her shield.

"I don't know." She really hadn't known. She knew a client complained, but a lot of the time she never met the client. She met the person they were serving. How could she have known he was the one who complained? "I took the case because my coworker was taking his girlfriend to a Golden Knights game. I was helping him out."

"You're saying it's a coincidence." Detective Geary smirked, which wasn't much of an improvement. "You might want to work on your story before you stop at the precinct."

She probably did want to work on her story. The truth was messy. It sounded like an excuse, and now she had to stop at the precinct. She didn't really have time to come up with a better story today.

Maybe tomorrow.

Could she possibly push it out till next week?

CHAPTER 14

THERE IS NOTHING SEXIER THAN A
FIREMAN THAT KNOWS HOW TO USE HIS
HOSE. ~ UNKNOWN

ROXY LEFT the darkness of club just as the security team opened the front door. Men slowly trickled in from the line outside the door, some in suits and some in shorts and tacky button-down shirts printed with beer cans and palm trees. Every day at the strip club was apparently like Black Friday at Walmart.

Rafe pushed through the group of businessmen and tourists grabbing lunch and stormed toward Roxy. She'd noticed he looked mad, but that was redundant.

"Did you know?" he demanded through his teeth.

"I said I didn't know." In fact, those were her exact words.

Rafe crossed his arms. She would've been impressed with the way they bulged, but he was being a jerk. "I know that's what you told them. I'm asking for the truth."

Her gut clenched from the words he just sucker-punched her with. She wouldn't like him lying to her, so she wouldn't lie to him. Not about this. This was huge. This was a man's life—and her life.

"Despite what everyone thinks of me, I'm not a liar." She pushed those words out with everything in her. She wouldn't let him see the pain. Her voice would *not* crack. She yanked the keys from her pocket and controlled the urge to throw them in his still angry face. She was the one who should be mad. She didn't know why any of this was happening around her. To her.

"See you around, Amato." Not. She would have to do a better job of avoiding Rafe and his properties. She'd managed to not see him for years. How hard could it be? Especially now that she knew they all thought she was lying. Not they, him. The tears bit at her eyes. She didn't know if they were upset tears or angry tears. Right now, she was just acknowledging angry—so she'd go with that.

She speed-walked away from him. Well, she might have been running. If her tears actually made an appearance, she refused to show him. He didn't deserve to see her cry. She made it all the way into the garage before he caught up with her.

"Hold on, Horne."

She pretended to not hear him. Had she done that from the beginning, she wouldn't be fighting the lump in her throat. She opened the driver side door and it thumped against something hard.

Rafe grunted.

Roxy bit back a laugh because if she let anything out,

even a laugh, she'd probably break down into tears. She stopped herself from patting the door in appreciation. Karma. Before she could slide inside the car, a hand wrapped around her fingers.

"Roxanna." The way he said her name liquefied her insides. His voice was soft. Kind. It melted the restraint that kept her emotions from spilling over the edge.

"What?" She kept her head down, praying that the keys in her hand would somehow make her invisible. Her eyes burned. *No crying. There's no crying in investigation.*

"Look at me." His thumb caressed her hand. "Please, Roxanna."

Fine. She lifted her eyes to his. There was more than remorse in the crinkles in the corner. There was concern in the scrunch of his eyebrows and the frown on his lips.

"I'm sorry. I should have known you wouldn't lie to me." His other hand swept across her cheek. His fingers were rough, but his touch was soft. It was the perfect combination.

Her eyes couldn't leave his—even if she tried. And she wasn't trying. "I'm not lying."

"I know." His hand cupped her cheek. "But they think you are."

She didn't care about them. She cared what he thought. She wanted Rafe to understand. Admitting that out loud was scarier than her impending date at the precinct.

"Are you okay, Roxy?" MacAuley's deep voice broke through all the words she refused to say to Rafe.

She bobbed her head up and down, breaking contact with the warmth of Rafe's hand on her face. "I'm fine."

"Geary can be a little abrupt." MacAuley's hands were in his pockets. He seemed upset, but she couldn't tell if it was because of what his partner had done or if it was something else.

"Abrupt?" Roxy snapped. Was that what they're calling it these days? "I was thinking he was another word starting with an A."

MacAuley grinned, but it was forced. Not that all-powerful smile from lunch. "Geary can be an asshole, too. He's just trying to figure out what happened."

"So am I," she pointed out.

"I know how much you thought you had riding on this, but it's your freedom now. Let us handle this." MacAuley sighed. "I promise I'll find out who killed Dunne."

"Okay." She crossed the fingers on the hand not in Rafe's possession. It wasn't lying if your fingers were crossed—playground rules.

MacAuley didn't look like he really believed her. Whatever. As long as he went away, it didn't matter what he believed right now. "Are you bringing her to the precinct?" he asked Rafe.

"Yeah." Rafe squeezed her hand and stepped closer

to Roxy. The intention was clear. MacAuley better back off. "Do you need anything else?"

Roxy would be disgusted by all the testosterone flying around, but she wanted MacAuley to back off. He was right. This was not just her job now. This was her freedom. And orange really wasn't her color.

MacAuley shook his head. Whatever he was seeing, he didn't like. Well, she didn't like being called a liar by his partner. "We should be done in fifteen minutes, then we're heading back to the precinct. I'll see you both there." MacAuley headed back inside.

Warm breath tickled along her temple. "I'll drive."

Drive. She pulled away from Rafe's body—which practically required the jaws of life. But there was no way he was dragging her to that interview. "Where?"

"To the precinct." He moved closer.

"I'm not going there today. Maybe tomorrow." She tried to angle into the car, but it was impossible with a large male body pasting her legs in place.

"You said you were heading to the precinct."

"I didn't say when I was going."

"I thought you didn't lie." The side of his lips quirked up. He was playing with her.

She kind of liked it. "I said I'm not a liar. Everybody lies."

"Really." The humor in his eyes was too much. It made her heart melt. Heck, it made her body melt. "How do I know you didn't lie to me?"

"Because I don't lie to you." The words came out before she could think about what that meant. Before she could stop them. Heat pooled in her cheeks.

Rafe's smile disappeared before his eyes went black. He pulled her into his chest before pressing a kiss to her lips. A soft gentle kiss that made her knees weak. Her head spun. Her heart stopped. Her body was alive with that gentle touch. Then he was gone.

"Let's keep it that way, Horne."

What? Keep what? Where? Her lips tingled. Her body jingled.

The confusion must have mingled with the flush on her face, because Rafe smiled. "If you're not going to the precinct, where are you going?"

Was she going? The fuzz in her brain cleared as she took in the parking lot at the Diamond Club. She'd interviewed the girlfriend, fought with the cops, and kissed Rafe with his soft lips. Well, her brain was caught up. But if she kept thinking about that kiss, there was a chance she'd fall back into the fuzz.

"Where are you going?" He smirked.

"Donnie had an office in Henderson. I thought I'd go take a look."

"Do you know where in Henderson?"

"I'm not sure. I need to do some research." Her computer and all her logins were back at the office. She could probably enlist Sarina's help, but Roxy didn't want to get her in trouble.

Rafe pulled out his phone and tapped the screen. "He has a building over on Water Street."

"How do you know that?"

"I've been doing my own investigation."

"Why?"

"You're not the only one who has something riding on this."

"Like what?" It wasn't his livelihood or his freedom. Nope, those were her crosses to bear. Why would he be investigating?

He slid his phone in the front pocket of his BDU's. He wasn't going to answer. She knew that even before he said, "How are you going to get in?"

"I got ways." She had no ways. She was banking on luck.

"I'll go with you."

"Why?"

"I, too, have ways. Ways that don't just include a rabbit's foot."

"I don't even own a rabbit's foot." *Ha!* She'd told him.

"Come on, Horne." He reached around her and ducked into her car. Before she could ask what he was doing, he walked away with her purse.

"Hey, that's mine."

He kept walking like he hadn't heard her, so Roxy had no choice but to abandon her car and go after him. Lights flashed on a giant black pickup truck, and after tossing her bag into cab, he climbed in the driver's seat.

The window on the passenger side rolled down. "Come on, Horne. We're burning daylight."

She sighed. There was no fighting him now. He had her bag as hostage. Maybe this was a good opportunity. He could teach her a few tricks— like how to do a proper B&E. She'd never broken and entered anywhere before. If she was going to make a go of the PI thing, she needed to acquire some new skills.

She climbed into the front set of the truck. A sinful smirk hit Rafe's lips before he pulled out of the spot. He had the look of a man who was ready to teach her a few skills, and none of those skills included lock-picks.

For a good opportunity, this was such a bad idea.

CHAPTER 15

RAFE DROVE his pickup past a line of large warehouses, and parked in a lot in front of a nondescript building. White stucco. Bright blue trim. Roxy did a quick count. Fifteen floors. She left the truck and waited while Rafe took his time getting out. They walked to the front door together, and Roxy stepped inside while Rafe held the door for her. There was a small foyer with an elevator on the left and a hallway on the right.

"What floor?" Roxy's hand floated over the elevator button.

"This way." Rafe grabbed her hand and pulled her down the hall, past closed office doors, to a metal door with a picture of stairs on it.

"What floor?" Roxy asked, hoping for a low number. Like one.

"Fourteen."

"Fourteen." Fourteen flights of stairs were at least ten

minutes of cardio. "Today's not my cardio day. Why don't we just take the elevator?"

"There are cameras in elevators. We don't want anyone to know we were here."

"Do we really care fourteen floors of stairs worth?"

He shook his head with a laugh. "Come on."

He opened the metal door and started up the stairs. One flight. Two flights. No problem. Three flights. Four flights. Bring it on. Her breath came in pants. *Feeling the burn.*

Halfway through the fifth flight, her muscles twinged. Just a little twinge. Her breathing was—maybe—a little labored. A little. *Stairs are easy.*

By the sixth floor, her legs were more than a little twingey. When was the last time she'd actually done cardio on cardio day? She needed to go back to the gym or at least climb some serious steps. Breathing was a problem. Her legs were lead beams, her muscles struggled to move them up and down. Okay, it wasn't that bad, but it still sucked.

She wanted to call uncle. She wanted to drop to the floor and plead for the torture to stop. But despite swearing she was on her last leg, her two legs kept moving up and up.

"Still alive back there?" Rafe climbed like a darn monkey. He wasn't breathing heavy. He looked like he was having a grand old time. Masochist. He stood at the landing of the seventh floor and pulled the door open.

"Are we taking a break?" Thank goodness.

"No, we're here."

"This isn't the fourteenth floor."

He smiled. "I might have been exaggerating."

She didn't know whether to kiss him or knee him in the balls. Since she could barely lift her legs, kneeing seemed like way too much work for so little reward. Anyway, she didn't have to climb anymore stairs.

That was a win in her book.

They entered the hallway and passed door after door. Lawyer's office. Flower delivery service. Accountant. They made it to the last door. No helpful sign. Nothing but a number. 712.

She tried the handle. Locked.

"Don't touch anything." Rafe pulled out two pairs of leather gloves. "Here."

"Where did you get these?" She took the pair he offered and slid them on.

"They were in my glove compartment." He put his on. "Never touch anything without gloves."

"Got it. Do you need a credit card? They picked a lock on TV the other day with a credit card." She slipped a credit card from the pouch on the back of her phone case. "Discover work?"

"This door only takes Visa." He produced a slim metal bar and a wavy metal pin from his wallet as he laughed. Smart ass.

"I meant because this card is thicker than most." She slid the card back in the phone case.

Rafe knelt on the tile in front of the door and stuck the metal pin in the lock.

"Wait. I want to watch." She could hear the sexual connotations in that statement.

His eyebrow lifted. Apparently, he could hear the sexual connotation too. "What exactly do you want to watch?"

"How you're picking the lock." She bumped his shoulder with her hip. "You perv."

"Not a perv. It's not my fault your mind was in the gutter. I was just interested in what you wanted to watch me do." His voice was all mock injustice.

She wanted to argue the gutter point, but her mind was in the gutter. She blamed him.

"That." She pointed at his hand at the door. "I want to watch you do that."

"First, you put the tension wrench in the keyhole." He held up the slim metal bar so Roxy could see the angled tip. "Tension wrench."

"Got it."

"You want to put the wrench inside, jiggle it to see which way the handle should turn. One way will have more give. Here." He slid the wrench into place. "Grab the wrench and twist back and forth."

She leaned over him. Her hand bumped his as she put her fingers where his were. She would like to say she felt nothing. But that was a lie. Not that it mattered, she was currently breaking and entering, so who cared. *His touch meant nothing.* See? No one cared.

"Slow down a bit." He guided her hand back and forth. "Can you feel how it gives a little bit when you slide it to the right?"

How the hell was she supposed to feel anything through the gloves and with his hand on hers?

"You want to keep pressure on the wrench and slide the rake into the top of the keyhole." He inserted the wavy pin. "Now you move the rake, tapping each pin up one at a time until you have them all lifted." His wrist jiggled as his fingers worked the rake thingy. The wrench moved. The lock popped open. "Easy."

Easy was how he made it look. All she'd done was put a bit of pressure on the wrench. That had been easy enough. If she just brought him with to wiggle the wavy thing, she'd be great.

He slipped the tools in his pocket as they entered the office. Although office might be a stretch. It was a room with a desk. Papers covered every surface and were piled on the side beside stacked boxes. A small flowerpot sat on the windowsill.

"Where do we start?" She ruffled the edge of the papers filling one of the boxes.

"Start there. I'll go through the desk."

This was her case. He was the locksmith. She was the

PI. "You start with the box. I'll take the desk." There. She told him.

He smirked. "As you wish, Roxanna." He switched places with her.

"*The Princess Bride?*" Roxy slid open the top drawer of the desk.

"It was my favorite movie."

"Was? Past tense?" How could anyone like *The Princess Bride* in past tense? Cinematic gold and he just tossed it to the side. She held her hand over her heart. "I was almost impressed by you."

Rafe didn't turn his head. "Was. Past tense."

"What's your favorite movie now? What could possibly dethrone the Princess Bride?" She sifted through the capless pens and loose paper clips before giving up and shutting the top drawer.

"Nothing dethroned it." He finished the first box, and moved to the next one. "I just grew out of it."

"How do you grow out of it?" Roxy opened the bottom drawer. Empty. Almost empty. She pulled out black tubing with a squeeze bulb on one end and a clear cylinder on the other. "What is this?"

His eyes grew wide. "You might want to put that back."

"Why?" She dropped it in the drawer.

"That's a penis pump."

Ew. Gross. She ran her gloves back and forth on her thighs until the cooties were gone—or, at the very least, aggravated. "You mean a pump to make a penis bigger." Donnie probably needed to do something to get that many women to jump into bed with him—without leaving cash on the nightstand.

"Yes."

Roxy stared at the drawer, hoping that thing wouldn't jump out at her. She never would have guessed that there was a pump for that. In fact... "How do you know what one of those are?"

"A penis pump?"

"Yeah."

"Instructions came with the penis handbook." He laughed.

Sexism was alive and well. They got a handbook. All the problems that came with women's plumbing, and there was no handbook. No instructions. Nothing.

Rafe nodded as he dipped into the third box. "Finding anything?"

"Besides the pump? No." That was it for the drawers. The top of the desk was remarkably free of paper, and had only a phone and a large desk calendar. She flipped open the calendar. There were a few scribbles. A lunch here. A dinner there. But then she found something interesting. It seemed interesting. Along the bottom of one of the pages. "Look at this. Presley, nine months. Seven-twenty." Presley. There was that name again. "Donnie's wife mentioned she thought Donnie's girlfriend was named Presley." Roxy ripped the piece of paper of the pad. *Presley. 9 months. 7/20.*

"I thought Amethyst was the girlfriend," Rafe said, abandoning the boxes.

"Maybe it's her real name?"

Rafe took the piece of paper. "No. We ran a background check when she got a job at the club. We would've known if she was called by another name."

"Maybe he had more than one." She took the paper away from him and shoved it in her pocket. She looked around the room. Maybe there was something else about Presley or Amethyst.

She crossed the flattened and stained red carpeting to examine the flowerpot on the windowsill. The plant was a brown, shriveled mess. When she looked out the window, two people crossed the lot to the front of the building. MacAuley and his partner.

"Cops are here. They just went in the front door. They'll probably take the elevator." She tried to keep the frustration out of her voice, but her legs still hated her from the trip upstairs.

"Probably." He restacked the boxes and opened the door. Glanced into the hall. "Let's go."

They ran down the hall. Silent, except for the sound of their shoes hitting tile. Fifty feet. That's all they needed to cover, and they'd be in the stairwell and away from the cops.

And she needed to stay away from the cops. They'd warned her. They'd named her a suspect. If they found her here, she'd never hear the end of it. Mostly because she'd be stuck in a jail cell where they would have twenty-four-seven access. She'd never be able to drop the soap again.

A ding came from the elevator. Not just a regular ding, the loudest elevator ding on the planet. They were only halfway to the stairwell. Rafe grabbed the nearest door handle and twisted. Nothing. Roxy reached for another one and the knob turned. "Here," she whispered as she slid inside. No windows. Nothing giving off light.

Rafe pushed her deeper into the room and shut the door. Her foot bumped a bucket and wood clanked against the wall. If it wasn't so damn dark, she was sure she'd be looking at a fallen mop.

"Shh..." He pulled her to him and whispered in her ear, "They're coming."

Her body was flush against his. She could feel all of his hard muscles. If she didn't get her mind out of the gutter, she'd be the one coming. Not just the cops.

"It should be just down the hall." MacAuley's voice was muffled through the door. "The key says 712."

Rafe smelled good. He smelled so good she almost couldn't hear the voices outside the door. All right, she could hear them, but she almost didn't care.

"Why won't you even listen?"

"If you said something worth listening to, I would." MacAuley's voice passed by the door.

His partner's voice stopped in front of the door. "She did it. She has motive and she found the body."

Found the body? As in her? Rafe's body tensed in her arms.

"Look, I know it's not Roxy." Apparently, it was about her. But at least MacAuley was defending her.

"Roxy? You mean Roxanna Horne, don't you? She's sketchy as shit and you can't see past the big tits."

Something hit the door with a smack. "Back off."

"You're seriously going to fight me over her. Are you sleeping with her?"

"Darren, you're crossing the line." MacAuley's voice was deep and threatening.

"I'm just trying to figure out what the hell is going on." The partner's name must actually be Darren. Surprising. She had been convinced it was Asshole.

MacAuley sighed. It was a loud one since she could hear it through the door. "I'm just trying to figure all this out, too. But my gut is telling me she didn't do it."

"For your sake, I hope you're right."

The voices disappeared.

All that was left was silence and Rafe's body against hers. Her heart thumped in her chest. Because he was so close or because she was hiding from the cops or because, apparently, the partner thought she was guilty—she didn't know.

The partner was ticking her off. What had she ever done to him? She didn't have murderer written on her forehead. No criminal background—well, not much of a criminal background, but peach schnapps made her clothes fall off. There wasn't a song about it, but that didn't mean it didn't happen. "He thinks I'm guilty."

"MacAuley doesn't seem to think so." Rafe didn't seem to be impressed with MacAuley's defense.

"Is there a problem?"

"No." He drew back and opened the door. He looked left, then right. "We should go."

They headed down the seven flights of stairs. She let the conversation go, but Rafe had to know she wasn't done with him.

CHAPTER 16

ROXY DIDN'T SAY A WORD. She hadn't said a word as they ran out of the building. She hadn't said a word as they ran to the car. Getting away from the detectives had been priority number one. But they were on the road now. Far away from the arguing detectives.

"So."

"So." Rafe idled the truck behind another car, his blinker blinking. Blink-blink. Blink-blink.

"What happened back there?"

"What happened where?" His fingers drummed on the steering wheel.

"Back in the closet." She could tell something happened. His body was wound tighter than a corset on a viscountess in a historical romance novel.

Rafe shook his head as he followed a car onto Boulder Highway.

"Come on, Rafe."

"What do you want me to say?"

"I could feel it. Back in the closet. What was the problem?"

"Dammit." His hands gripped the steering wheel. Knuckles white. "Do we need to do this now?"

"Yes."

He sped off the highway and found an empty lot. Then he slammed the car into park before turning to her. The setting sun haloed around his head. "Fine. Are you sleeping with MacAuley?"

"What?"

"He never answered the question."

"Probably because it's a dumb question." She crossed her arms. Did he really think she'd jump into bed with MacAuley? Rafe and she had kissed. It wasn't a marriage proposal, but she thought it meant something.

"If it's such a dumb question, why won't you answer it?"

"I don't even know his first name. There's no way I'm going sleep with someone when they won't even tell me their first name." She gazed out the front window. Then there was silence.

A lot of silence.

Roxy sighed. Loudly. "We should go. I need to get back to my car."

Rafe pulled out of the lot and headed back onto Boulder Highway. Roxy stared out the side window, watching desert pass by in a blur. The silence settled on the car, sucking all the air.

She wanted to be mad. Okay. She was a little mad. She wasn't some badge-bunny chasing after the first cop she found. And since they had shared not only a kiss, but Rafe's hands sliding up and down her body—she would like to think he'd known her better than that.

Apparently not.

The scenery switched from desert to tracts of houses. The stifling lack of noise inside the car didn't change.

"I'm sorry." Rafe stared at her, and then focused back on the road. "It's not you."

"It sure felt like me. It felt like you were judging me."

"Not you. I don't trust MacAuley."

"What the hell happened between you two?" Roxy turned in her seat to face Rafe. "He wasn't very forthcoming with information. All I know is he was your best man and friend and now he's not."

"You talked to him?"

"I tried. He said it's not his story to tell." She sighed. Men.

"Of course he did." His hand tightened on the steering wheel. "I told you I was married."

Roxy nodded. She knew that much. They had gotten that far into the story. But that left more questions than answers.

"Monique and I were together for one year. In the beginning, it was great. But then I got a promotion and she got a promotion. We were both successful." He said successful like it was four-letter word. "We didn't have much time for just the two of us. So, one night I came home, and I found them."

Them?

No way.

"That lying jerk." She'd believed MacAuley when he said that he hadn't slept with Rafe's wife. No wonder he didn't want to tell her the story. He was a cheater, cheater, friend mistreater.

"What?"

"I asked MacAuley if he pulled a Bridget Jones. Well, not really a Bridget Jones but a Daniel Cleaver..." Her voice faded as Rafe looked at her like she was from Venus, eyebrows scrunched together. How did he not get the reference? "You know, like Daniel Cleaver who was the best man at Mark Darcy's wedding and then slept with Mark's wife. He was like a total scoundrel. Even the mom said so."

Rafe shook his head and a smile tugged at his lip. "He didn't pull a *Bridget Jones*."

"Oh." She sat back and waited. She might have read the situation wrong. "Who did you find?"

"I came home and found my commander and my wife in my bed."

Whoa. "That sucks. Is that why you left Las Vegas PD?"

"No, I left Las Vegas PD when I found out that my supposed best friend knew about it and didn't tell me."

MacAuley was obviously the best friend in this scenario. "Maybe he just hadn't had time to tell you?"

"He knew for two years."

"But you were only married for one year."

"You can see how the math doesn't quite work."

"Why didn't he tell you before you married her?" *Don't say it wasn't his secret to tell. Don't say it wasn't his secret to tell.*

"He said it wasn't his secret to tell."

Well, that would explain the ex-best-friend thing. She sagged against the seat. How could a best friend think that was okay? She'd never do that to Sarina, and she'd be heartbroken if Sarina did that to her. There are some codes that shouldn't be broken. Hiding the last cupcake— totally okay. Hiding that the love of your life is a lying, cheating scumbag—not okay. And really, when it came to your BFF, the cupcake thing wasn't okay either.

Rafe left the highway and headed toward the strip, where her car was still parked at Diamonds Gentlemen's club. Since the cops were at the other building, they weren't at Diamonds.

No. They were at the other building fighting over her. "Do I look guilty?"

He merged and made a right onto Las Vegas Boulevard before his hand found hers. "Look? Yes. But you're not."

"But only you and MacAuley believe that."

"True. Despite MacAuley being a huge dick, he's a good cop." Rafe brought her fingers to his lips. The softest brush of lips. The slightest tickle of breath.

And her body was goo.

He dropped her hand and turned into the Diamonds' parking lot. "You have me. I might not be on the force, but I've got a few tricks up my sleeve."

He did have tricks up that sleeve—like those thick, well-defined biceps she felt in the closet. Not that she'd noticed.

Rafe drove through the lot, but he didn't stop by her car. "My car is right there." She pointed, but he kept going, pulling up to the exit on the other side. She spun her body in the seat to see if there was something wrong with her car. Nothing. "Umm. It's that way."

"Are you ready to talk to the cops?" He tapped his blinker and tick-tock filled the cab.

Cops? One thought she was guilty and the other was a jerk. "No."

"There are cops on your car."

She twisted as far as the seatbelt would allow. Her piece of crap sat there alone—well, surrounded by other cars. No people. "There's no one on my car."

"The blue Suburban two aisles over."

She counted two aisles and found the giant SUV with two people sitting in the front seat—a man and a woman. "How do you know they're cops? Maybe they're going to have a quickie."

"If they were interested at all, they'd at least be looking at each other. They're not making out. Their focus is outside the car."

"As in, my car."

"That would be my bet."

"What am I gonna do?" Now she didn't have a car. How would she get places? She had responsibilities. Not that she had a job she had to get to in the morning. But she had things to do... No, she didn't. Outside of this investigation, she really had nothing to do. The realization was sad.

"I can take you home, but there's a good chance they posted someone there as well."

She couldn't go home. She had no car. Given the text yesterday, Sarina was probably on-again with Cliff, which meant trying to sleep on the couch while listening to the headboard bang against the wall. There was always her mom, but since her partner Danielle was a doctor and usually on call, Roxy would be stuck dealing with her mother and her judgement. Her father's place wasn't much better. No judgement, just a woman the same age as her trying to get Roxy to braid her hair and call her mom. The choices were stupefying.

And by stupefying, she meant stupid.

"You can stay at my place."

"What?" Roxy was hearing things now. She could've sworn she heard Rafe say she could stay at his place.

"If you need a place to lay low for a few days, you can stay with me."

So that wasn't a figment of her imagination.

"Unless you want me to take you to the precinct. You have to face them sooner or later."

"I choose later." It was true, she had to face them. Eventually. But knowing they thought she was guilty? Knowing they might not let her leave? She needed to figure some things out before she entered their lair. She needed the upper hand. Preferably another name to replace hers at the top of their list.

"So where to?"

"Your place." The ramifications of those words hit straight to her core. Spending the night in Rafe's house with him was such a bad idea. They needed to focus on finding the bad guys, not on finding her G-spot.

Although looking at his hands—remembering the feel of those hands— she had a feeling he already knew where hers was. Just thinking about it made her body hum.

But they were just friends. Friendly friends.

She had to keep remembering that, no matter how much her G-spot wanted to be found by that man.

CHAPTER 17

TWENTY MINUTES LATER, Rafe parked his truck in a numbered space in an underground garage at the Pura Vida. The setting sun crept through the concrete poles holding up the building and painted the floor with flared stripes of orange.

Roxy glanced around. "You live at the hotel?"

"The condos." He got out and closed the door.

The truck alarm beeped as Roxy followed him toward the elevator. Rafe hit the up button. "What floor are you on?" Roxy asked when the doors slid open and they stepped inside.

"Eighth." He hesitated inside the elevator, his hand hovering over the panel. "Do you want to hit the button?"

"What?"

"Sorry." He hit number eight and the doors closed. "I'm used to people asking me what floor so their kid can push the button."

"Kids. How many kids do you get in Vegas hotels?"

"You'd be surprised."

She probably would be surprised. When she was a kid, her parents always warned her about the shenanigans that happened on the Vegas strip, usually as they drove by on their way to somewhere else. The lights and people were so interesting to a five-year-old. But after she snuck up to see what her parents were watching on TV one night, she was convinced shenanigans were gremlins, so she was always afraid to visit.

Rafe slid a card over the reader at one of the dark blue doors lining the hallway. With a click, the door unlocked and he pushed inside.

Afraid. That was a mistake. The hardwood floor in the front hall of the condo led straight into the living room with its floor to ceiling windows. Sun glistened on the buildings at the southern edge of the strip. The city looked practically angelic. "This is beautiful."

"The view is nice." Rafe walked past Roxy into a small kitchen. Cherry Shaker-style cabinets lined the side wall and wrapped around an island with a black quartz countertop and three bar stools. He pulled a package from the refrigerator and set a pan on the stove. "How do you like your steak?"

This was like speed-dating. Not that she'd ever done that, but you heard things. What was the question? "Steak?"

"Dinner."

"Medium." She took a better look around. A tan L-shaped couch faced both the window and the TV hanging on the righthand wall. A foosball table sat next to the kitchen. She could see an open bedroom door behind the table.

White, black and brown pillows lined the cherry headboard of a king-size bed made up with a brown and white comforter. The matching nightstand held a phone charger and a simple silver lamp.

His bedroom—if she wasn't mistaken. Her eyes moved back to the bed. Where he slept. Visions of Rafe stretched out naked underneath his sheets fluttered through her inappropriate head. Those inappropriate thoughts meant she had to stop staring at his bed before he noticed—or her nipples went hard. Whichever came first.

"Can I help?" She turned to Rafe just as he finished searing the meat and slipped the pan in the oven.

"Nope. I got it."

He hadn't noticed her gawking. Nice.

"Keep ogling my bedroom if you'd like."

Dammit.

"Or go inside and take a closer look."

Even though she wanted to take that look, there was no way she'd do it with him thinking she was ogling anything. She didn't ogle. If she did, she kept it private—where ogling belonged.

"Do want something to drink?" He slid a small pot of

water on the stove and started the burner. "I have Merlot, Corona and water."

"Corona, please."

He pulled out two bottles from the bottom shelf and used an opener before putting them on the counter.

She took the closest one and leaned against the island-slash-breakfast bar. "Do you have a condo at every hotel?"

"No. Just this one. If things pop off and we work too late and they have an opening, they'll give us a room for the night. Kind of like I did for you." He leaned an elbow on the counter and took a pull of his beer. "This is my home."

Roxy raised her eyebrows. "With throw pillows?"

Rafe shrugged. "The condos come furnished."

The throw pillows made perfect sense then, but that left another decorating question. "And the foosball table?"

"I didn't see the point of a kitchen table when I have the bar here, so I gave it to Marinda." He took another drink.

"Marinda?"

"My nanny."

"You have a nanny?"

"Had a nanny. My mom passed away when I was in third grade. Marinda was my nanny, and then my dad's second wife. She was like a mother to me."

"Is she still with your dad?"

Rafe laughed, a hollow unfunny grunt. "My dad doesn't keep people around. He's living in the highlands with his fifth wife and their three-year-old son."

"The southern highlands, where you lived in college." She remembered that house. Large and ridiculous. "There were pictures all over the house of your dad with a woman. Was that Marinda?"

Rafe took a pull from his beer. "That was her. She was around until after college, when my father decided he didn't need her. I just like to make sure she's taken care of."

"That's nice of you."

Rafe played with the mouth of his beer, winding the neck between his fingers. "I don't know about nice. She's my family."

"She had a friendly smile, from what I remember." It had only been one party, but she'd made sure to soak up the environment.

He cocked his head, mouth quirking. "You noticed that?"

It was Roxy's turn to take a drink before answering. "It was a small town. Everyone noticed everything."

"Like when you cut your bangs junior year?"

"I didn't cut them. Sarina did." Her bangs had been crooked. Short enough to stick straight out. She'd be mad at Sarina, but Roxy had forced her to do it. "How did you know that?"

"Small town." He smirked but didn't elaborate.

"Nice subject change."

"I liked it." He shook his head and set his beer down, turning around to dump a box of Minute Rice into the boiling pot. "What about your parents? Do they still hate each other?"

"Talk about noticing." Warmth spread through her chest. He remembered when she'd talked about her parents.

"It's a small town. Everyone notices everything." His smirk was almost predatory, so she almost threw up her hands and surrendered. Almost. If he wanted to snatch her up and eat her, she was game.

What was that?

Red clawed at her face at the thought of snatching, eating and gaming. Stop! His lips moved but she couldn't hear anything over the sexual innuendo rushing in her ears.

She needed to focus and get her mind out of his pants —or her pants. All thoughts needed to be pants-free—but not him. He needed to wear pants. Her too. They were still wearing pants. That was good. "What?"

"How are they doing?" The side of his lip edged up. "Your parents."

Oh yeah, them. How were they doing? "They're fine as long as they aren't in the same room. Did you know my parents weren't together? After my dad left my mom, she met a woman and fell in love... I guess that's how that works. I don't know. Anyway, my mom and Danielle are going strong, but my dad is dating someone named Stormy and she's two years older than I am. She wants to be besties and for me to call her Mom. I can barely call her Stormy. Who would do that to a kid? It's not even a name. It's a weather system. We were in high school at the same time. How do you call someone you went to high school with 'Mom'?"

If there wasn't enough red crawling up her neck before, now she could power the letters in the Vegas sign. As usual, she became socially awkward with him around. She rambled. Not that she was the picture of articulation when he wasn't around, but she seemed to be able to tone it down. Or maybe it was that no one noticed.

"I'm glad they both found someone. That's how that works if you're lucky."

"Weren't you married?" The heat receded from her cheeks as she held back an eye roll. The man was making her dinner and giving her safe harbor. He deserved steady eyes for thoughtfulness. "Were you lucky?"

"Not a chance. You've heard all about my marriage disaster. How about you?"

"I don't have a marriage disaster." That would require a marriage. She hadn't found anyone worth even attempting that walk of shame.

"You're lucky." He fluffed the rice in the pot before pulling out two plates. After portioning out two scoops of rice on each plate, he took the steaks out of the oven.

A couple knives and a couple forks later, they were

sitting at the bar cutting into the most tender steak Roxy had ever eaten.

"This is amazing. Where did you learn to cook like this?" She took another bite. And another.

"Marinda."

"Tell her thank you."

"I will." He attacked the steak and rice same as her, as if he hadn't eaten in months. "Did you always want to be a process server?"

"Since third grade." She tried, but she couldn't stop her eyes from rolling. No one wanted to be a process server. "Most kids wanted to be a doctor, mermaid, or a mermaid doctor. But not me. I dreamt of serving paperwork to angry people."

"So, if this isn't the dream, what is?"

"What's your dream?"

"You first." He took a drink of beer.

"Private investigator." She looked down and her plate was empty. When did that happen? "You know, like Sherlock Holmes, but with girl parts."

"Thank goodness for the girl parts."

"Your turn. Are you living the dream?"

He leaned back in the chair and moved his empty plate to the side. "The dream was to be a cop."

"You could find another police department. North Las Vegas. LA."

"Dreams change." He waved at the condo around

them. "Anyway, why would I leave here? I have a great job that pays me well, and I oversee security for twelve properties all over the United States. As soon as I think things are getting slow, someone comes up with a new scam and we have to adjust and find a new way to handle things."

"It sounds like this is the dream."

"It is." He smiled and stood. Taking the dishes to the sink, he rinsed them before putting them in the dishwasher. "Did you want to watch a little television? Or are you tired?"

"I should probably go to bed." Going to sleep in Rafe's bed sounded pretty good. She just needed to talk him into getting into the bed with her. Unless he was putting her on the couch. That thought made her sad—and not just because couches notoriously led to back pain. Either way, both of them needed their rest. "We need to find Presley tomorrow."

"Yeah, we should start early." He closed the dishwasher and hit the button. A slight hum came from the machine as he wiped his hands on a towel hanging from the handle of the stove. "Let me show you to your room."

Disappointment snaked through her. *Your room.* He turned down a hall to the right of the entry door. She hadn't even noticed the hall when they'd first come in. Which wasn't her fault. That view was killer.

She followed him down the small hall to a bedroom.

"I'll bring you some clothes." He disappeared from the room, and she was left alone. Where she would sleep. Alone. Not wrapped in Rafe's arms.

More disappointment, and not because of the room.

It was a nice room. Queen bed with a blue comforter. A small bedside table with a silver lamp. Over the bed, a painting with white flowers standing at attention across a black and mustard canvas.

"These should fit." Rafe came back carrying a toothbrush and travel toothpaste on top of a pair of sweatpants and a tee.

She took the stack from him and fingered the plastic packaging. "A toothbrush?"

"I have a few extras for when I travel." He pointed out the door. "There's a bathroom over there."

The clothes were nice. Thoughtful. But the toothbrush and toothpaste. It was too much. He was too much.

A bubble of gratitude skipped in her throat. "Thanks for this. Tonight. Everything."

"No problem." He headed toward the door but stopped and twisted his head to look at her. "Come get me if you need anything."

"I will." Or not. There was nothing she could possibly need that she would feel comfortable *coming to get him*. She watched him leave and stared at the open door.

She could ask for a glass of water.

She could ask for a shot of whiskey.

As long as she didn't ask for the one thing she really wanted. His hands. His body. Him.

He'd asked her to his place and didn't make one move. Didn't even try. That told her more than she wanted to know.

CHAPTER 18

ROXY LAID ON THE BED, praying to go to sleep, but God must have had bigger fish to satisfy. Her eyes wouldn't close. Her body wouldn't lie still. She wanted to blame being overtired, but she had a feeling it was being so close to that man across the condo and not being able to touch.

Even her body knew it was unnatural to deny herself a piece of that. But she wasn't denying herself. Was she?

A part of her wondered if he was interested. She thought he was. He seemed all kinds of interested in the closet today. The way his body covered hers? Okay, maybe she'd imagined it.

Then there was the kissing. But she wasn't in grade school. She was an adult. Kissing wasn't a promise. It was just kissing.

Overanalyzing her love life or lack thereof wouldn't help her sleep. She switched to counting sheep. Big fluffy balls of fleece. Jumping. One over the fence. Two over a bale of hay. Three over Rafe laying on the ground giving Roxy those come-hither eyes.

Maybe he was naked. Rafe, not the sheep. Were sheep already naked if all they had was wool on their bodies? How many sheep did you see modeling the latest barnyard trends? Although there was this documentary where the sheep were shaved down to their skin. That was probably naked in the sheep world.

She sat on the edge of the bed. This was so not working. She should've asked for that shot of whiskey when she'd had a chance. Rafe was probably sound asleep. She could try and find something to help her get through the night on her own.

The only light in the living room came from the view of the strip outside the window. Red, pink and blue lights washed onto the couch. The view was amazing. This was her city. Lights flashing. People splurging. She pressed her forehead against the window as the glowing city winked back at her.

"Shouldn't you be asleep?"

Her head bounced on the glass as her body jumped. Rubbing her forehead, she turned around. "Sorry. I was having trouble sleeping, so I thought I'd come out here and grab a drink." She tipped her head toward the glitz of the strip. "I got sidetracked."

Speaking of sidetracked. Rafe stood in front of her in a pair of sweatpants and nothing else. His bare chest was hard pecs and ridges that begged to be touched. "It's calming."

Calming? Her body was the furthest from calm. "What is?"

"The lights." Rafe edged closer to Roxy at the window, staring out over the twinkle of lights. "Being so high up and watching people go about their business. Go on with their lives."

"It makes me feel small."

"Yes. But there's something soothing about knowing there's so much world out there and we can only control our piece."

She didn't pull away as his bare shoulder grazed hers. "Do you have control over your piece?"

"I try." His eyes were sad as he looked out at the city. "Most of the time I do. But what happened to Donnie Dunne shows I don't have the control I need."

"You can't control everything, all the time." She slid her hand in his as her heart broke. He truly believed he had to manage his entire empire. Alone.

He shook his head. "It's my job. It helps that I only have to control my piece of the world."

She slanted her body toward him and rested his hand along her hip. "What happens if you lose control?" Her hand travelled up his chest and slid down his other arm.

"People get hurt."

"What happens if you have help?" She angled her body a little more toward his.

His hands both found their way to her hips, his fingers sliding beneath her shirt. He pulled her close, and her body hummed with every stroke of his thumbs on bare skin. She pressed her thighs together, trying to control the need pulsing through her body.

He dipped his head. His lips moved to her neck. His breath blazing a trail behind her ear. "I've never tried it."

"You should try." The air left her lungs in breathy bursts. Her arms wrapped around him, hands running the length of his strong back.

"Maybe we should change the subject."

"What do you want—" Her eyes closed. Her body throbbed. "—to talk about?"

His lips hovered above hers. "Let's not talk."

She could feel his breath and the slightest brush of his lips on hers. All-consuming want swirled in her body as he hovered. No talking. Talking was overrated. Kissing. Her lips tingled. She needed kissing.

She needed him.

His mouth found hers, his tongue slowly licking the edge of her lip. Her body flamed, on the edge of combustion. She could practically feel the orgasm tug at her core.

He was desire. He was want. He was everything she needed him to be and everything she'd never had before.

He rested his hands on her ass.

"Wrap your legs around me." The whispered order held a tad of desperation.

He rested his hands under her ass and lifted her legs

up to circle his waist. Her body rubbed against his in all the deliciously perfect places. He pulled her close and moved toward his bedroom, pausing right outside the doorway.

"Are you sure about this?" That desperation hollowed out his tone.

She understood. "Yes."

He carried her into the bedroom and shut the door.

CHAPTER 19

ROXY WOKE up the next morning with a smile on her face. Yes, she was smiling, and she didn't care who knew. Her body ached from the things Rafe did with his tongue. That tongue should be coated in gold and worshipped. Not to mention the things he could do with that body.

He was hot and bossy one minute, gentle and reverent the next. It was like he had her body on lock. He'd known what she needed before she even did. She reached her arm across the bed. Empty. No Rafe.

He'd left. She sat up, pulling the blanket up to cover her chest. He wouldn't have left her alone. She smelled coffee wafting from the open door as a clinking came from the other room.

The tell-tale sizzle made her stomach rumble. She grabbed the sweatpants and T-shirt Rafe had given her last night and slipped them on before heading into the kitchen. The smell hit her right in the gut.

Her stomach rumbled again. It probably said, "num, bacon," since that was what her brain was thinking.

The toaster popped. Toast sounded good, too. "You made breakfast."

"I did." He divided two pieces of toast and a handful of bacon between two plates and put them on the breakfast bar. He came around the front and wrapped an arm around her waist. "I figured you'd be hungry after last night."

"You figured right." She sank into his embrace. "We need to find Presley."

"We do." His lips found hers in a sweet kiss. "But first, we eat."

"Sounds good." She pulled away—reluctantly— and sat on the chair.

He circled the island and selected a couple mugs from an upper cabinet. After he poured each of them a cup of coffee, he sat next to her.

A bell tinkled.

"Is that your phone?"

He stood, his eyebrows arched. "No. It's the doorbell."

"Are you expecting anyone?"

"No." He checked the peephole on the front door. "MacAuley."

"Why is he here?"

"Probably looking for you."

"How would he know I'm here?" Visions of orange

jumpsuits and plastic trays filled her vision. They said you just had to knock out the biggest, baddest person in the yard. She just had to learn how to fight. Who was she kidding? She was totally going to end up being someone's bitch.

"Go into my bedroom and don't make any noise. I'll get rid of him."

She took her plate into the bedroom and partially shut the door. If she shut it all the way, it would be too obvious. Too obvious would mean being in police custody. A closed door would also keep her from hearing what they were saying.

She sat on the edge of the bed, put the plate on her lap, and got ready for the show. And prayed MacAuley wouldn't get curious and want to look around.

"What are you doing here?" Rafe's voice came through the door loud and clear. Thank goodness, or she'd have to stop eating and press her face to the wood.

"Came to say hi." MacAuley's voice drew closer. "Rafe, you act is if I never come to visit you."

"You don't."

"Eating breakfast?"

"Yes." Rafe didn't elaborate. Just kept it short.

"Two cups of coffee?" MacAuley must have seen her cup of coffee. Darn it. She forgot to bring it into the bedroom.

"I'm extra thirsty." Roxy could hear the sarcasm oozing from Rafe's tone. "What do you want?"

"I was wondering if you saw Roxy Horne."

"Sure. Yesterday at the club."

"And after the club?" MacAuley sounded annoyed. Which didn't bode well for Roxy.

"Why do you care?"

"Come on, man. You were there. She was supposed to stop by the precinct."

"Maybe she was busy."

"Busy at Donnie Dunne's office building?" MacAuley sighed. "Don't bother lying. There are tapes."

"Okay, I won't."

"Look, Rafe, I'm not going to ask if she's here. I don't care. But I have a murder investigation and I need her to come in. Every day she hides, she looks more and more guilty. I can only keep them at bay for a little bit longer, and then there will be a warrant."

"Why are you telling me this?"

"You know why." MacAuley's voice drew closer. The knobs on the foosball table rattled. Then they stopped. "What are you doing?"

"You lost the right to ask me anything a long time ago."

"I know." MacAuley sighed again and his voice was barely above a whisper. "I didn't have proof. If I had any proof, I would have told you right away."

"You should have told me anyway." The story Rafe told her earlier spun through her mind. MacAuley knowing Rafe's wife was cheating and not saying a word.

"So you could ignore me or hate me? You loved her, and I didn't want to be wrong." MacAuley hadn't known. Not for sure.

"Well, you weren't wrong."

"Yeah. I wish I had been."

Footsteps moved away from the foosball table, toward the front door. MacAuley's voice wavered in and out before she heard, "Make sure she gets to the PD by noon."

The front door closed. Only silence was left.

Carrying her plate, she butt-checked the bedroom door open. Rafe stared—at who knew what. MacAuley appeared to be gone. "He left?" Roxy asked.

"Yes." Rafe took her plate away from her and scraped it into the garbage, followed by his.

"Don't you want to eat that?" She'd wanted to eat hers. There was bacon.

"No." He rinsed the dishes and put them in the dishwasher. "We should get going. We have to find Presley."

"Maybe we should start with the wife."

"Okay." Rafe grabbed the towel and dried his hands before drying off the counter. He was quiet. The conversation with MacAuley had obviously hit him hard.

"Do you want to talk about it?"

He folded the towel and tossed it on the counter. "There's nothing to talk about. Did you want to take a shower before we head out?"

"Together?" She moved toward him. The morning

was looking up if they were going to redo a few of last night's highlights.

"We should probably take separate showers."

"Is everything okay?" *Are we okay?* She really wanted to ask, but it had been one night. She knew better than to expect professions of love after one night.

He smiled, but it was strained. He stepped up to her and slid his fingers through hers. "Everything is fine. I just want to clear your name, so we can get on with our lives and be rid of MacAuley."

He leaned in, pressing his lips to her temple. The kiss was soft. His lips lingered. The words made sense, but there was something else. Something she missed. She could feel it.

"Go take a shower and I'll meet you back here." Rafe let her go and walked into his bedroom, shutting the door.

She'd take her shower and clear her name. What else did she have to do at this point?

CHAPTER 20

AN HOUR LATER, they were both done taking separate showers— such a pity. Roxy wore the same clothes from the day before. It was like a walk of shame, but lasted all day long.

Not that she was complaining. The night she spent with Rafe was totally worth it.

She slid into the passenger seat of his pickup. "We should talk to Donnie's wife. She had the most information on Presley. Maybe she knows more than she thinks."

"It's a place to start." He turned onto Las Vegas Boulevard. Something was still off. He was distracted, and not in the good want-to-rip-your-clothes-off kind of way.

"Is everything okay?" That MacAuley conversation still ran through her mind. Rafe had been quiet since he showed up.

"Fine." Rafe followed the traffic down the boulevard,

avoiding the rush of people crossing the street. The good news was they all looked like they'd Vegased a little too hard last night. Which meant her walk of shame clothes looked classy.

He went a mile or so and pulled off the highway.

She looked around. "Why are we leaving the highway?"

The Southern Highlands, where Donnie's wife was probably rolling around the house with the trainer, was west.

Rafe idled on the shoulder. His fingers tapped at his phone. "I have an errand to run first. It shouldn't take long."

An errand? That was only slightly cryptic. What kind of errand took precedence over clearing her name? Before she could answer that question, Rafe hung a left at a light and drove a few blocks to a large tan building. Her stomach dropped into a flat cartoon pancake—without the cartoon hilarity.

She knew this building. It was a building she'd seen one too many times. But even if she didn't know the building, the sign would give it away. Las Vegas Metropolitan Police Department.

"Why are we here?" Disappointment balled in her throat and poked at her sinuses.

Rafe didn't say anything as they drove across the parking lot. Roxy grabbed for the handle on the door.

She'd never thought about jumping from a moving car before. It was a new feeling.

Her hand itched as he stopped behind a row of cars, waiting for the one at the front to park in an open spot. She was now in a non-moving car. Getting out would no longer be jumping.

"You look guilty. You need to go in and talk to them." Rafe's voice was barely above a whisper.

"To people who want to lock me up." Roxy's hand was no longer considering opening the door. She wanted to karate chop the man who'd abducted her.

"They won't lock you up."

"How do you know?"

"MacAuley said they just need to talk."

At least he looked torn, uncomfortable. She'd like to kick him someplace sensitive and see how much more uncomfortable she could make him. Just the thought kept the betrayal tears at bay. The rolling of her eyes helped. "Cops are known for telling the truth. They wouldn't lie to get a murderer off the streets." And the blatant sarcasm didn't hurt either.

Rafe shook his head. "You're not a murderer."

"You and I know that, but they don't. MacAuley and his partner practically had an MMA match in the middle of a random office building because they don't agree." Staring down Geary and his distrustful glare wasn't how she thought today would go. But that wasn't even the worst of it. Having Rafe stab her in the back and hand over to the cops wasn't on her list of things to do today either.

"MacAuley knows you didn't do it," Rafe said.

They were getting closer to the building, and who was standing in front? Rafe's ex/new BFF. MacAuley. Roxy almost punched Rafe in the arm. "You texted him."

Rafe sighed as he pulled up to the curb. "He's right. You need to talk to them."

"You sold me out." And lied. And abducted her. And hurt her. And... there were so many ands.

"It's not that dramatic. They just want to talk. MacAuley said he'll be there the whole time."

Not that dramatic? He slept with her and then took her to the police station against her will. That was pretty darn dramatic in her book. It was crappy. Who would do that?

Oh yeah. Rafe.

"I trusted you." She tried to hide the crack in her voice, but the reality of the situation jabbed in her throat. Her eyes burned with all the emotions she shouldn't be having. It was one night. One night didn't make trust. Why'd she thought it had?

"You can trust me." Rafe stopped the car in front of the building as MacAuley headed for the door.

Trust him? No. She couldn't even trust herself. She'd made a huge mistake letting him in. Not that she would have this conversation here and now. Not with MacAuley getting closer.

She didn't even know what to say. Where to start. So she didn't bother. She whipped open the door and slid out of the truck, making sure she didn't forget anything.

She'd already given up enough—her pride, her body, her trust. She didn't want to lose anything else. There was no way she would reach out to him for something she might forget. Or reach out for a ride. Or anything ever again.

"Roxanna. I can pick you up when you're done—"

He probably kept talking after she shut the door. She didn't know. Or care. He'd lied to her. Did what he wanted without consulting her. They were done.

"Roxanna Horne." MacAuley kept his hands in his pocket as he approached her.

"Detective." She didn't stop. She focused on the front doors of the precinct. She was pretty upset with him too.

"Hey, Roxy." MacAuley grabbed her arm. "What's the matter?"

She glared at his hand until it was removed from her body. If only she could shoot lasers from her eyes, then his hand would not only be removed from her arm, it would be removed from the planet. "What did you say to him?"

"What?"

She saw Rafe's truck out of the corner of her eye as it pulled away. Good riddance. "What did you tell him to bring me here?"

"The truth." MacAuley invaded her personal space

and not in a good way. It was an angry, pointy way. "They were close to issuing a warrant out for your arrest. You looked guilty."

"I'm not guilty."

"Then tell us what happened." He walked the few feet to the front door and held it open.

"Let's get this over with." She followed because she didn't think she could outrun MacAuley or the rest of Las Vegas' finest. Not because she thought the two men in her life were right.

Because they weren't.

CHAPTER 21

AN HOUR LATER, Roxy sat in a room with Detective Geary and MacAuley. It was about as delightful as she thought it would be—a little worse than a root canal, but better than waterboarding.

"Why did you go upstairs?" Geary's dark brown eyes narrowed at her.

"To serve Donnie Dunne his summons."

"Why were you serving him anything?" Geary hadn't seemed to change his mind about her so far. He was still mean. Although, that could just be his demeanor with everyone. "It wasn't your case to work."

"As I told you before, Skip wanted to take his girl-friend to the hockey game. I think he was looking to get lucky. He couldn't take his girlfriend and serve a summons at the same time. They haven't invented that technology yet. Since me taking his girlfriend on a date wouldn't ensure his *luck*, he asked me to handle the summons and he handled the girlfriend." Yeah. She was being a bit nasty, but she'd been listening to him ask stupid questions for over an hour.

"So, again, you're saying it was a coincidence?" Geary said the word coincidence like it had four letters.

She had a feeling agreeing with coincidence would be a bad thing. "If that's what you want to call it. All I know was I was doing my job."

"Were you also doing your job when you impersonated a cop and spoke to Donnie's wife?"

"I didn't impersonate anyone." Wasn't that a felony or something? "I never told anyone I was working for or with the police." Which was true. High-five to technicalities.

"You never told anyone you were security with the hotel?"

Geary kept asking questions, and MacAuley just sat there. He was like a good-looking statue.

"I never said I was security. I just said I was working with the hotel. It's not my fault no one questioned that."

MacAuley's mouth tipped up into a grin, but he still didn't say anything.

"So, you went upstairs..."

Roxy wanted to roll her eyes. She was so tired of talking about the night she found Donnie's body. It wasn't exactly something she wanted to relive. "Yes, I think we've established I went upstairs."

Detective Geary glared at her some more before

putting his face back in the notebook in front of him. "Let me get to the question. You went upstairs to his room. Then what?"

"No one answered, but the door was propped open, so I went in."

"Do you always go into rooms without an invitation?"

Only when I want to. She didn't say that out loud. She didn't think he would find it funny. "No."

"But you entered this room?"

"Yes. I had a job to do, so I figured why not try and do it."

"You walked in and then what?"

"I didn't see anything. Just a counter full of desserts. So I tried a brownie and Sarina came up to the door."

"Wait." Detective MacAuley finally found his voice. "You ate a brownie at the crime scene. You were serious about that?"

"It wasn't a crime scene, yet." She'd gone over this that night, so why they kept harping on the brownies she had no idea. Good thing, though. She could use it when she claimed insanity at the trial. "I had just walked in and there was nobody there, so I just took a brownie."

Geary shook his head as he wrote in his pad, then flipped to the next page. "What happened after you stole the brownies?"

"One brownie." If they were going to judge her, they might as well have the whole story. "And I didn't steal it."

"You didn't? Did you give it back?"

Roxy would be happy to give the damn brownie back. If it meant she could get the hell out of here, she'd toss her brownies all over the man.

"Did you eat anything else?" Geary shook his head as he wrote on his notepad.

"No, but in my defense, they were really good."

"Then what happened?" MacAuley's hand lingered near his chin as he tried to hide a laugh.

"I went into the bedroom and found Donnie at the end of the bed."

Geary turned another page of his notebook. "He was dead when you found him?"

"Yes." She avoided the obvious snarky response, since they'd probably lock her up and throw away the key, if she said no. Even if she ended that no with an *uh-duh, I'm kidding.*

"How did you end up covered in blood?"

"I was trying to get away from him and I tripped over the blankets on the bed."

"Why did you go see Donnie's wife?"

"I had a few questions." Geary acted as if a person couldn't ask questions.

"Was she able to help you?"

"Sure."

"What did she say?" Geary was actually fishing for information.

Maybe Roxy could make this into a quid pro quo situation. "So, you want me to tell you what she said to me, but you don't want to tell me what she said to you."

"We're cops investigating a murder." Geary huffed. "You're playing a game."

A game. Somehow her life was a game and their job was important. She could admit now that she really hated Darren Geary. Maybe his mother didn't breastfeed him long enough, or maybe it was too long. Either way, he was a dick. "What game? I have more riding on this than you do."

"You do?" Geary's voice rose, the anger apparent in a vein popping from his forehead. Like he had any right to be mad.

"I have a hell of a lot more riding on this." She might have been yelling. But screw this guy. "My life. My freedom rides on what I can find. I have everything to prove. If you don't find this guy, will the department stop paying you? No. Your life will go on."

"Seriously?" Geary stood.

"All right, we need to calm down." MacAuley held up both hands. "Everyone sit."

At some point Roxy had left her chair too, apparently. She sat. Which was probably a good idea.

"I need a minute." Geary pushed his chair back and left the room with a slam of the door.

The room was eerily quiet after that as MacAuley sat in the chair across from her.

"Why does he hate me?" Roxy asked after a moment.

"I don't think it's you."

"So he's a jerk to everyone."

"Not really." MacAuley sighed. "Why won't you let us handle the investigation? Honestly."

"At first, I just wanted to clear my name so I could go back to work." That drove her to ask questions and dig deeper. Clearing her name so she could pay her bills and avoid jail had been at the forefront of her mind.

"And now?"

"Same thing. I want to clear my name so I can go back to work and preferably not end up in county lock-up." She worried at her fingers. She hadn't even admitted this to herself yet and here she was blabbing to the police. But something about MacAuley made her want to trust him.

Something about Rafe made her want to trust him, too. And that had worked out so well.

"What else?"

"I like it. I'm enjoying tracking down the leads and talking to witnesses." To be honest, she was loving it. The intrigue. The questions. So many pieces, and she just needed to arrange them to find the answer. Not that she'd done that yet, but she was working on it.

MacAuley smiled and, for the first time in the interrogation room, he wasn't hiding it. She thought about wishing upon his eyes they were so twinkly. "What information did you obtain from Donnie's wife?" Before Roxy could argue, he put up his hand. "I'll show you mine. You show me yours."

"Are you playing good cop/bad cop with me?" Not that she minded, at the moment. She needed information, too.

The sparkle in MacAuley's eye faded. "I'm not playing."

"Okay. She told me that she was trying to lose weight because she wanted her husband to stop cheating. He was keeping half the hookers in thigh-highs. She seemed sincerely sad. Her bestie, not so much."

"You think Mandy did it. The aura-reading woman?"

"The night of the murder, Mandy and Adelaide stopped at the hotel to drop off his phone." Roxy was pretty sure that was suspicious. It raised a red flag in her book.

"That was early in the evening and Mandy only had minutes. She would have needed to know what room he was in and exactly how to get there in time to murder him, and you saw him after. It's not Mandy." Cop logic always got in the way.

That early evening piece was the part that kept tripping her up. Roxy saw Donnie alive later that night. "She could have gone back."

"But she has an alibi," MacAuley pointed out.

Damn alibi. MacAuley was right.

"Anything else?" he asked.

"Donnie was broke, and he was moving his wife to

Reno to start over. Except his pregnant girlfriend was also moving to Reno with Donnie to start over."

"Did the wife know that?" MacAuley kept asking questions, so she was clearly helping him. What about her?

"Why are you asking me these questions? Nothing I say is admissible." She'd seen enough *Law and Order* to know that hearsay wasn't admissible in court.

"True. But we might not have asked the right questions the first time. If we know what to ask, we might be able to get more information. The wife never mentioned she knew the girlfriend was coming."

"So I am helping." She couldn't stop the warmth spreading through her chest. She was aiding a real police investigation with real facts. All her *Veronica Mars* dreams were coming true. It was way cool. Her sixteen-year-old-self wanted to find Justin Timberlake and do a "Bye, Bye, Bye" fist pump.

"You are helping." MacAuley smiled. "Did Adelaide know about Amethyst?"

"Not really. The girlfriend thought the wife was an ex and the wife thought the girlfriend was someone named Presley."

"Who's Presley?"

Bummer. MacAuley didn't look like he'd come across a Presley in his search either. "We haven't been able to find her."

"Have you checked the file at M&J? They might have come across a Presley."

Why would her company have anything on Presley? "File?"

"Steve Brandt was the one who hired your company to watch Donnie. They've been on him for a few weeks, from what I've heard."

"Have you seen the file?"

"We're waiting on the warrant to come through."

They were waiting on a warrant. Well, Roxy didn't need to wait on a warrant. All she needed was someone with keys to the front door.

"Don't get any ideas." MacAuley moved forward in his seat, crowding her space. Like she would stop searching because he got too close. "What else did the girlfriend say?"

"That she'd gone up to the room that afternoon to take a nap. Donnie had rented the room using her employee discount. He was selling his company so they could move to Reno to be closer to her parents."

"We didn't get the impression she knew about his money problems, either." He shook his head. "Anything else you want to add?"

Why should she scratch his back if he wasn't going to scratch hers? "Anything you want to add?"

"You were right about Steve. You said he's hiding something. I think you're right."

"Did you figure out what he's hiding?"

"Not yet."

"You going to look into Mandy?"

"We're looking into everything." The words were right, but something told Roxy he wasn't taking her appraisal of the situation seriously. Mandy might be all sweet and aura-loving, but she had a dark side. And an alibi. Darn it.

Roxy's focus shouldn't just be Mandy. She had her own freedom to consider. "Am I still a suspect?"

"We're considering all angles, but not in my mind."

"Is that coming from Detective MacAuley or MacAuley MacAuley?"

"MacAuley MacAuley?"

"You said MacAuley was your first name."

MacAuley's chest rumbled as Roxy swore she heard laughter come through the west wall. "You know my first name's not MacAuley."

"I do. But if you're going to give me a ridiculous name and not tell me your real name, then you get to live with it."

"Fair enough." MacAuley stood, and opened the door to the interrogation room. He rested his hand on her shoulder as she passed him in the doorway. "I know you plan on continuing your investigation. But remember, whoever did this has murdered before. They'll do it again if you get in their way."

If she wasn't so intent on seeing this through, that little pep talk might have scared her. Especially since he never really answered if she was still officially a suspect. Which meant yes. "I'll be careful."

He nodded. "Keep Rafe close."

No thanks.

He laughed. "Trouble with Rafe?"

She might have made a face, or MacAuley was now reading her mind. "I'm here, aren't I?"

"What?" MacAuley dropped his hand.

"He didn't tell me we were coming here."

MacAuley sighed, and he truly looked sorry. "That was my fault. I told him to get you here by any means necessary. And see, it all worked out."

She hated when people made sense. She was enjoying her righteous indignation and didn't need logic to muss it up. Not that it was mussed. "It's that he didn't ask. He didn't talk to me about it."

"Maybe he thought you'd say no."

"Isn't that my choice to make?" Just thinking about it made her blood boil. How dare he undermine her like that.

"Yes."

"Right answer." She stepped away from MacAuley because, even in her agitated state, she could tell he smelled good. She didn't need the confusion brought on by a nice-smelling man.

"I'll show you to the front." He walked with her down the hallway and through the atrium to the front door. "Do you have a ride?"

She thought about the offer Rafe made—for all of two seconds. He was still a backstabbing jerkface. Okay, he'd been right that she needed to get it over with. She wasn't a suspect any longer. Much.

But he had no right to lie to her. He had no right to bring her here without asking. He might not be backstabbing, but she stood by jerkface.

"Roxy!" Arms wrapped around Roxy's body, pinning her arms in place. Sarina's blond hair embedded itself in Roxy's mouth.

Roxy shook her head and stuck out her tongue. But instead of getting rid of the hair, it just managed to suck more in.

"I was so worried."

"Whath are thoo doing heoir?" Ew. Now there was hairspray on her tongue.

"What?" Sarina pulled back, taking her mane with her.

Roxy scraped her tongue along her teeth. It didn't help. "What are you doing here?"

"I came to pick you up."

"How did you know I was here?"

"Rafe called, said something about you not wanting to see him."

Darn Rafe. Just when she was sure she was too ticked off to think anything nice about him, he did something sweet.

"See? Rafe's not so bad," MacAuley said.

Roxy couldn't help the eye-roll she gave him. "See you around, Detective."

MacAuley laughed. "Always a pleasure, Roxy."

Sarina's eyes grew two sizes that day. "I thought Rafe called because you two were together, but the look MacAuley gave you. Are you and MacAuley…?"

"No."

"Then you're with Rafe." Sarina pushed through the front door of the police station and headed toward the parking lot.

"No comment."

"When do we ever *no comment* when it comes to men?"

When the man was a complex pain in the butt that didn't make any sense. "Let's get in the car. I'm going to need your help."

"Anything." Sarina hit the locks on her orange Jeep and jumped in. "But changing the subject doesn't mean you aren't going to tell me about all the *no comment* you had with Rafe."

Roxy couldn't argue. They told each other everything. Spilling her guts would be a small price to pay to get Sarina to help her break into the file cabinets at the office.

CHAPTER 22

A TRUE FRIEND NEVER GETS IN YOUR WAY
UNLESS YOU HAPPEN TO BE GOING DOWN.
~ ARNOLD H. GLASOW

"WELL, you never have to see him again." Sarina pulled into the M&J Investigations parking lot.

Roxy had spent the entire trip from the police station telling Sarina about the most amazing night of her life, followed by the most embarrassing morning. Sarina oohed and ahhed in all the right places. And now she showed appropriate indignation on Roxy's behalf.

"He'd probably grind up birth control pills and put them in my food if he decided he didn't want kids. He wouldn't even ask me."

Sarina shook her head. "Good thing you're not being dramatic."

"How is that dramatic? He didn't ask me, just dropped me off like a toddler at preschool." Roxy sighed. "Let's not talk about him anymore."

Sarina parked toward the back of the lot. "Fine. What's the plan?"

"I need to get into the records room, and I need you to get me in there. Act natural, like you're supposed to be at work."

"That's easy. I *am* supposed to be at work."

"You left work to come get me?" Roxy's heart grew two sizes because her best friend had ditched her paying job to pick her up at the precinct.

"Always." Sarina grabbed her purse from the back-seat. "Stan was here when I left."

"He said he'd answer the phones?"

"Yeah."

"Did you have to offer a favor?" Stan was famous for asking for favors. They were generally creepy.

"Nope. He likes me." Sarina pointed to the side of the building. "Go behind the building to the back entrance. I'll check to make sure the bosses aren't around, and then I'll open the door."

"Okay. Don't forget about me." Roxy got out of the car.

"Have I ever?" Sarina entered the building before Roxy could answer that question.

Sarina had left Roxy at a bar one time, but she texted the next morning to tell her she'd left. Oh wait, that wasn't Sarina, That was her. Roxy.

The back of the building was dark because shade from the surrounding trees kept things creepy. Garbage cans overflowed, and a rotten milk smell tickled her nose. Lumps of color and caked dairy covered one of the garbage bins. The can belonged to the ice cream shop next door. They liked to toss the ice cream into the bin with a Jackson Pollock flair.

She moved toward the center of the mini mall, hoping the smell would unsour. No such luck. She snarled her way to the door that said Investigations and tried the knob. It didn't open. Of course not. It was important for her to stand here among the festering lumpy milk.

She leaned against the grimy wall and waited. And waited. She pulled out her phone. Twenty minutes since she'd checked the clock in Sarina's car. Sarina probably forgot about her. If Roxy didn't remind her, Roxy would be sleeping in the M&J garbage bin tonight.

A rustle and clink later, and the back door inched open. "Ready?"

"I've been ready."

"Keep it down. Everyone is here," Sarina whispered.

"Everyone?" Roxy walked in the back door, tripping over two cartons of old printer paper and a community bike left behind by someone a few years ago that no one had thought to throw out. The bike immediately slid down the wall with a thump.

Sarina picked up the bike and propped it back against the wall. "Shhh. Why don't we wait till they leave? Come back later."

"We need the information now." Roxy hated it too, but she needed a lead. She needed something to follow.

"Kat and Pete are in the break room."

In the front of the building.

"Stan is at the front desk taking calls."

Also at the front of the building.

Side note. Roxy didn't want to see Stan. If he caught her, he'd threaten to say something to the owner, and she'd owe him a favor. The last time Roxy had asked him for a favor, he'd said only for a picture of a nip-slip.

She'd said no, obviously. But she could only imagine what the favor would be for a little B&E.

"Skip and John are at their desks."

Which meant they were the other ones she and Sarina had to dodge. The file room was in the back corner, and Skip and John were currently in the other back corner.

Sarina shrugged. "Let's go in there and get the file. Then you can take me out to dinner. We'll drink, eat chocolate, and think of mean things to do the jerk who shall not be named."

Given the day Roxy'd just endured, all of what Sarina said sounded like heaven. Drinking. Eating. Man-bashing. Sarina had been there for every man-bashing session since Todd Krason in the second grade. He'd chased her around the bus, begging for a kiss. When she gave him one, he'd said Wanda Moore kissed better than her. That was the inaugural chocolate-infused man-bashing session.

"We need to be quick and quiet." Sarina peeked

around the wall separating the back area from the main room. She waved Roxy forward. "I'll take care of John. You'll have to deal with Stan."

Roxy took Sarina's place and looked around the corner. Stan sat at his desk on the other side of the room, staring straight ahead. Straight ahead. Otherwise known as straight at the records room. His eyes didn't blink. Seriously. Not one blink.

Was he dead? She watched his chest. Nothing. Then his breath stuttered in his throat, but his eyes stayed impassive. He was snoring. With his eyes open.

Roxy had no idea what he could or couldn't see with his slumber eyes. "Maybe we should just come back tonight?"

"Who will drive if we're drunk?" Sarina whispered.

Good point. "Okay."

Sarina handed Roxy the keys. "Go in and I'll take care of him." She motioned to John's open door. She'd been here long enough to know his eyes were always on the door and his staff.

"I don't know who opened the case."

"Well, figure it out. Fast. We don't have all day." Sarina walked into John's office. "John, I was hoping I could talk to you for a moment."

Roxy ducked her head as she slunk by his office and across the wide-open area under Stan's sleeping gaze. Why the duck and cover? She had no idea. It just felt like it was needed.

She inserted the key into the lock on the records room, trying to be quiet. Although she wasn't sure why she was trying because the laughter coming from John's office could drown out a bulldozer in reverse.

Roxy looked at Stan as she opened the door. His eyes didn't register. His chest kept moving to some internal rhythm. She slid into the dark room and locked the door behind her. No windows. The lights were out, and she couldn't turn them on. Not without announcing to everyone she was there. There was a gap at the bottom of the door.

She pulled out her phone and used it like a flashlight, careful not to aim the light at the door. There were tall file cabinets along all the walls, and short cabinets butted up against each other in the center of the room. Alphabetical. By client.

Who would want Donnie Dunne watched? Besides everyone. Adelaide Dunne. Roxy moved to the Ds. Dunford. Dunning. No Dunne.

If it wasn't the wife, then it was probably the partner.

Steve Brandt. She opened the file with the Bs. Branagh. Brandt. Steven. It was here. She opened the folder and pictures slipped to the floor. There were a lot of pictures. Loose pictures. Envelopes with pictures.

She held up her phone so she could see. Pictures of Donnie with his baby-momma at the coffee shop. Donnie shopping with his wife. Same. Same. Same. She pulled the corner on another picture. Long red hair. Donnie and

Gretchen, Steve's daughter. Alone with Donnie. Eating at Mon Ami Gabi.

Romantic. She slid the picture into her pocket.

Roxy didn't know they knew each other well enough to share a meal, let alone a romantic meal in Paris. Granted it was Paris on the strip, but still, anything French was romantic. Except French fries. There was nothing sexy about French fries.

She opened one of the envelopes. More pictures of Donnie. Nothing interesting.

The lock jiggled as someone whispered on the other side of the door. There was a giggle. Speaking of interesting. And terrible timing.

She needed a place to hide, but since it was a room with one door and all kinds of file cabinets, there weren't a lot of options. The door flew open and Roxy ducked behind the middle cabinets.

"I didn't think he'd ever stop watching this door." It sounded like Kat.

"John needs a hobby." But that didn't sound like Kat's husband.

"He has one. Sarina." Were they actually talking smack about Sarina in the records room?

Kat climbed on the middle file cabinet. "They should just do it and get it over with."

"John needs something to chill out."

A zip filled the air. Was he pulling down his pants? A belt hit the floor with a ping. She peeked around the corner. Pete's pasty white butt hung out as Kat scooched her underwear down to her ankles.

Ugh. Roxy inched farther along the cabinets and stuck close to the side. If she stayed far enough away, they couldn't see her. Right? Why couldn't you just close your eyes and be invisible? That should be a thing.

"Maybe John will screw that stick out of Sarina's ass." If Roxy wasn't hiding, she would so kick Kat's ass.

"Move down."

Kat's dress edged over the side and swayed back and forth. "Move to the right."

Bodies slapping. People grunting. Holy fornication. Couldn't they do this at home? Oh wait. They had spouses, so no. Couldn't they rent a hotel room like normal people? There was a semi-clean motel down the road that charged by the hour. They hadn't had a crab outbreak in months.

"I have a sales call." Kat grunted. "Faster."

The door whipped open.

"Rox...Ahhh. What is going on in here?" Roxy had never been so happy to hear her best friend's voice. Sarina slammed the door shut.

There was scuffling and zipping. The clothes were going back on. Alleluia.

"Don't you knock?" Kat sounded angry as she threw open the door. Blue balls would do that to a girl.

"This is the records room. Why would I knock?"

"Why would you burst in like a bat out of hell? Bitch."

Silent Pete and his mouthy sex partner left the room, and Sarina shut the door. "Roxy?"

"I'm here." Roxy stood behind the cabinet. "Thank you for saving me."

"Yeah. I got to see things I didn't need to see."

"Really?" Roxy didn't get that visual. Thank the heavens. But she was curious. "What did you see? Anything good?"

"I wouldn't call it good. More like old school porn," Sarina snarled.

This was why curiosity was bad. It killed cats. And it gave visual images of mounds of hair in places she didn't want to picture hair at all.

"Did you find anything?"

"Maybe." Roxy tapped the picture in her pocket. "We should go. I'll show you in the car."

Sarina opened the door and looked around the main office. "I have to stay here."

"Okay. I have to run an errand. We'll meet here at six?" Roxy handed Sarina her car keys.

"How are you going to get around?"

Roxy clicked the app on her phone. "Uber."

"Just take my car." Sarina shoved her keys back into Roxy's hand. "Bring her back in one piece."

"I will. Thanks." Roxy walked toward the back door.

"Anytime."

The office population had thinned, with people heading home or to watch their marks for tonight. Roxy spun the keys in her hand and decided to go out the front door.

One more interview and then her focus would shift to the twelve pack of beer she planned on buying. She was hurt. She was tired. She was heartbroken. Tonight would be all about heartbreak and drinking Rafe away.

CHAPTER 23

ROXY HEADED to the heart of suburbia. According to the file, Gretchen lived in a four-bedroom in Henderson. Roxy parked the Jeep in the driveway in front of a two-story beige stucco house with brown trim.

She passed a little boy running and screaming as she made her way to the front door and hit the bell. The neighborhood was alive with kids playing kickball in the neighbor's driveway. Bike spokes fluttered and tapped as kids raced down the sidewalk.

The door opened and Gretchen stood there wearing a *kiss the cook* apron. Her red hair was pulled back, away from a face covered in flour. "You're that woman who talked to my father."

"I am. And I was hoping to talk to you as well."

"About?" Gretchen wiped her hands on the apron.

"Donnie Dunne."

Gretchen nodded. "Do you want to come in?"

"Thanks." Roxy came inside and followed Gretchen into the living room.

Ivory walls, tan furniture, and a bin of toys in the corner. Wooden signs—*Family* and *Love*— hung among a multitude of photographs.

"What can I do for you today?" Gretchen settled on one end of the couch.

Roxy moved the peach and blue pillows and joined her.

Boots clomped in from a back hall. "Mrs. Ramstad."

"Sorry." Gretchen turned from Roxy to the man. "What do you need?"

"We'll finish the drywall tomorrow. But we're quitting for today."

"Thank you."

"See you tomorrow." The workman stomped out the front door, followed by two men and a woman—all covered in drywall dust.

"Sorry. We're adding an addition to the main floor. They're finishing up my father's bedroom and bathroom."

"That's nice of you to bring him into your home." Nice didn't even cover it. Roxy couldn't imagine living with her parents, again. Not that it couldn't happen, but the ramifications of why she'd need to move back in with either set of her parents wasn't something she wanted to think about.

"He's done so much for me. I couldn't turn him away."

"Does your husband mind having your dad here?" Was there a husband?

"He loves my dad, and we could use the help."

The front door swung open. "Mom. Can we jump on the trampoline?" A red-haired boy covered in dirt ran into the house. It was impossible to tell where the dirt began and freckles ended on his adorably chubby face.

"Okay, but only two jumpers at a time."

The little boy's face lit up with a smile. "Okay."

"Miles, only two of you on that trampoline at a time."

"I know, Mom." Miles ran out, slamming the door.

"Sorry." Gretchen shook her head and ran a hand over her stomach. "This is a madhouse. Always."

"Miles is adorable." Like an Internet kitten meme. Looked just like his mom. "Is he your only child?"

"No, we have two sons. Nate's outside riding his bike somewhere." Gretchen grabbed at her stomach. Her face took on a troubling green hue. "Can we go into the kitchen?"

"Sure."

When Roxy followed her to the other room, Gretchen leaned over the sink, splashing water on her face. Slowly, her face turned a normal color as she ran a towel over her neck. "Sorry. Can I get you anything?"

"No, thank you." But Roxy had a feeling Gretchen

could use something. Saltines. Water. EPT. "Are you feeling okay?"

"Yes." Gretchen sighed and tossed the towel onto the counter. "No, I'm not. Don't say anything. I'm waiting till we see my husband's family next month. Not that it really matters anymore. I'm pregnant."

"Congratulations?" Roxy assumed that was a congratulations type of announcement.

"Thank you. It really is a good thing. The first three months are usually hard for me, but I've never been this sick in the second trimester. It's weird, but the doctor says it's normal." Gretchen sat at the white kitchen table, the color returning to her cheeks. "You wanted to talk about Donnie Dunne?"

"Yeah." Roxy really should have thought about how she was going to phrase it. But here she was, and she had no idea. "When I spoke to your dad, I didn't get a chance to talk to you. Did you have any contact with Donnie before he passed?"

There. Easy peasy. Give Gretchen the chance to tell Roxy what happened. Unless she lied. *Don't lie. Don't lie.*

Gretchen stared at her hands as she twisted her fingers together. The look of a lie. Darn it. "I met with him a few weeks ago." Her words stopped, but her fingers kept bending and weaving. Something was obviously on her mind—or she was trying to knit her fingers together into a scarf. But the words weren't coming.

Roxy knew about the meeting, so Gretchen hadn't lied. But she also wasn't speaking. Maybe she needed a nudge. "Why?"

"Please don't tell my father." Gretchen sighed. "Donnie was my dad's best friend way before they became business partners. Donnie was my godfather, for goodness sake. I wanted to try to reason with him. He was upsetting my dad."

"What did Donnie say when you talked to him?"

"What you'd expect. That he was fixing it. That my father was confused."

"Confused?"

"My dad caught him skimming money from the company. Donnie said it was a misunderstanding. But my dad had the numbers. He'd found the irregularities and he was working with Harold Maas to figure out exactly how much."

Harold, the financier Donnie's wife mentioned. He had a name. Well, he always had a name, but now Roxy knew what it was. "Where does Harold work?"

"He's a lawyer at Maas and Brickman." A lawyer. A lawyer that both Donnie and Steve were using.

Roxy didn't know rich people, but was that normal? "The lawyer that Donnie was using?"

"He might have gone to Harold, too. They were all college friends. They were in the same fraternity."

"I'm too sexy" buzzed from Roxy's phone in her pocket. "Sorry." She pulled it out and looked at the screen. Rafe. Which she already knew because that was the ringtone she'd given him.

That needed to change. His sex appeal had dropped a few notches when he brought her to the cops. Snitch. Snitches get stitches.

The chair Gretchen sat in scraped against the floor, taking Roxy out of her thoughts of giving Rafe a few wallops that would require stitches. Gretchen stood up. "Is that it? I have to get dinner ready."

"Yes, thank you." Roxy walked toward the front door. "Congratulations on the little boy or girl."

Gretchen's face lit up. "Girl. My mom's going to flip. She'll finally have a girl to spoil rotten with dresses and dolls."

Roxy smiled and left out the front door. The sun was sliding down. She had a half hour to get to Sarina and an hour till beer would be in her belly.

Her phone vibrated with "I'm too sexy" again. She hit ignore. She wouldn't talk to him. Not today. And if she was lucky, not tomorrow.

Next week she was busy, and next month wasn't looking good either. She just had to remember that when she was drowning the betrayal with beer and chips.

CHAPTER 24

BY THE NEXT MORNING, Rafe had called four more
times. Roxy sat at Sarina's table, wearing borrowed
pajamas covered in little cats with wands, and ate a bowl
of Fruity Pebbles while looking at her texts.

He wanted to talk. She didn't. So they were at a
stalemate.

"He texted."

How did Sarina know?

"It's so sweet." Sarina had a goofy grin on her face
that Roxy was about to slap off.

"Whose side are you on?"

"What side?" Sarina shook her phone. "Cliff was
looking for me last night."

"I thought you two broke up." Hoped. Prayed.
Begged the universe was more like it. Roxy would almost
rather her best friend take Rafe's side than have her
talking to Cliff. Almost.

"We did." Sarina sighed as she dropped onto the chair next to Roxy. "He's trying to get me back."

"Is it working?" *Please don't be working.* When it came to Cliff, Sarina had made some bad choices in the past. Roxy couldn't live through another round of heartbreak. Well, she could. She'd get Sarina through it like she always did, but she couldn't promise she wouldn't hunt Cliff down. She was already suspect numero uno in one homicide. Why not make it two?

"Please. Give me a little more credit than that." Sarina giggled as she stared at her phone and grabbed the spoon from Roxy's cereal. She slipped a spoonful into her mouth and her grin dissolved. "Eww. This is mush."

"You want me to make you your own bowl?"

Sarina shook her head. "Nah, this is fine." She ate another spoonful.

Roxy's phone rang. Rafe. She hit ignore and flipped the thing over onto the other side of the counter.

"What are you doing today?" Sarina asked.

"Checking out the lawyer, Harold Maas."

"Did you find his office?"

"Not yet." That was on the list of things to do today. That and ignore her phone. She had a full day planned.

Sarina's fingers flew over her phone. "He's over on Mojave. Not a great neighborhood. Are you sure you don't want me to tag along? Just wait till I'm done working."

"You're going in?"

"I talked John into buying me a personal printer yesterday. I should probably go in."

"When you were distracting him, you talked him into buying a printer?"

"Yeah. Didn't I tell you?" Leave it to Sarina to find a way to benefit from a covert operation.

"No, you forgot that part."

Sarina shrugged. "I didn't want to talk about work. You were dealing with boy troubles and all."

"Well, at least something good came from yesterday."

"That's the spirit." Sarina poked at her phone.

"I need to get dressed and then let's hit the road." Roxy rinsed her bowl out in the sink. It was still early, but she had things to do.

"Why don't we sit and watch TV before we leave?" Sarina fell onto the couch in her living room. She pointed the remote and the television sparked to life. "*Today* should be on soon."

"Don't you have work to do?"

"Nope." Sarina's phone rang in her pocket. She looked at the screen, her finger hovering over the answer button. "Do you know anyone with the number 690?"

"No!" Roxy lunged at Sarina, knocking the phone out of her hand before her best friend could accept the call. She ended up diving onto the floor at Sarina's feet. Ouch.

"What the heck?" Sarina leaned over and retrieved her phone, rubbing the screen with reverential concern.

"Sorry." Roxy rolled to her knees and sat on the couch next to Sarina. Her side hurt and she was pretty sure her theatrics would leave a mark. "Can I see your phone?"

Sarina held her fallen comrade just outside Roxy's reach. Like Roxy would do anything to her precious phone—well, anything more.

A vibrating sound came from Sarina's hand and she read the screen, angling it so Roxy couldn't see. "Ah. Rafe. You could've just said that."

"You were going to answer a call from a number you didn't know. Who does that? I had to stop you."

"He called yesterday to make sure you were picked up. I knew the number, sort of. Anyway, he wants to know my address." Sarina stared at the vibrating nuisance in her hand.

"Why?"

"His first question was 'is she there?'" Sarina smiled but didn't attempt to text. "I'm thinking he's looking for you."

"Tell him I'm not here. Better yet, don't tell him anything," Roxy said, heading for the bedroom. "We should leave." She didn't know why, but she had a feeling Rafe could somehow triangulate Sarina's phone just by sending a text. She didn't want to be anywhere near this place when his stupid truck showed up.

In the bedroom, Roxy removed her cat pajamas and pulled on her clothes. Well, partly her clothes. She'd left a pair of jeans here at some point, but she had to borrow a shirt.

"Why?" Sarina asked, coming into the bedroom.

"I need to pick up my car and get going on this investigation." Roxy said as she sat on Sarina's bed and pulled on a pair of socks. "If you get dressed, I'll even buy the doughnuts."

"Deal." Sarina threw on her clothes for the day and, even though she'd done it in record time, still managed to look put together. Sarina picked up her purse and keys. "I'm ready."

They were off before Rafe figured out where Sarina lived.

CHAPTER 25

AN HOUR LATER, Roxy had her car pointed toward Harold's office. She avoided the spillage of rush hour as she stuck to the fringes of downtown and drove past the Las Vegas Detention Center.

A few miles down, she found the building. Well, more like a storefront. The small white-brick building had two large, dirty windows with Criminal Law in bright red letters, and a dull-gray shark hanging next to a brown wooden sign that read Maas and Brickman.

Maybe these guys didn't know that being seen as a shark was a bad thing. Or maybe they were in on the joke. She parked in front of the windows and opened the creaky wooden front door.

The office was dark, not much light from the filthy windows. The front desk was meticulously clean, albeit devoid of human presence. An as-seen-on-TV sign hung behind the desk, with a picture of dark-haired man in a collared shirt. She'd seen him before—his commercials played at the hockey games.

A woman in a long plaid skirt and black socks shuffled toward the front. Her stockinged feet rubbed against the scuffed floors. Her white blouse was tucked into the high-waisted skirt. She adjusted the glasses on her nose and sneered. "I'm sorry. I didn't hear you come in. I would have been out front if someone had a scheduled appointment at this time. You don't have one."

High-waist didn't seem to like Roxy even though she hadn't had much time to form an opinion. It was more likely high-waist didn't like anyone.

Which didn't bode well if Roxy wanted to get past her to see Maas. She had a feeling she'd need to butter up the troll to get over the bridge. Not that high-waist was a troll—that was just mean. But that didn't stop it from being apropos. Roxy needed to butter her up. Maybe use a little humor.

"I snuck in like a tiger." Roxy laughed.

The woman stared at Roxy like she was speaking another language. Maybe she just didn't get the joke.

"You know, because tigers don't sneak."

Still nothing.

"I mean, Tony the Tiger ran around saying, 'They're great.' So, he didn't sneak. The marketing team must have gotten that from somewhere. Right?" She was totally crashing and burning. The woman didn't crack. Not one giggle, grin or guffaw.

"Maybe—" Roxy licked her lips "—he wasn't truly representative of all tigers."

The woman sat at her desk and woke her computer. "Do you have an appointment?"

Roxy thought they covered this. "No."

"What do you want then?"

Cheery thing, wasn't she? "I need to talk to Harold Maas."

"Make an appointment."

Roxy was about to tell the troll where she could shove her appointment. But that wouldn't get her over the bridge. And yeah, she was embracing the troll metaphor. The woman earned it.

"May I please make an appointment to see him?" She stopped before adding the pretty please and the sugar on top. She was hovering on sarcasm and Roxy didn't think the woman would appreciate it.

"For what purpose?"

"To meet with him." That might have been sarcasm. What other purpose would there be to make an appointment to see someone?

"Obviously." The woman rolled her eyes as she looked at the screen of her computer. "Why do you need to meet with him?"

"I need to talk to him about Donnie Dunne."

"You are?"

"Roxanna Horne."

The phone on the woman's desk rang. She picked it

up and listened before putting it back down. "He can see you now."

"Okay." Roxy wanted to look around for the listening or recording device. That was the only way Maas could have heard what they were talking about. But she had a feeling if she made any sudden movements, she'd be kicked to the curb.

Of course, that didn't answer why he was letting Roxy back with just a mention of Donnie's name. But that would just get added to the long list of questions Roxy had these days.

High-waist led Roxy around her desk and into a back hall. Offices lined the way, and they both stopped at the last one before the back door.

"Mr. Maas, Roxanna Horne to see you."

Roxy held out her hand to shake his hand—if that really was him. He didn't look anything like he did on television. His dark hair was gray. What was once a wrinkle-free face was now covered in character.

Maas motioned for her to sit in the brown leather chair across from his white marble desk. She looked behind her, but the troll must have gone back over the bridge to harass other citizens.

The office was an interesting mix of dark woods and glitz. The fluorescent light bounced off the gold pencil cup and the flaking gold sconces. Jewel covered art hung on the wall. It was like if Liberace shopped at the dollar store.

"Lovely to meet you," Maas said. "You were there the night Mr. Dunne was murdered."

"I was."

So that was why he was so quick to let her back. He knew she was at the hotel. "What are you doing here now?"

"I wanted to ask you a few questions about Donnie." She sat, sinking into the worn leather. "Why did he come to see you?"

"What we talked about is private and covered under privilege." Maas steepled his fingers.

"Even now, after he died?" She needed to get him to understand. To help. "I want to find who did this."

"I'm sympathetic to your cause. Donnie and I had been friends for years. I want this person caught."

"Then help me." She leaned forward, hoping he'd see the desperation. She was out of leads.

"All I can say is it had to do with his children."

"You mean child." The big baby bump currently residing on—in? with?— his girlfriend.

"I know what I said."

Children? "Oh wait, you're right. Amethyst's baby, and the one he had to give away."

"Who told you that?"

"That he had to give one away? Amethyst."

He shook his head. "Don't believe everything you hear."

Like Roxy was missing something. And apparently she was. "So, he didn't have to give away his first child?"

"I really can't talk about this."

"Why?" She wanted information on a dead man. Didn't privilege end when the person privileged wasn't here anymore?

"He's not the only one I'm representing on this matter."

"Does this have to do with Steve Brandt?"

"I definitely cannot and will not tell you that." Maas's tone had changed from one of intrigue to that of annoyance.

Which meant she didn't have a lot of time. "Who is Presley?"

His eyes widened, before his expression became neutral. "Who told you that name?"

"Donnie's wife said he was having an affair with a woman named Presley. We're looking into her to see if she was the scorned mistress."

"He was not having an affair with her."

"Who is she?"

His face went back to no emotions as he stood. "I don't know. It was lovely to meet you."

Apparently, the meeting was over, and she hadn't learned anything else. "Mr. Maas, I have nothing. I want to find out who did this to Donnie. If you have any information you can share, please do."

The lawyer shook his drooping head. "I can say this. Presley isn't his mistress. She's his daughter."

His daughter. "The one he had to give away."

"I'm not at liberty to discuss the nature of their relationship."

"Can you tell me where to find her?"

"I'm sorry. I can't." He stepped around his desk and disappeared through the door. "I only told you about her because she wasn't a scorned mistress. She isn't someone you need to look into."

"How do you know?"

"Because she doesn't know he's her father."

"Could she have found out? Wanted to speed up her inheritance?"

"I don't know what you know about Donnie, but he was broke. There was no inheritance. Even if there was, she wasn't the type to look for handouts."

"You know her." She wasn't asking. It was obvious he not only knew her. He liked her.

He led her down the hall, where the troll sat at her desk looking almost smug as he practically ran her into the front door. Although there was no reason for her to be smug, so maybe that was Roxy's imagination.

He turned to Roxy and raised his hand. "Thank you so much for stopping by."

"Thank you for taking time to talk to me." She headed to the door, but she wasn't done yet. She needed more information. Not that she was going to get it. Today.

She grabbed a Post-It and a pen from the troll's desk. She wrote her name and number and gave it to Maas. "Please reach out to me if you remember anything else you can tell me. One more thing, do the initials SBM mean anything to you?"

"I don't know anyone with those initials."

He flipped the paper in his hands as Roxy left. She wasn't holding her breath that he'd give her a call. But she really hoped he would. Because right now, the only thing she knew was that Presley was his daughter and she didn't even know it.

She could basically be anyone.

CHAPTER 26

WHEN CRIME BUSTING IS EASIER THAN YOUR PERSONAL LIFE, SOMETHING HAS GONE SERIOUSLY WRONG. ~ LAURELL K. HAMILTON, BULLET

SINCE SHE WASN'T TRYING to dodge the cops anymore, Roxy headed to her apartment. Thanks to Rafe. She tried to muster the appropriate amount of snark as she thought that, but she was having trouble. She pulled into the parking lot and turned off the engine.

Rafe stood in the next row of cars, leaning against his pickup truck.

She didn't want to see him. She was still mad, but she didn't feel the fury burning deep inside like she had before. That needed to be fixed. If she didn't taste that fury, she'd never give him the tongue-lashing he deserved—and not the good kind.

She could slam her door and restart the engine. Run away. But that wasn't really her style—now that he'd seen her. If he hadn't seen her, she'd be a curled puff of air like in the cartoons.

She could pretend she didn't see him and head to her

apartment—that was only slightly cowardly. Or she could face him, head on. Be courageous.

Roxy grabbed her purse, slammed the car door after she exited and hoofed it to her apartment. Cowardly? Yes. But the lion from *The Wizard of Oz* had nothing on her, and she was okay with it.

She made her way to the stairs leading to her second-floor unit. But there was a muumuu standing in her way, taking up the width of the stairs. There was no way around without knocking the muumuu to the ground. Problem was that she liked the woman attached to the muumuu.

Ms. Potter stood there with her hands on her hips. She wore one heck of a frown. Ms. Potter, not the muumuu.

"It's so nice to see you, Ms. Potter." Roxy injected her voice with an excitement she wasn't feeling.

"You said you'd drop off the check. You promised. Even the nutter in 1B paid on time."

"I'm sorry I'm late, but I get paid tomorrow." Which was true. She wouldn't get paid again for a while after that, but that was a problem for next month. "I'll have the money tomorrow."

"You're not having gambling problems again, are you dear?"

"I'm not gambling." Roxy's "gambling problem" was back when she was making minimum wage. She went with her dad to the bingo hall and lost the money for rent.

It happened once—okay maybe twice—but she didn't sling the daubers anymore.

"Is there a problem?" a male voice asked.

Why? Why was he here to see this? What had she done in a previous life to deserve this? Rafe approached Ms. Potter, all professional in his black suit pants and white collared shirt unbuttoned down to the bottom of his throat. His sleeves were pulled up, showing muscled forearms. And his hands? Don't get her started on his hands. It made her hot.

Again, why her?

"Well, well, who might you be?" The old woman turned to Roxy. "You didn't say you had a bloke."

"I don't have a bloke." She had a one-night stand that ended in a backstabbing. "There's no problem. I'll get you this month's rent by tomorrow."

She gave Ms. Potter a look to move along. Nothing to see here. But either Ms. Potter was ignoring Roxy's rounded eyes, or she couldn't see them through the lust she obviously had for Rafe.

In fact, the old lady beamed at him and fluffed her hair like she was on the pageant circuit. "What's your name?"

"Rafe, ma'am." He held out his hand and shook. "It's nice to meet you."

"The pleasure is all mine." She batted her eyelashes.

Roxy had never seen Ms. Potter bat anything. Well, except for the raccoon that tried to take up residence in the hallway last year. Then the old woman swung a bat like she was in a cricket match. But this? This was weird.

"I should get to my apartment. I have work to do." Roxy nodded and inched by Ms. Potter. Her feet slapped the steps as she escaped.

How she was actually going to escape anything, she had no idea. Eventually, Rafe would get past Ms. Potter and then he'd be knocking on Roxy's door.

Maybe she could move? Totally not an overreaction. Right?

She unlocked her front door and slid inside the apartment, closing the door behind her. Halfway to closed the door thumped something, or someone, and wouldn't budge.

She looked down at a black boot between the door and the frame. She pushed, but nothing. He and his big foot weren't budging. *Well, neither am I, pal.* She stuck her face in the gap. "Can I help you?"

He rolled his eyes. Rolled his eyes! "I just want to talk."

"Maybe start by not rolling your eyes at me. That's not a good way to get me to want to talk to you." She pushed on the door and internally danced a jig when he flinched. Payback was awesome.

"I'm rolling my eyes because you're flattening the hell out of my foot and your face is in the door. All I have to do is move my foot and you'll have black and blue lines along the side of your face."

He was totally exaggerating. But she pulled her face back so she wouldn't get her cheeks smashed. Just in case. "Thank you for telling me that. I've moved my face, so you can remove your foot."

Another push on the door and he winced. She was enjoying this way too much and not at all, at the same time. He was a walking, talking representation of her stupidity. And he just stood on her doorstep—mocking her—telling her how dumb she was to trust him. She'd liked him, that was why she'd spent the night with him. She'd thought he'd liked her.

That was where the stupidity always seemed to find her. She thought guys were into her. She thought they liked her. Stupid.

"I can't move my foot, not until you let me in."

"Why?"

"We need to talk." He was almost pleading.

"We really don't." Her arms were getting tired. She turned and leaned her shoulder on the metal door. Eventually he had to get tired. Right? "There's nothing to say."

"There is." His voice was bourbon and velvet. Warm and smooth. Hearing the dejected tone as he bumped his forehead on the door made her even more tired. Talking for a few minutes wouldn't hurt anything. Just her psyche.

That was already suffering anyway.

She pulled away from the door, letting it fall open. Rafe passed Roxy and closed the door, taking all the oxygen from the planet. He seemed to take up all the space and all the air.

They stood there—Roxy trying to breathe and Rafe making it look oh so easy.

Rafe studied the room, probably seeing the dust bunnies foraging on the furniture. Well, the parts of the furniture not covered by clothes. Bad news? Her clothes were all over the place. Good news? It was mostly dresses. No undergarments.

"Nice place." The first time he stopped by and her apartment was impersonating Las Vegas Boulevard on New Year's Day. His words didn't lift the stress from the room.

"How did you find my address?"

He couldn't seem to meet her eyes, embarrassed, maybe. "I have my ways."

"Stalk much?"

Rafe ran a hand up his neck and a short laugh burst out. "Sorry."

"For what?" The list was getting longer.

"For stalking you."

Not that she really cared if he stalked her or not. "You're forgiven. Is that all?" She wasn't in the mood to be found by him right now, so she'd forgive him anything if that meant he'd go away.

"I'm also sorry for what happened earlier."

Maybe she wouldn't forgive him anything. "Okay."

"I didn't want the cops to hunt you down. When

you go to them, things are still cordial. MacAuley is the lead on the case and they were working on getting a warrant. If that would have happened, that interview would have gone differently. Did they give you a hard time?"

"No, they didn't. Well, Detective Dick might have been an ass, but MacAuley was fine."

"Which I knew he would. I wouldn't have let you go if I thought he'd hurt you."

"They weren't going to hurt me, but they could've arrested me." She'd still be rotting in a cell, wondering how the hell it happened. Knowing deep down it was her own fault for trusting Rafe. Anger gutted her stomach. Or maybe it was sadness that he could just hand her over like luggage.

Rafe shook his head. "MacAuley said they didn't have the evidence to arrest you, but that every minute they didn't talk to you was giving Detective Dick more ammunition." He laughed. "I like that name, by the way."

Roxy couldn't believe this guy. It wasn't like cops didn't lie— everyone did. Just last week, she'd told her mother the stew she'd made was edible. Stringy chicken that a dog wouldn't eat. Lies happen. "And you believed him?"

"Yes, I did. I still do. If he was lying, you'd still be in custody. I was trying to protect you." Rafe stood inches from her.

How he'd gotten that close, she had no idea. But she

didn't want him near her. "You lied to me to protect me?" What a crock.

"Yes."

"You didn't protect me. It was my choice to turn myself in or not. My. Decision." Her blood pressure spiked a knot into the back of her neck. Her fists clenched, and she fought to keep them glued to her side and not swing them at his *protective* face. "You took that away."

Rafe leaned his head back and sighed. "You're right. I was wrong to take you to the station without making sure you were on board first. That was an asshole thing to do."

"It was." It wasn't much fun being mad when he was agreeing. Her fists unclenched as he paced, shaking his head.

He finished back where he'd been, closing that gap but still not touching her. "What can I do to make it up to you?"

"You lied." She didn't say it, but she didn't know he could ever make this up to her. "You took away my choice."

The look on his face told her that the words hit exactly where she was aiming. You didn't take away a woman's choice. You didn't take away anyone's choice.

"I didn't even think about it that way. But that's not an excuse. I'm sorry." His breath lingered along her cheek as he leaned forward. Still not touching her.

"How do I know you won't do that again?"

"I might be an idiot, but I can learn. I can see what I did was shitty." His eyes found hers with a look that tore out her heart. "Tell me how I can make it up to you." The regret in that one look was enough for her to want to reach out. Tell him it would be okay.

But it wouldn't be okay. Not until she knew. "Don't ever do it again." She couldn't move forward without trust. And right now, that trust was fractured.

"I won't."

"I mean it, Rafe." She felt the tears sliding down her cheek. She didn't care if he saw them. He needed to know. He couldn't do this again.

She couldn't handle being lied to. Her father had lied to her enough in her lifetime. She was stuck with her dad. She wouldn't purposely get into a relationship with someone like that. No thanks. "No lying," she told him. "No not telling me something for my own protection. Don't ever take away my choice again."

"I won't." He lifted his hand and slid his thumb under her eye, wiping away the tear. "I swear."

She closed her eyes and tried to find the anger or the hurt. But she was empty. Maybe it was the tears, or maybe it was that Rafe knew now what he did wrong and he promised to never do it again.

He leaned in. "May I kiss you?"

She looked into his eyes, wondering why he was asking. He had to know she wanted him.

"You have to say yes or no, Roxanna. This is your decision."

Did she want him to kiss her? She was still mad—a little. She was still hurt—a moderate amount. She still liked him—a lot. She wanted to see where this could go. "Yes."

His lips met hers and her knees nearly mutinied. The kiss was raw and intense. That magical tongue found its way to her mouth. His hands slid up and down her back, bringing her closer and closer.

His body was everywhere and not nearly as close as she wanted him to be. A loud gurgle stopped Rafe mid stroke. He pulled back and lifted her chin with his hand. "Was that your stomach?"

"Yes."

"Why don't we grab some dinner?"

"Really?" She was warm and willing, and he wanted dinner?

"Really." He pulled away, slipping his phone from his pocket and clicking on the screen. "We have all night to make up. Let's make sure you have the energy to enjoy it."

He was right. After he plied her with dinner and dessert, she had more than enough energy to make up properly.

CHAPTER 27

ROXY'S EYE PEELED OPEN. An arm lay across her chest. Her back was pasted against the chest of the man who'd kept her up all night. Her body ached. Her hair was probably a rat's nest.

Yet she couldn't keep the smile off her face. Not that she could see her face. But her cheeks felt like they were about to explode. And she was okay with it. Everything about this moment was delicious and warm, like just-out-of-the-oven chocolate-chip cookies.

Her cellphone vibrated on her dresser. The telltale buzz cut through the silent room. She held her breath. She didn't want to wake Rafe or lose the warm cocoon. She was snuggly and the air outside was cold and angry.

Her phone silenced and then jumped again. She looked around the room for the time, but she didn't actually own a clock. She needed the thing in the red plastic case that wouldn't shut up. But to get to it—she was back to the cold and angry.

Then it did it again. Damn phone. Roxy inched the blanket off her body and slid down, lifting his arm as she inched her chest underneath. Which shouldn't be exciting. But somehow it was.

Ignoring the enjoyment her body was feeling, she scooted her butt closer and closer to the edge of the bed. Her legs bent as she crept lower.

"Where are you going?" a gravelly voice asked as that arm travelled down her body and pulled her back into the warm chest.

"My phone's ringing."

"And?" His mouth found the top of her head with a soft kiss.

Her legs stopped moving. Her body stopped scooching. She wanted more kisses. In more places.

Her phone buzzed again.

Little kiss-blocker.

"I have to get that. It hasn't stopped ringing."

"Fine." His vise-like grip loosened.

She grabbed the phone flashing Sarina's picture and hit speaker. "There better be an emergency."

"There is. The cops are here." She whispered into the phone. "They found the murder weapon."

"Okay." Roxy still wasn't feeling the urgency.

"Here. They found it here. At the office. They're heading to your house."

"Wait. Why?"

"You were their main suspect and now they found the murder weapon at your job. Do the math."

"How much time do we have?" Rafe's voice suddenly came from right behind Roxy. When he got out of the bed, she had no idea.

"They left about ten minutes ago."

Rafe tapped her shoulder and took the phone when she held it out.

"Thanks. We have to go." He hit end on the phone. "Get dressed."

Roxy wasn't really into the whole domineering guy thing, but at the moment, she didn't have time to care. She threw on a pair of yoga pants and a T-shirt. She stuffed a bra into her purse along with her phone and threw it all over her shoulder.

"Let's go." Rafe somehow was dressed and ready.

She ran through the living room and stopped at the door. No cops in the peep hole. She threw open the door and held it for Rafe. "Where are we going?"

"Far away."

"What about your place?" She locked the door and followed Rafe down the stairs.

"We can't go to the hotel. Too many cameras."

"My parents?"

"The cops will go there next." Rafe hit the locks for his truck. They both jumped in as sirens sounded off in the distance.

Roxy sat up. "My mom wanted me to watch one of her friend's houses. The cops wouldn't know to look there."

"Okay, but how do we get in?"

"I used to babysit for their kids. I know where the hide-a-key is."

"So, we're adding B&E and squatting to the list." Rafe drove down the side streets, farther and farther from the sirens.

They sat in silence. Miles and miles of silence. Too bad Roxy's head wasn't quiet. She couldn't seem to figure out why the cops were after her again.

Well, she got the whole murder weapon thing. But how did the weapon end up at her office?

"How did the murder weapon get to your office?"

"That was what I was just thinking."

"Did you figure out an answer?" He smirked as he entered the expressway.

"I've got nothing."

"Where we heading?"

"Blue Diamond, right outside Red Rock."

A half hour later, Rafe pulled into a dirt-covered driveway. The nearest house was a mile or so away. The house looked the same. Spanish tile roof. Salmon stucco walls with a white-trimmed bay window in the center. It was just like she remembered.

After getting out of the truck, Roxy followed the front walkway past the small fountain in the center of the yard and past the flowers lining the front of the house. Under a small plastic wannabe rock, she found the key.

The front door opened on a dark front hall. Not that it was dark enough outside to need lights, but all the curtains were pulled closed. The house smelled dank, like the curtains weren't the only things that hadn't been opened in months. She walked further inside and met eyes. Eyes set in a face a good foot taller than her. Large eyes staring.

A scream ripped from her lungs as she jumped, her back hitting a wall. Rafe ran in the house, pulling a gun from his hip. He hit a wall switch and light flooded the hall. Once the sparkles and pops cleared from her eyes, she saw it. Those eyes.

The eyes stared back. But that wasn't the worst of it. A large brown paw was raised high over her head. Sharp teeth snarled at her. Her heart froze. Everything froze. Her breath sputtered into icicles on her lips.

But the bear didn't move. The arm didn't lower. The snarl didn't deepen. The eyes were dead. This wasn't how she remembered the Schmidts' house.

Rafe came back, all the lights in the house now blazing. "I don't see anyone." He didn't know. He didn't know she'd just screamed at an eight-foot-tall giant stuffed bear. He never had to know.

"I thought I saw something move over there." She pointed to the living room behind the bear. "But it must have been light or something."

Something big and brown. She made her way into the living room. More eyes. More animals stuffed and mounted.

A taxidermist's life for me hung on the wall.

Oh goodness.

Of all the hobbies for her parents to have... Please let them never find this one. Stuffed dogs in various states of play. An owl. A bird that looked suspiciously like an eagle, but couldn't be because weren't they endangered? All with the appropriate fangs, teeth, and claws. Stuffed to the snout, with piercing eyes that looked real. And creepy.

"Are you sure you're okay?" Rafe kept his head on a swivel, looking for the imaginary thing that moved when they'd walked in the door.

"I'm fine. I must be seeing things."

He holstered the gun that had come in handy scaring the stuffed animal. "I'll lock up." He looked out the front door. Right and left. Then he shut the door and locked the locks. "I'll check the windows."

He ran up the stairs as she wandered into the kitchen. White tile floor. Faded wood cabinets along one wall. And a stuffed raccoon on the counter. On the food counter. Where. They. Put. Food.

"Oh, hell no." She took a Christmas towel from the handle of the stove and wrapped it around the raccoon's body, careful to drape the excess fabric over the critter's eyes. She slid the entire thing into an oak cabinet in the dining room. She shouldn't need the dining room. She peered around the corner at the living room and all the animals. Maybe she could move all the stuffed demons there. Let them all stare at each other and leave her alone. But they'd never all fit in the dining room. *Dammit.*

Yes. She was aware she was thinking about hiding animals that were no more than dolls at this point. But that didn't stop the eyes from following her. It didn't stop how real they looked. At one point, they were real.

And she was sleeping here. Probably alone. Rafe had a gorgeous apartment in a high-rise, and a job. Eventually, he'd have to get back to both of them.

She pulled her cell phone out. Whether he stuck around or not, she couldn't have her mom showing up at the door. Not if they were going to christen each room. Eyes stared at her from the dining room. Maybe they wouldn't christen that room. She remembered the giant bear. Or maybe not the living room.

She flipped through her contacts and found her mother's number. "Mom."

"Roxanna." Why was it her name sounded so sexy on Rafe's lips, and annoying as microphone feedback at the bingo hall coming from her mother's mouth? "Should I avoid the news?"

"In general, or because I might be starring?"

"Roxanna..." Her mother sighed. There were so many implications in that sigh. So much disappointment.

Before her mother got any ideas of actually expressing her disgust, though—.

"I'm just calling to tell you I'll take care of the Schmidt's cat for a couple of days."

"What? Why?"

"Well, you asked me." Very true.

"I find it hard to believe you'd travel out that far west without needing something."

Also true. "I do need something. Don't tell anyone where I am. No matter what."

"What might matter?" Her mother sounded skeptical. How astute. Astute? Roxy's internal dialogue got all formal when her mom was on the phone.

"Even if the cops come."

"Dear God. Please tell me the police will not come to my house."

"I can't control the police, Mom."

"Roxanna Penelope Horne." Whole name. Not good. "What have you done?"

"I haven't done anything." Much. "But they are looking into a murder and they have to look at all the people. I didn't do it. Just know that."

"I know that. But why can't you have normal problems, like Danielle's kids? They just called to borrow money to buy a car."

Buy a car? She needed a car. "Is that an option? I could use a new car."

"I gave you a car."

"When I graduated high school." Which was—ugh, don't bother with the math.

"Well, sell it."

"No one is interested in my piece of junk car." This conversation was going nowhere. Which was normally how Roxy's interactions with her mother went. "Seriously, it needs a new starter. You could loan me the money…"

"I could have, but you want me to lie to the cops, so that is all you get."

Hmmm. She somehow got the short end of that stick.

"Oh, by the way. There's a cake in the fridge. It's from Mrs. Schmidt's baby reveal party."

"Mrs. Schmidt is sixty years old. How is she having a baby?"

"Her son. Don't be obtuse."

Roxy had devoted her life to being obtuse—according to her mother. Didn't mean she wanted to listen to it. "Well, Mom. Thank you for perjuring yourself, so I don't end up in jail."

A long breath came across the line.

"And thanks for the cake." She hung up after her mom said good-bye with the sound of, most likely, wine being poured in the background. Not a bad idea.

She walked back to the animal-free kitchen and opened the refrigerator, where the promised cake waited. Putting it on the counter, she removed the plastic wrap. A spoon or fork would be good. Drawers clanked as she opened them one by one, looking for silverware and praying there were no stuffed animals. She finally found a large serving spoon with slots. Big, but it would fit in her mouth. She really should put that on her Tinder profile—when she got a Tinder profile. Not that she had plans for a Tinder profile.

A second later, sweet sugar hit her tongue and her heart rate slowed. This cake was the only thing standing between her and a full-blown meltdown.

"Did you want to sit and eat that?" Rafe. He stood in doorway watching her.

The spoon stopped inches from her mouth as humiliation crawled along her skin. She'd been shoveling in frosting like she hadn't eaten in months. But even so, she didn't care. Those bear eyes were still staring at her, even though the bear faced the other way and was down the hall. "Not really. Did you want some?"

He went for the spoon in her hand and she nearly bit him. You don't mess with a woman's spoon when it's filled with cake. Was he crazy? She pulled a drawer open, motioning to serving spoons that weren't currently covered in HER cake.

Roxy shoved more ooey-gooey goodness in her mouth and scooped up another bite, her spoon bumping against his as he infringed on her piece of the cake.

"Do I get some?" He took his bite and stuck his plastic serving spoon back in.

"You're getting some," she pointed out around another a mound of frosting.

"Some, but you're going to go into sugar shock."

He made it sound like a bad thing. Sugar shock sounded good right about now. Maybe she'd sleep through the nightmares that were bound to plague her all night. It wasn't just the stuffed animals. It was the cops and making sure they didn't find her. She couldn't handle waking up to a SWAT team alarm clock.

But she had to. They were after her. Not Rafe. He didn't need to put himself in harm's way any longer. And even though she'd love to have him stick around, she couldn't ask him to stay. "Thanks for dropping me off. You should probably go to work." Nonchalant. Relaxed. She was totally cool with him going to work.

"I took a personal day."

She almost shimmied her hips as she dipped her spoon into the cake. "Really?" She wanted to think the day off was to be with her. Maybe? "Why?"

"Because the first thing MacAuley's going to do is track me down to find you." He licked the spoon in what should have been a normal action, but somehow, her brain made it feel salacious. Which didn't match the words he was saying. "I don't feel like dealing with MacAuley's shit today."

He didn't want to stay here with her. He just didn't want to deal with MacAuley. Great. Not that she didn't appreciate the company and all, but she wasn't a charity.

Thoughts of grabbing a fistful of cake and cramming it in her face like a one-year-old bounced through her mind. But she was an adult. And dignified. She ran her spoon through it again. "You can leave whenever you want. You don't have to stay here if you have other plans."

"What other plans would I have?"

"I don't know." Plans to stay away from MacAuley. Which wasn't the same as plans to hang out with her. They were two totally different plans. They might intersect at this very moment, but it wasn't the same.

"I have no plans. But I'll leave if you want me to." His spoon hung over the cake as he watched her. His eyes searching for something. She didn't know what. But he just kept staring.

So she just stopped looking at him. She knew he could see the self-esteem drain down to her toes. She knew he could tell she wasn't worth getting into all of this trouble. She shrugged as she finished the first piece of cake. She was being ridiculous. Deep down, she knew it. But she also wasn't some charity case. He shouldn't be stuck here if he didn't want to be.

Rafe rested a finger underneath her chin and gently lifted her gaze to his. "Do you want me to leave?" He looked so deep in her eyes that she swore he saw her gallbladder.

"I don't want you to leave," she admitted.

"Then I won't."

"Why?" She couldn't understand. He was putting

himself in danger. He was aiding and abetting a fugitive. Even if *abedding* a fugitive was on his list of things to do, he could get anyone in his bed. He didn't have to help her.

"Why what?"

"Why do you want to stay? You could be arrested."

"I could." Leaning down, his lips drifted along hers. Once. Twice. Just a ghost of a kiss.

Her lips tingled in anticipation of more.

"But I'm not leaving you alone with this. Not if I don't have to."

Her heart about jumped out of her chest. He wouldn't leave her alone. Her body pulsed as his breath lingered, mixing with hers.

Sugar. His breath smelled like he'd been dipped in whipped cream. That was totally unfair. His kisses were like drugs normally. But now kissing him would be like French-kissing candy. And she was a fructose fanatic.

Closer. Her eyes shut as his lips met hers. Soft and slow turned to deep and hungry. She couldn't get enough —she wanted more—she wanted it all.

She wanted him.

He bent forward, and his hands wrapped around her thighs. He picked her up, then moved out of the kitchen and down the hall, walking toward the large bear. She didn't want to break the kiss, but she could feel its eyes. She swore it was thinking bad things about her. She pulled from Rafe's lips and glared at the bear. It was still angry.

Her eyes must have been the size of saucers. She swore it had grown. Even though her body was on fire from Rafe's touch, she couldn't get past all the eyes. And claws.

She leaned into his skin and smelled frosting. Her insides wept as she said, "I can't do this with them watching."

He stopped in the hall. "There are no animals upstairs."

She smiled. No animals. Thank heaven. "Then what are we doing down here?"

He grinned and adjusted her position, giving his legs wider range. After he carried her up the stairs, he found a bedroom and flipped on the light.

Not one animal. No eyes.

She reached behind him and slammed the door as they cocooned themselves inside. His lips found hers. Her body found the bed. His body laid on hers as they removed clothes and spent the night thanking heaven in various octaves for a bedroom without stuffed animals.

CHAPTER 28

THE NEXT MORNING, Roxy dumped kibble in the cat bowl and filled the water dish. Winston hadn't actually come out to see her yet, but the cat was old and was probably trying to hide from the stuffed critters.

After the cat dishes were filled, she sat at the kitchen table eating the cake from last night.

"I can make eggs."

"Why?" She was achy in all the best places and eating frosting from a giant wooden spoon. It was like paradise. On top of that, she was watching her very hot boyfriend... well, they hadn't labeled it. Lover? Yuck. She hated that word. Boy-toy. That worked. She was watching her very hot boy-toy make coffee.

It was like she was bouncing around on her very own personal ninth cloud.

"An egg is at least food."

"Cake is food. It even has eggs in it."

He shook his head as he filled a mug with coffee. He sat on a chair next to the table and took her spoon—they still hadn't found the drawer with normal sized silverware—and took a bite of what was left. "This is good."

"It is." She stole her spoon back. "You're lucky I'm in a good mood, or this spoon would be stuck somewhere unpleasant."

His lips quirked in an adorable smirk. "Good thing I managed to put you in a good mood, then." He leaned over and ate the cake off her spoon. "Multiple times."

"You do understand multiple times does *not* equal multiple bites of cake. Right?" She pulled the plate out of his reach.

He stretched his hand across her body for the spoon, but she wasn't having any of that. "Not even one bite per orgasm?"

They were pretty good orgasms... but this was cake. The pout on his lips as he looked at the plate on the other side of the table made her weak. Who was she kidding? When it came to him, she was always weak. "Fine. One bite."

"Per. Meaning I get two more bites."

"Weren't you going to make eggs? Eat some real food and leave my fake food alone?"

"This is more fun." Maybe for him. Not for her. She offered the spoon to Rafe and watched his lips wrap around the tip. He pulled away and stray frosting lined the corner of his mouth.

She fought to keep her tongue inside her head. It wanted to reach out and lick someone until his lip was shiny like a new penny. But then his tongue came out to play, slowly wiping his lip clean. Dear heaven, that was hot.

"What's with this cake, anyway?" he asked. "Why did they leave it in an empty house?"

"It's a gender reveal cake. It's how you tell people if you're having a boy or a girl. Apparently, Mrs. Schmidt's having a granddaughter." The piece of cake left on the plate was decorated with a white chocolate circle. It was round, with a weird crest. She knew that crest.

Like the cake in the hotel.

Rafe must have had the same thought. "So, Amy's having a girl."

Roxy shook her head. "No, she isn't. She and Donnie are having a boy."

"But the cake in the hotel room was pink. At the risk of being a sexist, isn't that a girl color?"

He was right. If the cake wasn't for Amethyst, who was it for?

"Whose cake could it have been?" Rafe kept saying what Roxy was thinking. It would be creepy if Roxy didn't think it was so darn cute.

Roxy had to think about that. She ate more cake while she thought. "Steve's daughter is having a girl. Gretchen was meeting Donnie to talk about something important. But she's not telling anyone about the baby's sex yet. How would Donnie have found out?"

"Do you know anyone else who's pregnant in this group? Maybe it was someone else." Rafe's eyes were glued to last bits of cake on the plate.

He could glue all he wanted, but they were hers.

"Maybe, but doesn't it seem strange that Gretchen was having a girl, and there's a girl reveal cake in his room?" She lifted the spoon to her mouth and his gaze followed.

The heat built as his eyes grew heavy-lidded. "Could be a coincidence."

"Is that what you think?" She stopped the spoon's ascent and licked her lips. Her words were suddenly more breath than voice.

"No." He pulled the spoon away from her and sucked the last bits clean off.

"Hey!" Empty. It was empty, and he just took it. "You owe me cake."

"We should go talk to her." Rafe licked his lips in a move that should have been sexy, but he stole her breakfast.

Roxy narrowed her eyes. "*I* should go talk to her."

"Why don't I get to go?"

"Because you stole the food from my mouth. Douche move."

"That was, wasn't it?" His tone said he felt bad for

the move, but the smirk on his lips said he was just a douche. He took a sip of coffee.

She refrained from tipping it down the front of him. It would be fair play to steal his breakfast, but he didn't have any other clothing. She'd never get a darn thing done today if he ran around Vegas without a shirt.

"If you're coming with me, let's go, food-klepto." She tossed the spoon into the sink. She'd deal with the dishes later.

"We going to see Gretchen?"

"Yeah. I don't believe in coincidence."

Rafe laughed. "You're starting to sound like Detective Geary."

No. She did *not* sound like him. "That was mean."

"He doesn't like you much."

"Tell me something I don't know." She sighed. Having Detective Dick hate her wasn't exactly making her life easy these days. It could be because she called him Detective Dick. But probably not. She'd never said it out loud. To him.

Rafe leaned in—inches from her face. His finger softly lifted her chin. "I had a huge crush on you in college."

"What?" She nearly choked on the word. *He'd* had a crush on her? Since when? How? She'd had a crush on him. He hadn't known she'd existed. Well, he'd known, he hadn't cared.

"You wanted me to tell you something you didn't know." He shrugged. "I didn't think you knew that."

She smiled. He'd had a crush on her in college. "After everything that happened, I didn't think that you cared about me at all. I always thought you started that rumor going around that I was sleeping with all your friends. Like the only way you'd be with me is if I was easy—not that you liked me."

"I told everyone you were only with me. They just didn't listen." Rafe leaned in and his breath tickled her cheek. "I wanted to come and find you, but that's when my sister started having trouble in school and I left campus to help out." He brought her fingers to his mouth. "But make no mistake about it, you were always on my mind."

She licked her lips as he stared at her like she was dessert. The look he gave her would lead to one thing. That one thing wasn't heading to Gretchen's to get answers. As he shifted closer, she found she didn't care.

His lips pressed lightly to hers. It was soft and sweet and so damn hot her underwear might have gone up in flames.

"Let's go." He pulled away. "We should hit the road if we're going to talk to Gretchen before Geary finds you and stun-guns your ass."

Her underwear couldn't care less about Gretchen. Or stun guns. But her mind knew better. She didn't want to tangle with Geary again. Not after they found the murder weapon at her work. He probably had an APB and checkpoints set up throughout the city just to get her.

CHAPTER 29

I USED TO JOG BUT THE ICE CUBES KEPT FALLING OUT OF MY GLASS. ~ DAVID LEE ROTH

RAFE ROLLED up to Gretchen's suburban home in Henderson. The kids were nowhere to be found. No bikes. No screaming. Endless quiet down an empty street.

Roxy jumped out of his truck. He followed her to the front door and rang the bell.

The door opened. But instead of Gretchen in an apron, Adelaide's BFF, Mandy stood in the doorway in a purple tie-dyed sleeveless dress with a hem that arrowed down in the center to her ankles.

"Mandy?" Roxy looked at the house again to make sure she didn't ring the wrong doorbell. Nope. Gretchen's house. She was pretty sure anyway. "Is this Gretchen's house?"

Mandy nodded. "My daughter. Yes, this is her house." Mandy turned to Rafe and her smile grew. He had that effect. " You're from the hotel too."

"I'm Rafe Amato, head of security." Rafe held out his hand and Mandy took it.

She held it for too long and flipped his hand over, rubbing her finger along his palm. "You have a gorgeous aura. Bright red. Passionate."

His lip curled up. "So I've been told."

Who would have told him that? She'd found out a few days ago she was a blue. Whatever that meant.

Mandy held his hand as she invited them in the house. "Can I get you something?"

"Is Gretchen here?" Roxy wasn't sure what Mandy wanted to get them. Water. Tea. Pot.

"Gretchen! Your friends are here."

"I told you I'm busy." Gretchen came up behind her mother. Her glare for her mom turned to a grin when she saw Roxy and then Rafe. The usual apron was around her waist. "Do you have a few more questions?"

"I do."

"Why don't you invite your friends inside?"

"I will, Mom." Gretchen sighed. "Can you please go check on the kids in the back yard?"

"Do you need my help?" Mandy disappeared through the sliding glass doors to the backyard.

Roxy almost felt bad for the woman. But since she was still at the top of Roxy's list, she didn't feel that bad.

"Come on in." Gretchen led them to the living room, where she sat in a chair and Roxy took the couch.

Gretchen looked over at Rafe standing in the corner. "I don't think we've met."

"I'm Rafe, a colleague of Roxy's from the hotel." He moved toward her to shake her hand but managed to send a smirk to Roxy. Yeah, she might have said she worked for the hotel. Sue her. Although he might actually be able to do that, so please don't.

Gretchen took in a deep breath and let it out. "I'm sorry about my mom. We don't exactly see eye to eye on things."

"Things?"

"All of my choices. My entire teenage years. She doesn't like that I'm letting my father move in."

"Does she live here too?" Welcome to Roxy's nightmare.

"No. I couldn't live with my mother. We would kill each other. I've always been more of a daddy's girl."

"I tried to be a daddy's girl once. My mom wouldn't let me." The woman had literally stuck to Roxy like glue. Which probably worked out, because a year later, her father had left for his new family.

Gretchen laughed. "What can I help you with?"

"We just had a few more questions." Rafe had perched himself back in the corner.

"Sure."

"Did you see Donnie at the hotel the night he died?" Roxy wasn't sure that was the most tactful way to ask the question. But it was hopefully effective.

"I didn't."

"Were you supposed to see him?"

"Yes. It was weird. He asked me to stop by, something about good news to share with me. I figured they found a way to get him out of whatever he'd gotten into. So, I went to his hotel room, but when I got to the door, no one answered." That explained the pink cake, but someone had eaten the cake.

"I don't know why you went there. Why would anyone want to spend one minute with that man?" Mandy needed a bell. She was sneaky.

"Mom." Gretchen stood. "Can you please keep an eye on the kids?"

"I just..." Mandy's eyes glistened as her voice shifted to a whine. "I just don't want you near that man."

"He's dead, Mom." Gretchen shook her head. "I won't be going anywhere near him again."

Mandy sighed. "I know. I don't know why you and your father insisted on dealing with him."

"I was trying to get him to do right by Dad. They used to be such good friends." Gretchen somehow made her mom speechless. Given the short time Roxy had spent with the woman, she had a feeling Mandy didn't do speechless.

"I just worry about you, honey. You're my little girl. Your father could barely handle that man. I didn't want you around him. I'm trying to protect you."

"Mom, I'm an adult now. You don't have to protect me."

"You have kids. You know how it is. You want to protect them. You've always been so obstinate. Even when you were born." Mandy sighed and wiped at her eyes in dramatic fashion.

"When you were born?" Roxy asked, curious despite herself.

"My mom complains I didn't want to come out. I was like two days late, but she acts like I was weeks late." Gretchen shook her head.

"One other thing." Roxy took advantage of the lull in their discussion. "Do you or anyone you know have a jacket that says SBM?"

Gretchen shrugged. "Everyone has one."

"Everyone?" In her thirty-one years, Roxy had seen the jacket once. Yet somehow everyone had one.

"The whole club."

"There's a club?" Maybe it was that damn club Sarina kept trying to drag her to.

"Mom has one. It's for the Scrapbook Mavens club. SBM. Why?"

Mandy had a jacket. Imagine that.

"Is someone missing their jacket?" Roxy watched Mandy's face, but she didn't give anything away. She was good.

"Mine is at home. I think Nia is missing her jacket."

Mandy didn't look like she was lying. She was the obvious choice for bad-guy.

Which meant Roxy would be doing another interview today. "Nia?"

"Nia Maas."

Maas. She'd heard that name before. "Any relationship to Harold?"

"His wife."

The lawyer's wife. Another person to add to the mix. Eventually, they had to find the real bad guy. Right?

Unless it turned out that Detective Geary was psychic and, somehow, Roxy killed Donnie without knowing it. Her mom swore she had multiple personalities. But that was never proven.

So the chances of Roxy being the killer were slim. Thank goodness. But at the rate things were going, she wouldn't prove it until three years into her stint at Florence McClure.

CHAPTER 30

EDUCATION IS LEARNING WHAT YOU DIDN'T
EVEN KNOW YOU DIDN'T KNOW. ~ DANIEL J.
BOORSTIN

AN HOUR LATER, Roxy sat in Nia Maas's large home. The house was black beams and glass. Contemporary and huge. Exactly what you'd expect from a local lawyer with commercials during the hockey game.

Rafe had propped himself against the wall. Something about that man and walls.

Nia was on the couch across from Roxy. She was around five feet tall, with beautiful light brown skin and straight black hair. Her curves were perfectly placed. Her bare feet were tucked beneath her as she leaned against the arm of the couch. She was runway ready, but also relaxed. Zen.

Which made sense. Her house was immaculate. She was immaculate. Not one hair was out of place. Flawless makeup. It would have been like Roxy was looking in a mirror, if Roxy wasn't naturally a disaster. Nia wouldn't be the main suspect in a murder investigation. She was too elegant for that.

"You're investigating Donnie's murder." Nia shook her head. "It's such a tragedy. He had a baby on the way."

"A little boy." Roxy nodded. It was a tragedy.

She smiled, but it was sad at the corners. "He would've liked having a little boy to play catch with."

"You knew him well?"

"Not well. He's friends with my husband and Steve. They all went to college together."

"When was the last time you saw him?" Rafe asked from his perch.

"Adelaide, Donnie, Mandy and Steve came over for dinner a few weeks ago."

"Mandy and Steve? Aren't they divorced?"

"They are." Nia laughed. "But they got joint custody of the friends."

"Was the dinner unusual?"

"Not really. Same old drama. Adelaide was quiet. Mandy was stressed. But between the divorce and Steve's money problems, you can't really blame her."

"Steve had money problems?"

"He had partner problems. Donnie was having money problems and dragging Steve down with him."

None of this was news. Roxy was no longer feeling the wind in her sails. She would have to move out of state and change her name. She didn't want to lead her life on the run, but it was either that or making license plates.

"How about your Scrapbook Mavens jacket? Do you have one?"

"I do."

"I've heard so much about this jacket. I'd love to see it." And touch it. If Nia didn't have her jacket, it might be sitting in the evidence locker at LVPD.

"Of course." Nia glided to the front closet. She pulled out a black jacket. "Adelaide bought these for us."

"I heard yours was missing."

Nia handed Roxy the jacket and sat back on the couch. "That's what I told Adelaide. But it wasn't lost. I forgot it. We don't wear the jackets very often, just scrapbook nights, so she gets a little upset when we forget it. With everything going on with Donnie, I didn't want to upset her."

"What was going on with Donnie?" The more Roxy learned about Donnie, the less she liked him. Thief. Adulterer. Leprechaun—and not in that cute Lucky Charms way. What Nia's friends saw as "everything" might be different from what Roxy saw.

"They were moving to Reno, away from Adelaide's family and friends. He was losing his business. That stuff takes a toll on a woman, and with all the fighting she did with Mandy, I didn't want her to fight with me, too."

"Adelaide and Mandy were fighting?" Roxy slid her finger along the jacket like she'd wanted to do at the crime scene. It didn't disappoint. It was soft and thick. "About what?"

"I'm not sure. I'm assuming it had to do with Donnie. There were whispers." Nia's voice dropped.

Donnie and Mandy? Ew. Roxy wanted to gag. Mandy had made it clear she hated Donnie. Would she have slept with him? Why would Adelaide still talk to her? "What kind of whispers? Was Mandy sleeping with Donnie?"

"Oh God, no. Nothing like that. Mandy never forgave him for dumping her in college. But it all worked out. She got Steve, who was so much better. They had a kid and got married."

Had a kid and got married. That wasn't usually the order. It was usually marriage then child. Not that Roxy was judging. She'd freaked over her share of broke condoms. Mistakes could happen. Thankfully, they hadn't happened to her. But still no judgement.

Roxy needed some clarification here. "Mandy had Gretchen before they married?"

"Yeah, apparently, it was a big scandal, and she wasn't sure who the father was, but it all worked out. Well, except for the divorce and all."

"So, in college, Donnie and Mandy were dating, then she found out she was pregnant and started to date Steve?" Rafe asked from the corner.

Roxy had almost forgot he was there.

"No. Yes. It depends who you ask. She started dating Steve, and eight months later she gave birth to Gretchen. Mandy said she was a premie, but come on, the baby was over nine pounds. She claims it's Steve's but the numbers don't match up. And back in the day, everyone did the math."

"Do you know someone named Presley?"

Nia shook her head. "Should I?"

"No." Roxy stood from the couch and handed Nia her jacket. "Thank you so much for talking with us."

Nia took the jacket. "I hope you can find who did this."

"Me too." Roxy and Rafe left, and Roxy waited to say anything until they reached his truck. "What do you think?"

"I think we're getting close," Rafe said, getting right in her space.

"One minute I think we're getting close, but then—not." She sighed. "I don't get it. Mandy has an alibi. She looks like the poster-child for peace. But there's something about her."

"What's her alibi?"

"She was with Adelaide and Nia at a scrapbooking weekend. Although she also said she was with Adelaide when she dropped off his phone at the hotel."

Rafe hummed under his breath. "So she was at the hotel that night."

"But she said she waited in the car," Roxy pointed out.

"Are you sure?"

"She said she did. Maybe I need to check with Adelaide again."

"Maybe." Rafe leaned in, his lips so close... And his phone rang. "Dammit." He looked at his phone. "I have to take this. He touched the screen and put it to his ear. "Amato."

Sounds came from the phone. Maybe a man's voice. But it was too hard to hear the words.

"Was anyone hurt?" Rafe walked farther away, frowning. "Okay. I'll be there in an hour." He hung up and lowered his head.

"You have to go," Roxy guessed.

"I have to go." The regret in his voice matched the feelings in her gut. "Can you wait till tomorrow to check with Adelaide?"

"Can you wait till tomorrow to go into work?"

"I'll take that as a no." Rafe took the meaning exactly as she'd meant it. What she had to do was just as important as what he was doing.

"I need to talk to her."

"Fine." He opened the driver's side door and dug in the center console. He found something inside and slid it into her hand. Mace. "Keep this with you. Use it if you need to."

"On the cops?"

"Refrain from using it on the cops." He laughed. "Although it would be pretty funny seeing MacAuley lit up. I won't be with you today so keep yourself safe."

"I managed to survive thirty-one years without you. I can make it for a few hours."

"Humor me." He touched her cheek, pushing a runaway hair back in place.

"Okay." She followed as he circled the hood and opened the passenger door.

"I'll take you to your car."

"Thanks." She climbed in, her hand slid along the hot metal. She'd like to think that she was strong and independent, that she didn't need a man. But a part of her wanted to skip going to Adelaide's house, just skip everything she had to do, and hide in the Schmidts' house until Rafe came home.

Home. But it wasn't his home or hers. She wouldn't be able to go to either of their homes until this was all sorted out. And sorting it out meant talking to Adelaide.

At least she prayed it did.

CHAPTER 31

IF YOU THINK NOBODY CARES IF YOU'RE
ALIVE, TRY MISSING A COUPLE OF CAR
PAYMENTS. ~ EARL WILSON

THIRTY MINUTES LATER, Roxy sat in Rafe's truck, parked down the street from her apartment building. He'd gone to check if the police had anyone sitting on her apartment, waiting for her.

"Are the cops posted outside?" Roxy asked when he got back.

"No cops." He winced. "But you might want to check out your apartment. Ms. Potter is packing up your stuff, muttering something about owing rent."

Roxy's heart sank. "She what?"

"Why don't you let me loan you a few bucks to tide you over?"

"You're sweet." She kissed his cheek. "Go to work. I'll call you when I'm done with Adelaide."

"And the money?"

"No thanks." She ran toward her building. It would be so easy to take money from Rafe, but they hadn't even defined what they were yet. She didn't know how he'd be as her loan shark. Nothing about that situation made her feel good. She'd rather be homeless.

Given the overflowing box on the front lawn, she might just be homeless. She looked inside. Her wine glasses stuck out between her underwear. Great.

She ran up the stairs and Ms. Potter was hunched over a cardboard box on the floor. At least the woman was packing up her crap before throwing it on the lawn.

"Ms. Potter!" Roxy felt the urge to pull out the newly gifted mace in her pocket, but she refrained. It wasn't for minor annoyances, only for bad guys.

"Oh, hi dear."

"What are you doing?" Roxy managed to refrain from saying "stop touching my stuff."

"You were going to pay the rent. Then the police came round and you didn't, so I figured you were moving. I don't want any more codswallop. I told you."

"I have the money. I'm not moving."

"You're not?"

"No. Please, Ms. Potter give me a chance. I have something I have to work out, but I want to live here. She ran to her bedroom and opened her bottom drawer. Ms. Potter hadn't gotten that far yet.

She pulled out her checkbook and prayed that M&J direct-deposited her check like they always did. Being suspected of a felony didn't negate money owed, did it?

Either way, she had no choice but to fill out a check. "Here. I'm sorry it's late."

Hopefully it wouldn't bounce.

"Okay, honey." Ms. Potter folded the check and slid it in her bra. She looked at the half-filled box. "I guess I'm done here. Oh, there's a box on the lawn you might want to fetch."

Since it had her stuff in it. Yeah. She wanted to fetch it. She'd rather it not be on the front lawn in the first place. She didn't say any of that out loud. It wasn't Ms. Potter's fault Roxy forgot to pay her rent.

In her defense, she'd been rather busy—ironically, with her other defense. Roxy sprinted down the stairs and stuffed her underwear back in the box. Since it had been lying around the front lawn for local perverts to fondle, she might just have to toss these. Not might.

She carried the box inside. Ms. Potter stood in the middle of the living room. "Do you need anything else Ms. Potter?"

"Oh no." She patted her bra, where she'd shoved Roxy's check. She stood there, watching the door.

"I'm not going to have time to unpack today." Not that Roxy thought Ms. Potter would want to help, but she just stood there. "I have to leave." Translation: you have to leave.

"You know, the police said I should call if you come round again." Ms. Potter eyed the door.

"It's all misunderstanding." Roxy grabbed her keys and headed to the door.

"I'm sure it is, dear."

The tell-tale sound of sirens wafted closer. "You called the cops."

The old woman at least looked remorseful as she stared at her flowered house shoes. She didn't look like she'd wanted to call the cops, but that didn't change the fact that she had.

Roxy ran down the stairs, Ms. Potter stuck to her heels. Her house shoes smacking against her bare feet. "They just want to talk to you."

"I don't want to talk to them."

"But they're both very nice and very handsome."

Which might be very true, but that didn't mean Roxy wanted to do the perp walk between them. "See you later, Ms. Potter."

She tried to angle into her car, but the canister in her pocket stopped her. She pulled the mace out and shoved it in the glove box. She said she'd take it, that didn't mean she wanted to use it. She turned the key. *Sputt... Sputt...Sputter.*

Dammit.

She rubbed the dashboard and kissed the steering wheel. "Come on, baby. If you don't start, I'll end up in prison, and you'll end up in some auction where they'll chop you up for parts."

The engine caught. She shifted into drive and took off, heading away from the sirens and, hopefully, toward some answers.

CHAPTER 32

A FEW MINOR siren-induced freakouts later, Roxy pulled up to Adelaide's house. Roxy knocked on the double doors, almost expecting to see Mandy, but thankfully, Adelaide answered.

"I'm sorry to bother you again," Roxy said, "but I wanted to ask you a few more things."

"No problem." Adelaide stood in the doorway. "Will this take long?"

From what Roxy could see from the front door, the house looked the same. Fewer people. No BFF. No trainer. "Not at all. You had mentioned you'd gone to the hotel to deliver Donnie's phone."

"I did."

"What did Mandy do while you went to the front desk?"

Adelaide leaned against the door jamb. "She waited in the car."

"She didn't come in?"

"No. I walked to the front desk, gave them the phone and the room number and left."

"Then you all went out to dinner," Roxy said. Adelaide nodded, and Roxy continued. "What happened after dinner?"

"We came here and opened a few bottles of wine and played games."

"Was Mandy here the whole time?"

"What is this fascination with Mandy?" Adelaide crossed her arms over her chest.

Roxy needed to shift direction before Adelaide decided she was too loyal to Mandy to answer. "I'm just trying to get to the bottom of this, and I'm going through and accounting for everyone's time."

"Mandy went upstairs about nine. She wasn't feeling well." Adelaide's eyes clouded. "We'd had a fight."

"A fight about what?"

Adelaide sighed. "She didn't want me moving to Reno and leaving her alone."

"She wouldn't be alone. She has her daughter."

"She and Gretchen don't get along very well. Gretchen has always been more of a Daddy's girl. She barely tolerates Mandy." Adelaide shook her head. "It's hard for Mandy to be so far removed from her daughter. I sometimes forget that."

"You two made up, though. Right?"

"We always make up. We're best friends."

"The night of your scrapbook party, did anyone else leave? Go to bed early? Head home?"

"No, we turned on the TV and had a Hallmark movie marathon."

Which went great with wine. Even Roxy knew that. "Did everyone have their Scrapbook Mavens jacket that night?"

"Nia didn't wear hers, but everyone else did."

"Did everyone leave with their jacket the next day?"

Adelaide bit her lip as her eyes glazed in thought. "I think so."

"I've heard so much about these jackets, and my scrapbook club is looking to create something like that. Do you mind if I see yours to get an idea?" Roxy kept an eye out for lightning. There wasn't one true thing in that sentence.

"Sure." Adelaide disappeared for a second and reappeared with her SBM jacket. It was exactly the same as Nia's except for the size. Nia's was a small, and this was a medium.

"Did you order different sizes for different women?" Roxy knew the answer but wanted to hear it from Adelaide.

"You have to, so they'll fit right."

"That must have been hard to keep track of if everyone is different."

"It wasn't too bad. Patrice and Nia wore a small.

Enya and Mandy wore an extra-large. I needed a medium."

Now that Roxy knew what the women wore, she needed to check the size of the jacket—unless the cops had already put it in evidence. In which case, she was screwed.

"How big is your group?" Adelaide watched as Roxy petted the jacket. It was soft. Sue her.

"My group?" Her group? Roxy's fingers stopped as her mind stopped tallying her to-do list and moved back to the conversation. "Oh. Five women."

"That shouldn't be a problem then. What scrapbook events do you attend?"

Crap. Roxy wasn't sure if this was a trick question. Were there such things as scrapbook events? Adelaide didn't look like she was trying to trap Roxy. No matter. They needed to get back to the jackets.

"Where did you get this logo done? It's so pretty." Flattery. Flattery worked every time.

Adelaide glowed with a huge smile.

Yep, working.

"I designed the logo myself. The font was all me." Adelaide reached over and ran a hand over the embroidery. "Isn't it great? You can't even tell it's not part of the jacket."

Roxy oohed and ahhed appropriately—given she'd already seen this jacket. "Thank you so much for letting me take a look." Roxy handed the jacket back to Adelaide.

"I hope it gives you an idea of what you'd like for your group."

"It does. Thanks." Roxy turned toward her car.

"If you ever want to join us for one of our nights, call me," Adelaide said to Roxy's back.

Roxy waved. If she ever got an urge to scrapbook, she'd make sure not to call this group. She was pretty sure there was a killer running loose. She slid in her car and drove away. As soon as she was a few miles away, she had Siri call Rafe.

"Are you home already?" Rafe's voice was hushed.

"No, I was hoping I could get into the crime scene. I need to see the size of that jacket."

The men's and women's voices in the background went muffled, then silent. He must have left the room. "The police took all of that away as evidence."

"Shit."

"Why don't you head to the house? I'll see if I can get something out of MacAuley."

Her heart warmed. "You'd call him for me?"

"I would, but he's already here. They're looking into a robbery."

"Has he asked about me?" Usually when she asked someone if a boy asked about her, she'd be devastated if the person said no. Today, she was praying for a no.

Rafe snorted. "Of course he has. He thinks I know where you are."

"What did you tell him?"

"That you used me for sex and ran."

Despite everything, Roxy grinned. "Did you tell him you were heartbroken and couldn't go on?"

"Something like that." Roxy was sure she heard him roll his eyes. "Go to the house. I'll stop by later to check on you."

"Fine. I don't know what I'm going to do without you there." She pouted. She could admit it. That house was creepy and boring.

"You'll find something to do."

"Amato, we have something here," a voice sounding vaguely like MacAuley said in the background.

"I gotta go." Rafe hung up.

She headed back toward the weird house that had no food in the refrigerator. The rearview mirror showed her more pouting. Enough. The bright lights of Smith's Food and Drug blinked ahead. She couldn't do anything about the weird house. But she could fix the no food.

Maybe buy some ice cream. Or cake. Or cooked chicken tenders. Or maybe she'd get it all. She'd earned it today. Sleuthing took energy, especially when hiding from the cops.

CHAPTER 33

ICE CREAM. Cake. Ice cream. Cake. Maybe Roxy should have gotten an ice cream cake. Or maybe she'd make an ice cream cake and then she could eat both. *Compromise rocks.*

She sat a scoop of ice cream on top of the chocolate cake she'd bought. The chicken fingers were long gone. So was an episode of *Outlander*. Bingeing Jamie Fraser and eating junk food was a good idea.

She grabbed her bowl and glass of wine. *Might as well bring the bottle.* But she'd run out of hands. She put the bowl on the counter and slid the bottle into the front pouch pocket of her sweatshirt-pajamas. She picked up the bowl and, with her hands full, she headed back through bear country into the living room.

She'd spoken with the bear, and they had a truce thing going. If she didn't go near him, he wouldn't give her the dead-eye. In the living room, though, an owl stared at her from the right side of the fireplace, a raccoon on the left. She might have a truce with the bear, but the other animals were more than happy to glare their bad juju onto her.

She scurried past them—careful not to spill her wine or drop her ice cream and cake— and wrapped herself in a blanket after plunking her loot down on the side table. She'd made it. The animals couldn't surprise her if she was on the couch. At least that was what she kept telling herself. It was either that or hide under the bed upstairs. And under the bed didn't have Jamie Fraser.

Jamie. Roxy snuggled into the couch with her bowl of ice cream/cake and glass of raspberry shiraz. She clicked play and the screen came to life with the long-haired Jamie. Num.

Winston finally accepted her in his house and showed his cute kitty face.

"You'll protect me. Won't you, Winston?" She rubbed under his chin with her free hand.

He moved closer, circling the couch cushion, finally settling into a ball at her hip. His purring vibrated against her leg but she couldn't hear it over the sound of Jamie's voice. But then again, who could hear anything over him calling Claire "Sassenach".

It made her lady bits happy. Maybe a bit too happy. Where was Rafe when she needed him? She spooned ice cream and cake into her mouth and watched as Claire and Jamie got married. More happy bits.

Something thumped on the front porch. *Thank goodness. He's home.* She set her bowl on the side table. Winston glared through half-open eyes as she jostled his happy bed. "Sorry, Winston," she called as she jogged to the front door, turned the porch light on, and whipped the door open.

Nothing.

"Hello?"

No one. Damn it. She was hearing things. Great. Next, she'd be wandering around the house with her mace—which she'd left in her car—checking corners and under beds for ghosts.

She closed the door and settled back on the couch, checking the time on her phone before she started the show again. Ten p.m. Rafe should be home soon. How long could a robbery investigation take?

She restarted the show. It might be the second time around, but she didn't want to miss one minute of Scottish goodness. Hugging her bowl close, she picked up the spoon and returned to her happy place. More *Outlander* sexual tension. More happy. The cat nuzzled in closer as she brought the spoon to her lips.

Another sound. Louder. This time, she was sure she'd heard it.

She looked toward the front door, but all she saw was the side of the giant bear. Thankfully, he wasn't moving. Who was, then?

Roxy quietly slid her bowl onto the side table as the

sounds of 1743 Scotland filled the house, making it hard to hear anything else. She hit pause and waited. Nothing.

She would swear she'd heard something.

Snatching the poker from the fireplace, Roxy gave the owl a second look before shooing Winston off the couch. If she believed in ghosts or reincarnation, she would swear the stuffed dead animals were coming after her. But she didn't. That didn't mean she wasn't creeped out.

Another sound, and then loud pops. The cat disappeared in a flash of fur. The front window shattered. Roxy dropped the poker and ducked in front of the couch. Another shot. More breaking glass. She crab-walked to the hallway, inching her way to the kitchen, where there didn't appear to be broken glass.

Pop.

A bullet pierced the front door, hitting a hall lamp and cracking it into bits. She slid behind the kitchen island and prayed. A lot.

Pop.

She covered her head with her arms and thought about how she could use a cop about now. Or maybe an ex-cop. She searched her pants for her phone. Dammit. It was on the side table. In the living room. Where there were gunshots.

Or had been gunshots.

The house was eerily quiet. Not one creature was stirring. Which meant Roxy needed to stir. She needed that phone.

She peered around the island. The front door was closed, but bits of the lamp were all over the hall floor. Maybe she could go around the other way, through the dining room.

She crawled next to the dining room table and peered around the wall into the living room. Not a sound, inside or outside.

She stumbled across the carpet, glass shards poking her feet. Not that she cared at this point. A few cuts were better than dead.

She dialed Rafe just as the front door swung open. His voice came through the line. "Amato."

"Rafe." Her voice shook and then stopped. She couldn't say another word. She couldn't do anything as she watched a gun appear. She saw the black barrel before she saw the person holding it. She swore it was smoking.

"Roxy, are you okay?" Rafe's voice faded as Roxy's arm dropped to her side.

The gun was aimed down the hallway. She had time. Sliding the phone into the kangaroo pocket of her pajama shirt, she backed toward the shattered front windows. She hiked her right leg over the bottom of the frame and a jagged piece of glass tore at her skin. She bit her tongue to keep the scream inside.

"Roxy, I know you're here," a female voice called out.

She wobbled, glass tinkled to the floor, and she froze on one leg, closing her eyes and willing herself invisible.

"Where are you?" The voice sounded familiar. And it was getting closer.

She tipped forward until her right foot landed in the front yard. Glass scraped along her left leg as she pulled it out of the house. Tried to, anyway. Her toes caught, and when she freed herself she fell forward onto her knees.

Bright light flowed from the busted windows, streaming onto Roxy as she knelt on the ground. Her hand lifted to her squinting eyes as they tried to adjust to the beam from a flashlight in the window. She needed to get up. To run.

"I found her," the voice said. "She's in the front yard." A figure approached Roxy. No gun. Just black clothes and a black hood. "Let's go." Plastic-gloved hands helped Roxy to her feet—which was not an easy task because the gash on Roxy's thigh blazed when she put pressure on it.

"Lean on me. I got you." The woman seemed so nice. She was helping Roxy get inside.

Probably to kill her, but that fact didn't match the voice. Roxy leaned on her shoulder to keep pressure off her leg. "Who are you?"

"Just come inside." The woman helped Roxy into the house and closed the front door before leading her to the couch. Roxy collapsed onto the cushions. The stranger took off her mask and leaned over Roxy. "Looks like you hurt your leg."

Mandy. Roxy knew it. She wanted to gloat. But there

was no one to gloat to. And given the fact that the woman had sprinkled the house with bullets, Roxy didn't think gloating was in her best interest. "Mandy, what are you doing here?"

"We should probably get you something for that," Mandy said, peering at Roxy's leg.

"Mom, leave her alone." Gretchen came out of the kitchen. She had a gun in one hand and a can of spray-paint in the other. She shook the can and handed it to her mother. "Start writing."

"Do we have to do this?" Mandy glanced at the bare wall and then the can.

Gretchen waved the gun. "This has to look gang-related. Tag the wall."

"I meant, do we have to kill her?"

"We talked about this. We can't just let her go. She's getting too close and she's going to call her cop friends. Hurry up." Gretchen pointed at the wall.

Getting close to what? Roxy wasn't sure what the hell was going on. It didn't help that her leg hurt like hell and she was still gawking at the gun in Gretchen's hand. "I'm not getting close to anything. And I have no cop friends. If I did, why would I be hiding?"

"She has a point." Mandy stopped tagging the Schmidts' wall with jagged block letters. "She's not going to the cops. She's here. Hiding."

"Until they catch her. And they will catch her. Then what? She'll start talking."

Mandy moved toward her daughter. "They'll catch her and think she did it. I put the weapon at her work. Everything points to her. We don't have to do this."

"Shut up, Mom. Get back to work." Gretchen pointed the gun at the wall. "Get that done, so we can go."

"I'm the prime suspect," Roxy pointed out. "They're coming after me. If you kill me, it'll look suspicious. Detective Geary doesn't believe in coincidence." Thank God for that. He might actually catch these two. Unless she could find a weapon.

The fireplace poker glinted in the flickering light from the television. She needed to grab that before Gretchen pulled the trigger.

Gretchen turned the gun on Roxy. "I'm sorry, but we need this to end. With the money Donnie owed to the gangs, and the fact that you killed him before they could get it back, there's no coincidence."

"Donnie owed money to gangs?" *Keep them talking.* Roxy inched to the right, hoping it looked like her leg hurt.

"He owed money to everyone. Having him owe money to a few gangbangers isn't a stretch. Nor is it a stretch that the woman he screwed over when he complained to her bosses killed him."

Roxy was being set up. One of the gangs were being set up. Given Geary's hatred of Roxy, it wouldn't be hard for him to believe. MacAuley might go along, because he'd probably believe it, too. The only one who might not believe was Rafe. But hopefully he was smart enough not to say anything. She didn't want him getting in the middle of this.

None of that answered why they'd killed Donnie—or better yet, why Gretchen killed Donnie. Mandy didn't seem to have a deadly bone in her body.

Roxy shifted another inch. "But why did you kill him? If it was an accident, the police would understand." It had to be an accident. Gretchen was a sweet mother with two little kids. Suburban moms didn't kill. They brought snacks for Little League.

Gretchen made a noise that had Roxy rethinking the "sweet mother" thing. "He wanted money. The creep actually tried to blackmail me. He said he'd tell my father that he wasn't really my father. That sleazeball wasn't my father. No matter what the DNA test said."

"You're Presley." Roxy eyed the fireplace poker. She inched over a little more. She'd need to dive two feet. Two feet didn't seem all that far, unless there was a gun pointed at you, a gun with bullets that could travel a hell of a lot faster than that.

"My mom and dad changed my name to Gretchen when I was born. Apparently Donnie always wanted a daughter named Presley. My mom was trying to get him back—not the best idea, given she was married to another man at that point. But she was young and dumb. We've all been there. Anyway, it didn't work. So my mom told

Donnie he wasn't the father. Donnie didn't care and Steve became my father."

Gretchen smirked. "Donnie actually invited me to the hotel. I lied when I said he wasn't there. He was. When he said he'd tell my father he knew I wasn't really Steve's daughter, I lost it. He had already taken everything from my dad. He wasn't taking me too. He wouldn't take my mother's mistake and rub it in his face."

"When I was pregnant," Mandy said, "I thought Donnie and I would run off with you after you were born, but he wasn't ready to settle down. He never was ready." Mandy finished tagging the wall. "I don't know how he found out about you, but what you did to Donnie was an accident. We can go to the police."

"The police won't see it that way." Gretchen looked around. "Did you forget anything? I don't want you leaving anything behind this time."

The jacket. Roxy turned to Mandy. "That was your jacket. You were there."

Mandy shook her head. "I was there earlier when Adelaide dropped off the keys. I ran up to the room and tried to talk him out of what he was doing. I tried to get him to do the right thing."

Except he didn't. Given everything Roxy had learned about Donnie, she wasn't all that surprised.

"There's no other way." Gretchen cocked the gun. "Mom, go outside. I'll finish up."

"But—"

"Go!"

This couldn't be how things ended. Roxy was being taken out in a fake gang fight. She was too young. There were things she had to do. There were things she had to see.

Tears slid down her cheeks. This was it. She'd never get to feel Rafe's touch again. Never hug her parents. She'd never get dragged to a horrible club by Sarina. Or get chased by servees again.

CHAPTER 34

IT'S NOT THAT I'M AFRAID TO DIE, I JUST DON'T WANT TO BE THERE WHEN IT HAPPENS. ~ WOODY ALLEN

THIS COULDN'T BE IT. This wasn't how she was going out. She needed to postpone.

Mandy didn't want to do this. Roxy could see it in her eyes. She was against the whole thing. Roxy just needed to give Mandy time to Mom-up and nip this in the bud. Get Gretchen talking.

"How did you find me?"

Gretchen sighed. "Does it matter? I followed you and your boyfriend when you left the house."

"You can't shoot me like this."

Gretchen scowled, but the gun stayed leveled at Roxy. "Why not?"

That was a good question. There had to be a good answer. Maybe. "Because this is a drive-by, right? That's why you shot through the windows. You have to shoot me from farther away and from outside, or the crime scene won't look right."

Roxy was reaching. Hell, they tagged inside the house, so nothing of what she said was true. Nothing made sense. But maybe, just maybe, she could get them to hold off until she could figure something out.

"You're right." Gretchen sighed again and waggled the cocked gun.

Mandy's eyes widened. She hadn't left. She was still here. "Gretchen, darling, we can just leave. We'll go away."

"No, Mom, we can't." Gretchen glared at her. "Can you please go outside and get the car ready?"

Mandy shook her head. "We need to rethink this."

Gretchen yelled, "There's nothing to rethink," and the hand with the gun waved out to the side. Away from Roxy.

This was it. This was her chance. Roxy dove to the floor and grabbed the poker. She slammed it into Gretchen's knees as a shot went off. Roxy didn't have time to figure out what it hit. She yanked the poker back, and somehow the metal hook caught on Gretchen's arm.

That same arm that held the gun currently aimed at Roxy. Shit. Another yank freed the poker, and Roxy scrambled to her knees. She used every ounce of strength to bring the poker down on Gretchen's arm. The gun flew off, who knew where, and Gretchen fell to the floor with a scream.

The gun. It was right there.

Roxy dove for it, but so did Gretchen. She grabbed Roxy's ankle. "Mom, give me the gun," Gretchen groaned.

It was like she had superhuman strength. The more Roxy kicked, the tighter Gretchen's grip. Roxy needed leverage. She kicked out with her other foot, landing a heel to Gretchen's face. Her grip loosened. The gun sat next to the front door—feet from Mandy.

"You girls stop it!" Mandy stared at Gretchen and Roxy with terror written on her face. She yelled like they were toddlers fighting over a toy.

Roxy wrenched her leg away and staggered to her feet. She stumbled, her fingers so close, she could almost feel the rubber grip. But before she got there, Mandy picked up the gun.

Oh. Hell. No.

The bear. They'd made their peace. Now she needed his help. Roxy pivoted like a drunken pole dancer and got behind the bear. Shoved as hard as she could. Nothing. Heavy sucker. She wedged her butt between the wall and the bear. Braced her legs and pushed. The bear rocked. Again. It didn't take more than a few seconds, yet it felt like a lifetime before the bear tipped away. Roxy heard a loud thump and a yell as the bear knocked Mandy to the floor, pinning her in place.

"Help me." She raised a hand to Roxy.

Like hell.

Roxy's breath stuttered in her chest as she leaned down and grabbed the gun. That took way too much work because now she was dizzy. She turned to the living room and aimed.

No Gretchen.

Roxy pointed the gun like she'd seen in the cop shows and crept around the wall into the dining room. In the kitchen, red pooled along the floor in staggered puddles. She jumped around the island.

Nothing.

Dammit. Roxy snuck to the other kitchen doorway. Little patches of blood smeared the floor, but that could have been from Roxy's bloody feet when the shooting first started.

She kept the gun up as she crept down the hall where the bear lay on the floor, Mandy squirming underneath.

"Bitch," Gretchen yelled.

Metal slid against Roxy's throat. She dropped the gun as her hands flew to her neck. Gretchen pulled Roxy closer, yanking the poker harder against Roxy's throat. Gretchen's body pressed into her.

Lungs burning. Head spinning. Roxy flailed her arms, trying to reach behind her. She slammed a fist into Gretchen's face. The poker dropped to the floor with a clang. Roxy fell to her knees, the air sputtering into her lungs in large gulps. She turned her head.

Gretchen, complete with crazed eyes and bloody nose, rushed toward her.

Not today, crazy. Not. Today. Roxy grabbed the poker as she stood up, and swung it like a tennis racket. The metal crunched into Gretchen's face and she fell backward onto the floor.

Gretchen didn't move.

Shit. Roxy didn't mean to kill her.

Gretchen's chest rose and fell. Not dead. Thank goodness. Roxy might not like the bitch much, but she didn't want her kids to be half-orphans. No one deserved that. Especially now that Roxy could breathe.

The front door swung open and another gun appeared. For the love of...

"Police."

Roxy lifted her hands above her head. "I'm not armed." She pointed toward the gun. "Get that thing out of here."

MacAuley came through the front door. "Are you okay?"

She might have nodded, but she wasn't sure. Her head spun, and she dropped her hands just in time to keep the floor from hitting her face. Her body ached. Who knew fighting crazies would take so much out of a person?

MacAuley stepped over Mandy and picked up the gun. "Amato, get over here."

Roxy eased her sagging bones to the floor. MacAuley's eyes glinted with worry even though the guy had to see this stuff all the time.

"No need for concern. You don't still think I'm the bad guy, do you? 'Cause I'm not the guy." She tried to lift her hand to point, but her arm was so tired. So, so tired. Fighting with these women had taken it out of her. "They're the guy."

"Does it hurt?" Rafe walked toward her looking way paler then he should.

She giggled, a breathy laugh that made her side burn. "You should see the other guy."

"Does it hurt?"

"Why do you keep asking that?"

Rafe and MacAuley exchanged glances.

"EMT." A woman carrying a large bag stood at the door. Good. She could make sure Roxy hadn't accidentally killed anyone. Although it wasn't all her fault. The bear did his part.

"What about the bear?" Rafe looked at her like she had two heads. "There's a bullet hole over here."

A bullet hole? Who was shot? The bear? "I didn't shoot the bear. I found him like that. Don't try to pin it on me."

She wasn't the guy.

"Lie down." Rafe helped her lie flat on the floor. Her side burned. She felt around for why. Wetness. She pulled her hand back. Blood. Her blood. Her vision went fuzzy at the edges.

"Roxy, stay with me, sweetheart." Rafe's voice was strained and so far away. He was disappearing.

Or maybe she was.

The darkness moved from the edges and closed in on her.

CHAPTER 35

BEEP. Beep. Beep.

Someone had better turn off that awful beeping, or she was going to throw whatever it was into the fiery pits of hell.

Roxy's eyes slid open to a white ceiling. Slowly, her body was coming online. Her fingers twitched. Her toes wiggled. Her head throbbed.

Did she mention that beep? Where the hell was she? She turned her head. A white wall. In front of that, a machine with a little screen showing a red squiggly line that bounced up and down to the beat of the beep. She lifted her hand. A white plastic clip was attached to her middle finger.

"Oh, thank God." Roxy couldn't see her, but she knew her mother's voice. "I was so worried."

Her mother didn't just seem worried, her eyes said she hadn't slept in a while.

"Don't say that," her father's disembodied voice scolded. "We're supposed to keep her spirits up."

"Paul, keep your comments to yourself."

"Don't fight in front of the children." Roxy's voice was scratchy.

Her father leaned over the other side of the bed. He looked like he hadn't seen a bed in months.

"How long have I been here?" Roxy croaked.

"A couple days." Her mom tried to smile, but it didn't exactly raise Roxy's spirits. "Do you remember what happened?"

Roxy propped her arms on the bed and tried to push herself up. Her chest was in a vise. She couldn't move. The pain she felt just contemplating moving was enough for her to be thankful she couldn't move any farther.

"Don't get up." Danielle walked in, complete with her doctor's coat.

Thank goodness. The normal parent.

"Welcome back. It's nice to see your eyes open." Danielle hit something on the bed and the back rest slowly angled Roxy's body upward.

Her side pulled and pulsed. "That's enough." It was barely enough to see everyone in the room, but her side didn't care.

"Sorry." Danielle stepped away from the bed. "How are you feeling?"

"Like I've been shot." Roxy laughed, a small giggle, before the pain made her stop breathing. The pain was bad when she moved. So she just wouldn't move anymore. Ever.

Her mother blubbered off to the side, large tears streaming down her face. "My baby. Shot."

"It's okay, Mom. I'm okay." Roxy had no idea if she was okay, but she figured her mom needed a little encouragement. And Roxy was talking, which sounded like an improvement over the last couple days.

"It's not okay. That woman tried to kill you."

"The good news is she didn't." Roxy thought that was funny, but no one laughed. Maybe she'd broken her sarcasm in the scuffle with Gretchen.

Danielle checked the beeping machine and typed in the computer. "How are you feeling?"

"Fine?" She was pretty sure she was fine, but it really depended on the definition. She was alive, so that was something.

"You don't sound convinced."

"Well, my side hurts, and it feels like there's a vise around my hips."

"Let me fix that." Danielle readjusted the blanket under her, jostling her hip and everything attached to it.

Pain. Light-blinding pain zipped past her eyes. She groaned. Which was impressive since she wanted to scream obscenities.

"Sorry. I'll have the nurse give you some pain meds." Danielle flipped the blanket up onto Roxy's stomach and loosened tape on her side. Which Roxy couldn't see, but the tickle of the adhesive coming off her skin and the sound told her what was happening. Danielle hummed. "You're healing well."

"What happened?" Exactly. She remembered bits and pieces. The whole getting shot part was a bit fuzzy.

Danielle covered the wound on Roxy's hip and pulled the blanket down, without wedging it underneath her. "You were shot in the hip. The bullet nearly grazed your spleen, but it managed not to hit any vital organs. We also stitched a laceration on the posterior thigh and there was some swelling on your neck."

There was more, but the Cliff Notes version was she'd be fine. Which, really, when you woke up and found out you'd been shot and had other various injuries, "you'll be fine" was the headline. Burying it just meant losing the audience.

"I need to ask a few basic questions," Danielle said, and launched right into them.

Roxy was pretty sure she got them all right. Her age. The current year. She was rocking this test.

"Do you know who this is?" Danielle pointed at Roxy's mom.

Roxy went to say the words, but—nothing. All of a sudden, he was there. The only thing she was rocking was googly eyes because Rafe leaned against the door jamb of her hospital room. His arms were crossed, making the muscles bulge. He looked awful. He looked worried. He looked like he hadn't slept in days.

Which was ironic since Roxy, apparently, had literally slept for days, and she probably resembled a coked-up Medusa clone.

Rafe walked in and stood off to the side. "Sorry to interrupt."

Those brown eyes. The way they caressed her body as he took her in wasn't an interruption. Well, it was, but who cared. There were worse ways to fail the doctor's mental stability test.

Danielle moved to block Roxy's view of Rafe and cleared her throat. "Can we get back to it?"

"Sure." Roxy could feel the red crawling up her neck —from her eyes creeping over Rafe's body.

A glimmer of a smile ghosted along his lips.

It was bad if he couldn't find joy in her embarrassing herself.

"Who is this?" Danielle pointed to her dad.

"My dad."

Danielle gestured to her mom. "And this?"

"Your wife."

"And this gentleman behind me?"

"Rafe." Her eyes met his and no matter how hard she tried not to get sucked back in, she did.

He was here. In the hospital. Their relationship hadn't been defined, but there was no way it was close to hospital-visit territory. Maybe a nice fruit basket, but actually standing there like he owned the place? No. That wasn't the stance of someone who'd showed up five minutes ago to drop off a card.

"Well, Rafe. It's nice to meet you. I'm Danielle, Roxy's stepmom." She took her wife's hand.

"I'm Roxy's mother, Olivia."

"Pleasure to meet you both." Rafe dipped his chin in acknowledgement, but then his eyes were back on Roxy.

"I think we should give them a few moments to catch up." Danielle typed out some information on the computer as a nurse walked in with a syringe. "He'll give you a little something for pain."

The nurse took the syringe and pushed it into her IV. He updated her chart before he disappeared.

Her dad kissed her forehead. "We're going to get some coffee. Stormy is so worried about you. She's in the chapel burning incense."

Stormy was worried? Roxy was worried about Stormy playing with matches.

Her mom wrapped her in an awkward hug. "I'm so glad you're okay." She pulled away and disappeared with Danielle out the door.

The room was quiet. Only her and Rafe. He kicked his leg out and walked to the bed. So slow and casual. It didn't match the intensity in his eyes. He put his arm over her head on the headboard and bent down.

"Roxy," he whispered as his head dropped down inches from hers. "I thought I lost you." Just saying the words seemed to cause him pain. He closed his eyes and touched his forehead to hers. His breathing a ragged in and out.

Part of her wanted to be happy he cared. Another part hated seeing him broken.

"I'm not lost." Her voice hitched in her throat, the grief nearly choking her.

His lids opened, and her pain was mirrored back in his tired eyes. "I saw the windows blown out and the bullet holes— then all the blood and— your eyes closed..." His breathing deepened as he shook his head against hers.

"It's okay. I'm okay." She raised her hand to the scruff on his face. He must not have been to work in a while. She couldn't imagine him showing up to lead his team like this. "We're okay."

He nestled his face into her palm and sighed. "I'm sorry."

"For what?"

"I shouldn't have gone to work. I should have gotten to you faster. If anything would've happened to you..." He lifted her hand from his cheek to his lips. Warm breath slid along the palm. Soft lips hovered along her skin.

"Nothing happened."

"It did. You were shot." His eyes were haunted.

"You got me medical attention, and I'm going to be okay."

He took a deep breath and pulled away, sliding his fingers through hers. "I'm glad you're all right, Roxanna."

She was too. Then she remembered him and MacAuley at the house. "Were you hurt?"

"No, by the time we got there, Mandy and Gretchen were incapacitated."

"Winston!" Fur had whizzed by her when the shooting started. She'd throw up if anything happened to Winston because of her. "Did they hurt the cat?"

"Winston hid upstairs. No injuries."

"Thank God." Her fingers were still wound with hers. She liked it. A lot. He'd found her. "And thank God you came home when you did. Why did you bring MacAuley with you?"

"Your phone." He pointed to the rolling table next to the bed. There was a bouquet of flowers on it, and also her cell phone, plugged into an outlet.

"My phone?"

"You called me when I was on my way. When I realized what was going on, I called him, and we came to you."

"I forgot I called you." Her lips felt funny and her eyelids starting drooping.

"There was a lot going on."

A burst of energy hit her as she remembered the mother-daughter duo. "Those two were crazy. Gretchen killed Donnie because she was his daughter. Mandy cheated on her husband when they were dating or something like that. But he was an ass." The drugs the nurse gave her were kicking in, and her eyes were getting heavy. "Oh. And Mandy planted the gun at the agency. And the bear saved me. And the owl winked at me."

Rafe smiled. "The owl winked at you?"

It made her happy. Inside, at least. She wasn't quite sure what her face was doing. It was too tired. "Hmmm?"

Were they talking about something?

"Go to sleep, sweetheart." He rested his lips on her forehead. He lingered there. So soft. So warm.

She wanted to open her eyes and wrap her arms around him. She wanted to tell him how happy he made her. How her whole body lit up from his touch. But her eyes wouldn't open. Her mouth wouldn't say words.

She slipped away thinking about those lips.

Best dreams ever.

CHAPTER 36

WHAT THE DETECTIVE STORY IS ABOUT IS NOT MURDER BUT THE RESTORATION OF ORDER. ~ P. D. JAMES

FIVE DAYS Later

Roxy limped into the police station, her hips and leg wrapped up mummy-style while she healed. She'd been staying at her mom's for the past few days, and it had been a nightmare.

Between Danielle helicoptering around and her mom asking if she was bleeding on the couch every ten minutes, she was more than ready to go home. To her own bed. Without a live-in doctor and furniture-dictator mother.

She understood, and it was nice they cared as much as they did. But even understanding didn't help waking up to her mother turning her over to check the bandages —more than likely checking the furniture—but whatever.

And it wasn't once. Multiple times. Roxy hadn't had a whole night's sleep since she'd arrived at their house four days ago.

At least when she was on the drugs she could sleep. Day or night. But now she was off the tough stuff. She was tired and bored out of her mind. The bad news was, she hadn't seen an episode of *Days of our Lives* since college. The good news was, she turned it on, and she was able to understand everything like she hadn't been gone for almost 10 years. She was pretty sure they were on the same story line now that they were on back then.

That gave her something to do for an hour a day.

"Roxy." Detective MacAuley's face hadn't been around harassing her in days. She almost missed him. "How are you feeling?"

"If I don't make any sudden movements, I'm fine."

"Where's Amato?" He looked around the room. "You didn't drive. Did you?"

"No." She could barely passenger these days. "Rafe is on his way. He's parking the truck."

"Well, we'll take you back, and I'll have him wait." MacAuley crossed the room and talked with one of the front desk officers. He came back and escorted Roxy to an interrogation room.

She hated those rooms. They were cold and sterile. And it meant she would get yelled at by Detective Geary. She hesitated at the door. No Geary. Maybe today was her lucky day. Maybe he won the lottery and quit the force.

She slowly lowered herself into the chair. Standing was okay. Sitting was all right. But moving between each position hurt. It was getting better. She didn't need to scream when she moved anymore. Progress.

She waited for her body to get used to sitting. The pain ebbed as she held her breath. Finally, she let out a long burst of air.

"Are you okay?" MacAuley looked concerned—almost pale. Like her head would spin around and vomit pea soup. Or worse, like she was going to cry.

"I'm fine. Those sudden movements, though." She smiled, and it didn't even have a wince in it. Her body was calming down. The pain subsiding.

The door opened and Detective Geary appeared, carrying a manila file folder. Dammit. No lottery winner. Which meant she'd have to listen to him yell. She wasn't in the mood—not that she was ever in the mood for yelling, especially at her—but couldn't she just catch a break?

"Ms. Horne." Geary was using the scary voice, which didn't bode well for Roxy.

"Detective Geary."

"How are you feeling?" He said the words as if reading from a book.

Like he cared. She wanted to cross her arms and sneer. But she didn't. "Fine."

"We wanted to talk about Donnie Dunne."

"Didn't you get everything you needed when I called Rafe and they confessed?"

Geary looked at MacAuley with a confused expression.

"We didn't hear them confess." MacAuley shook his head. "We couldn't hear anything they said."

"Then why did you come?"

"Rafe heard you scream."

They didn't have the confession. They only had her word against the mother-daughter killers. Who probably had plenty to say about Roxy. None of it good. From the look Geary and MacAuley were sharing, she was still a suspect. After everything she'd been through, they still thought she could do something like that.

Geary sat down and opened the folder. "Let's start with the gun at your place of employment—"

"Mandy put it there so they could frame me. Gretchen killed her father. Not me."

"Why don't you wait for me to ask the questions instead of jumping in?" Geary sighed. "Steve isn't dead."

"Her real father, Donnie." They didn't even know about Donnie being the father. She was so incredibly screwed.

"We're still waiting on a paternity test to validate that." Geary stared at Roxy. "Now, when did you find out they'd tried to plant the evidence at your office?"

"When they tried to kill me in a mock drive-by."

Geary wrote something inside the file. "Was that the night we found you in the Schmidts' home?"

"Yes."

"Why did they paint gang symbols inside the house, if it was supposed to be a drive-by?"

"You'd have to ask them." She wondered the same thing. Their plan had holes. Hopefully, the police were trying to fill those holes with the truth.

"What else did they tell you?"

"That Gretchen killed her dad, and Mandy did what she had to, to help cover it up."

"Anything else?"

"The SBM jacket is Mandy's. She went up to the room when Adelaide brought Donnie's phone to the hotel. She wanted to talk him out of trying to blackmail money from his own daughter."

"Thank you for your time." Geary stood.

Wait. What? "That's it? You believe me? Even without the phone confession?"

"That's it." Geary tapped the manila folder on the desk and walked toward the door. He was much more pleasant this time. Not that this level of pleasant was so hard to achieve when everything prior had been nothing but contempt. Today it was more like apathy. "You're free to go."

He left. She was going to miss that guy. Not.

Roxy stared at MacAuley but didn't get up. For two reasons, really. One, she wanted to know if she was still a suspect. And two, those sudden movements sucked. She wanted to put that off just a little longer. "Am I still a suspect?"

MacAuley shook his head. "No. The ice cream place put up cameras in the back of the store because they were having trouble with raccoons living in the garbage can. We have Mandy putting the knife in the can."

Saved by trash pandas. Who would have thought those things would turn out to be a blessing?

"Once we got them to talk," MacAuley continued, "they confessed to everything. The paternity, the blackmail, the murder. Except to hear Gretchen's take, it was Mandy's idea."

"Well, considering Mandy didn't want to kill me and Gretchen did, I'm Team Mandy." All the way.

"Mandy didn't want to kill you?"

"No, she kept saying there were other ways. They could move away. Even when Mandy got the gun, she didn't use it."

MacAuley leaned back in his chair. "Then why did you push the bear on her?"

"Because she did whatever Gretchen told her to do. It was only a matter of time before Mandy would have used the gun on me just to shut her up."

"Interesting."

"What's interesting?"

"To hear Mandy and Gretchen tell it, Mandy is some evil mastermind that engineered this whole thing." MacAuley leaned forward.

"I get the feeling Mandy would do anything for her daughter. And Gretchen has kids. Mandy probably doesn't want her grandchildren growing up without a mom." Roxy felt bad for the kids. It wasn't their fault any of this happened, but when it came down to it, they were the ones who would suffer.

"The husband has already filed for divorce. He never thought his wife could kill someone."

"In Gretchen's defense" —Roxy couldn't believe she defending that wack-job— "Donnie was a horrible person. He had the ability to make the crazy come out of anyone."

"Not that I'm arguing, but that doesn't make what she did right. In fact, she was pretty coherent when she tried to kill you." As coherent as Gretchen could get anyway. "You know you can leave anytime."

It was time to get out of here. Before they changed their mind. "I know. I just wanted to make sure I wasn't a suspect. And to see why I was brought in."

"We needed to see if you knew anything we didn't already know."

"Did I?"

"Yeah." He grinned. "We're going to interview Mandy again. See if she's the evil mastermind she's pretending to be."

"Good." Roxy pushed the chair back and stood. Aches. Pains. Winces. Once all the drama subsided, she wobbled to the door. "Thanks for believing in me."

"Thanks for not listening and helping." He stopped the door before she could open it completely. "But in the future, when we say back off, back off. You wouldn't have gotten shot if you'd have listened."

"But you wouldn't have caught the bad guys."

"You have no faith. We would have apprehended the criminal, and it wouldn't have nearly killed Amato. He was a basket case when we found you."

"I feel bad about that." Rafe had been so attentive since the hospital. He obviously felt guilty that she'd been hurt, and the reality of the whole death thing made her appreciate him more.

"Hold on to that feeling if you ever find yourself wanting to play detective again."

"I'll try." She would. She wasn't dumb enough to make a promise to never interfere again, though. When you were a lead suspect, you did crazy things. Not that she had plans to be a suspect again. She could check that one off her bucket list.

She passed the cops fluttering around the precinct, and MacAuley stayed at her side.

"You can go back to your desk.," Roxy told him. "I know my way out."

"Yeah, but I've seen you grit your teeth when you limp. I don't want you to fall. Rafe would have my ass."

Which was kind of sweet. Even if he pretended it was for Rafe's benefit, she knew better. He cared.

They passed the front desk in the main atrium, where Rafe leaned against the wall. He jumped forward when he saw her. "Everything go okay?" Rafe wrapped an arm around her.

She had a feeling all she'd have to say is that Geary was a jerk, and Rafe would kick his ass. That was tempting, but she didn't feel like sticking around while they arrested him. And she'd have to bail him out. She didn't have bail money on her. "It went fine. I'm not a suspect anymore."

"It's about time the Las Vegas PD got their head out of their asses." Rafe smirked as he looked directly at MacAuley, taunting him to disagree.

MacAuley leaned into Roxy. "Give me a call if you get sick of him." Then he turned to Rafe. "Amato."

"Keep going, MacAuley." Rafe didn't look too thrilled with him at the moment.

Roxy wasn't sure the whole bail thing might not still happen.

"Yeah. I've got important cop stuff to do. You sure you don't want to come back?"

"Positive." Rafe glared at MacAuley's back as he walked away. "Dick."

"That dick always believed in me."

"Yeah, he has his moments, but overall, he's just a dick."

She wanted to argue, but honestly, these two were like diet soda and Mentos. Not lethal, but definitely messy. Roxy followed Rafe as he led her to his truck. He'd managed to get a front spot. No wonder it took him so long to get inside. He probably had to wait for the spot to open up.

He paused next to his truck and moved a piece of her hair from her eyes. "Where to next? Should I take you home, or would you like to come to my place?" He leaned in, his breath a wisp along her ear. "I bought cake."

Cake. She had been living with her parents since the hospital. Going home sounded good, until she really thought about it. Her apartment probably had moldy cheese and stale cereal, but that was about it. On top of that, she still had boxes stuffed with her crap all over the place.

Her check had bounced because the direct deposit didn't quite cover it. Which meant Ms. Potter had called, ready to box up the rest of her stuff. Roxy wasn't proud of the fact that she needed her mommy to bail her out, but she still had a place to live. She still had her job, where they'd agreed to let her shadow one of the private investigators once she was back on her feet. She would finally start working toward her license. She'd get her life in order, clean up her apartment, learn a new trade, and pay off her debt to her mother.

But not today. Today, there was cake. And Rafe. The look in his eyes was promising so much more than that.

She couldn't have sex yet, but they were creative people. They'd find something to do with each other that would be almost as amazing.

She leaned into his lips. The kiss was everything. Hard. Sweet. A kiss that bubbled through her chest and landed in her toes. "Your place it is."

EXTRAS

Thank you for supporting an independent author. It would be great if you could leave a review or a rating wherever you purchased this book, or on Goodreads.

Would you like to know when my next book is available? You can sign up for my new release email list at http://www.vanessamknight.com or like my Facebook page at http://facebook.com/vanessamknightauthor.

Vanessa M. Knight has always enjoyed writing, and once she found mystery and romance, she was addicted. She props her laptop in the suburbs of Chicago with her family and menagerie of four-pawed claw-babies (AKA cats and dogs.) That laptop has partnered-in-crime to write contemporary romances with a dash of humor and splash of snark.

When she has a few moments to spare, you can find her singing off-key (but she assures everyone it's still considered singing), reading, kickboxing, or killing a few brain cells as she stares at the many sitcoms and dramas available through the Internet and TV.

For more information on Vanessa, including her Internet haunts, contest updates, and details on her upcoming novels, please visit her website at www.vanessamknight.com.

Busting In

Busting Out

Busting Through

CONTEMPORARY NEW ADULT

Ritter University Series

Major Renovations

What Happens in College...

Christmas Breakdown

Rushing In

Sophomore Slump

The Make-up Test

www.ingramcontent.com/pod-product-compliance
Lightning Source LLC
Chambersburg PA
CBHW011127190726
48289CB00012B/2942